SCUM

AND
OTHER TALES

Richard Bellush, Jr.

ROBERT D. REED PUBLISHERS • SAN FRANCISCO, CA

Robert D. Reed Publishers
750 La Playa Street, Suite 647
San Francisco, CA 94121
Phone: 650/994-6570 • Fax: -6579
E-mail: 4bobreed@msn.com
www.rdrpublishers.com

Editor: Jessica Bryan
Book Designer: Marilyn Yasmine Nadel
Cover Designer: Julia Gaskill

ISBN: 1931741190
Library of Congress Control Number: 2002102658

Printed in Canada

This book is dedicated to

Dick and Robina

To whom I owe everything

CONTENTS

BROWN ACID

The warning came repeatedly from the stage, "Do not take the brown acid!"

I should have listened but I didn't. It was raining. I was hungry. I was wet. I was cold. My bladder was full. There were people everywhere. I mean everywhere. When walking, you had to place each step with extreme care to avoid some body part. Mud and blankets and coolers and garbage filled the small spaces among the flesh. Often you couldn't keep your balance without using your hands as additional feet. The result was a general lurching movement that looked as though a giant game of Twister was being played on the entire farm.

The music was great but it wasn't that great. The only times I was comfortable was when I was high or making love. The latter wouldn't happen without the former because my old lady wouldn't get it on in front of everybody unless she was stoned. You know that if she was doing something I was too. So, yeah, I took the acid.

Everybody else just got sick or paranoid for a while. Not me. It really did a number on me. I wish I had never heard of Woodstock.

I'd dropped acid before plenty of times. I started when I was 16. It is embarrassing to be such a cliché for my generation, but I had gone to an auditorium at a nearby college in Madison and heard Timothy Leary speak. The man spoke of achieving a higher consciousness through chemistry. He seemed to speak directly to me. There was more to life than the petty materialistic concerns which so obsessed our parents, he said.

1

Right after the lecture he went back to a mansion in New York where he lived with an heiress who was one of his protégés. I thought about what he said all that evening while floating in the pool in back of my folks' house. I remember the stars were crispy bright that night. Ursa Major was the only constellation I could name for sure. It occurred to me that it might be fun to learn more about stars.

Two days later was Saturday. I took a train to NYC with a buddy and bought some caps in Washington Square. The dealer was an NYU student earning cash for college tuition. We were stupid teenagers. We dared each other to drop the acid on the train ride back home. We knew we were being stupid, but that was better than being chicken. At first we thought the dealer had ripped us off because 20 minutes went by and neither of us felt a thing. Then I handed the conductor my ticket and saw the afterimage of my hand hang in space across the entire sweep from my shirt pocket to the aisle. The view outside the window became a swirl in a pattern like cream makes when you pour it into coffee.

"Oh wow!" Ron said. "This is pretty cool, Aardvark!"

I guess I should explain the name. Critics ask me about it all the time and I make a point of not answering. Mystery makes mystique. The truth is simple enough. My first day of high school a varsity linebacker I accidentally brushed grabbed me by the back of the neck and ground my nose in the dirt. From then on I was Aardvark. I couldn't shake the name so I just went with it. Professionally it has been an asset. Folks remember me.

It was plain that LSD affected me differently. My friend described the world as having sharp crystalline edges and vivid colors, but he by no means was incapacitated by his high. The world I saw belonged in another galaxy. Maybe another universe.

I'm not sure how we made it to my house from the train station. I have a vague recollection of being led by the arm as the people we passed transmogrified into every one of the major Warner Brothers cartoon characters. We somehow avoided attracting the notice of the police, even though I remember shouting at Porky Pig something about wearing pants in public. The effects wore off by the next morning. My parents said nothing to me about my behavior. To this day I don't know whether they didn't notice or shrugged it off.

After several subsequent embarrassments at my hands, my friends learned to keep me out of public view whenever we got high. They enjoyed my company because I was entertaining. I listened to frivolous lyrics by Cream and expostulated loudly at their profundity. I laughed uproariously at the madcap humor of Ed Sullivan. One time I dismembered an orange in fascination and then cried for an hour in horror at what I had done. The laughter of my friends on that occasion boomed like cannon fire.

My sex life improved. To be more accurate, it started. I don't know if sociobiologists are right about girls being attracted to the strongest males. Maybe that's the case when they want help raising kids, but I wasn't very strong back then and I did OK. I think most times, as Cindy Lauper later insisted, they just want to have fun. As soon as I became known in school as a boy with acid to spare, I had girlfriends to spare.

Generally, LSD is a major distraction away from sex, but if you can keep your mind on the act when high it is an experience all its own. My first time I was convinced I was making it with a giant ripe plum. I never told that to any shrink for fear he would tell me what it meant. It can't be anything good.

Already I was a pretty good painter and amateur cartoonist. You can see elements of my later style in what I did then. I lacked originality at that point though. My sketches and splashes were nothing special.

I was one of the fools who bought tickets to Woodstock. More foolish still, I didn't keep them as collectors' items. I paid $18 each which by the standards of the day was an outrageously high price. Now they are worth thousands.

My girlfriend Vicky, who was a year older than I was, drove us upstate in her VW Bug. We ran out of gas in a huge traffic jam several miles from the concert site. Somehow everyone seemed to know the way to the concert even though it had been relocated at the last minute to some town named Bethel that I had a hard time finding on a map. It was 50 miles from the town of Woodstock. We pushed the car off the road onto the lawn of a small ranch house. I talked to the owner. He wanted $50 to let us leave it there. I had to sell almost all of my stash to the freaks still caught in traffic in order to raise the cash. I kept some caps. As it turned out, I didn't keep enough.

Vicky and I hiked the rest of the way. We approached the site over a field that was nowhere near an official gate. There was no one to take our tickets. We were not alone. About a dozen other kids were there and more were approaching. A few of the rowdier ones pushed over the makeshift fence to the applause of the rest of us. We all entered the grounds. The MCs on stage yelled about that sort of thing for a while. Eventually they gave up and declared Woodstock a free concert, as though they had a choice in the matter. I wanted to keep some distance from the stage where we could have some elbowroom, but Vicky wanted to be as close as we could get. So, we staked out a blanket space up front.

Because my stash was so low, I went around bumming for extra drugs. Back then people were pretty generous with what they had. Some dudes gave me a red pill and a brown one. I gave Vicky the red one.

I never was on a trip like that. The world didn't go surreal. Instead my perspective became all crazy. When I looked at the stage, it was like I was on the stage. I was Melanie singing *Beautiful People.* I could see the audience out there including me and Vicky. I could see me. I could feel through the clouds and through space to the surface of the moon. I could feel the mountain ranges, the craters, the plains, and the valleys on the surface. I swam through the Atlantic with tuna and was entangled in a net. I returned to the stage and for a while became Arlo Guthrie singing *Coming Into Los Angeles.* I picked myself out of the crowd and returned to me. I grabbed a handful of dirt and saw microscopic creatures living inside. I became an amoeba and stretched out my membrane to absorb a piece of decayed organic matter for food. I became a biology teacher in some California classroom I never had seen before writing the word phagocytosis on a blackboard.

I don't remember much of the concert after that until Joe Cocker took the stage. I remember rain. I remember becoming rain droplets in the clouds and falling back on myself. I remember exploring the solar system. On the third day I was mostly back to myself. I was pretty sick. The sickness might have helped restrain my mind from traveling by holding my attention on my own bodily sensations. My first totally sane view was of Vicky making it with a dude on the next blanket.

I lost it again for a while during Hendrix. It's a shame. I hear he was good. Vicky, like most of the audience, was gone by then. She was kind enough to pin a note to me that said "I'm splitting." After the concert, I hitchhiked back to Chatham, NJ.

My mind never was right after that, but the experience gave my artwork a special edge. It made my career. While very much a part of the psychedelic scene of that time, my work was nevertheless distinctive. I made my first sale to a poster company before I graduated high school.

I enrolled at Syracuse in order to get a 2S deferment from the jungles of Southeast Asia. Even as a Fine Arts student my work became highly commercial. My warped "inside out" perspective appealed to many in the counterculture. Since these people by and large had plenty of their parents' money to spend, I socked away a good little nest egg. I never was as big as Peter Max or as significant as Warhol, but my stuff sold. It was a rare head shop or boutique in the early '70s that didn't have Aardvark T-shirts, Aardvark paper airplane books, and Aardvark posters.

My success didn't help my grades. I wonder to this day if my professors resented me for my success or if they really thought my work was trash. At least they didn't fail me. I never did get an A in my field of study though.

You may be surprised to learn that I never dropped acid again. Certainly everyone assumed I was a total head. I didn't need to be. I could re-induce a brown acid style trip just by meditating. Better yet, I could end it pretty much at will. Sometimes it was harder to stop if I had any THC in me, so I cut down on my weed smoking too. I was concerned that taking acid again would send me over the edge for good.

The first inkling that I might be in for trouble anyway came in the Spring of 1971. The South Vietnamese had launched an offensive into Laos. Nixon coordinated the attack with a major renewal and escalation of the air campaign against North Vietnam. An anti-war mobilization demonstration was planned for Washington, DC, on April 30. This was intended by the organizers to be peaceful. It was an open secret that the next day, May Day, more radical activists would follow up the peaceful demonstration with an attempt to shut down the government.

The plan was simple enough. They would block DC traffic to prevent federal workers from reaching their jobs.

Six Syracuse students including myself crammed into a Chevy Nova and drove to DC. There were four guys and two girls. I had to sit in back with two other guys. None of my car mates were really my friends. We just had been sitting and talking at the same table in the cafeteria one day and decided we wanted to go.

Parking in DC was impossible. It is not that big a city and private garages easily are overwhelmed by events such as this one. We found a private parking lot in Virginia and ended up walking along the George Washington Expressway and across Arlington Memorial Bridge.

The demonstration was exhilarating. Hundreds of thousands of people, mostly young, crowded onto Constitution Avenue. They spilled over into the Mall and onto the Ellipse and all the way to Capitol Hill. It was a human sea of protest. The crowd was well mannered and peaceful. The culture of peace and love had been bruised by the events following Woodstock, but it was still alive. This would be its last big outing.

The six of us camped out on the Washington Monument grounds that night. The scene was familiar. A near solid blanket of human beings covered the ground between Constitution and Independence Avenues. A haze of marijuana smoke filled the air. Loud live rock music blared from the stage backing up to Independence.

Police were on hand but they were not in any way obtrusive. There was no effort to interfere with drug use. I entertained myself for a time by watching a thoroughly stoned young blonde help a cop on Constitution Avenue direct traffic. He was remarkably tolerant. He pled with her a dozen times to stop, but never lost his temper.

"Please get out of the street, miss. You are going to get hurt."

"No I won't. You need help." She waved directions to a bus that, if followed, would have directed it into the wall of a Roman style federal building.

"Thank you miss, but it's my job. Please go to the sidewalk."

Eventually the blonde grew tired and complied. "OK. You're a good cop!" she exclaimed as she patted his back.

"Yeah I know."

We found a spot up close to the Monument where we had a good view of the grounds. It was then that I began to lose it. It must have been the similarity to Woodstock that triggered the experience. I became the sound waves radiating from giant speakers and colliding with the eardrums of 50,000 people. I became the Washington Monument and felt the break across my midsection where construction had been halted for many years a century before. I sunk beneath the grass and became underground electric cables stretching out to a nationwide grid and pulsating my electro-magnetic fields at 60Hz.

I remember very little of the ordinary events that occurred in the immediate vicinity of my body that night. I have little recall of the passage of time. Apparently I had collapsed on my back. No one bothered me. They probably assumed I was tripping. They were right.

I snapped back into normal consciousness thanks to the stink of tear gas. It was just before daybreak. The Metro Police, the National Guard and federal troops had surrounded the Monument grounds. Gas canisters exploded in the air as Guard units began a sweep.

Literally thousands of people were herded into trucks and hauled off to RFK Stadium. The Stadium was one of the few structures able to hold that many people, so it had been appropriated for use as a temporary jail. Many of the campers managed to escape. Wanting no repeat of Kent State, the authorities had placed strict limits on the use of force. I ran with a clump of 20 young people who collided with a holding line of Guardsmen. More than half of us pushed through. Groups of police in their Civil Defense gear were in back of the Guard. They managed to grab a few more of us. They were more forceful than the Guard was. One cop grabbed my shirt and tore it but I kept running and got away. He grabbed some other freak.

As I ran I was a demonstrator face down on asphalt with cuffs behind my back. I was a cop wrestling with a bearded freak while shouting at him to give up. I was a Metro bus driver stopped at an intersection blocked by hippies. I was the diesel engine of the bus, and I could feel a saboteur reaching inside me to break my fuel line. I was the *Eyewitness News* cameraman in a helicopter filming the events from overhead.

The pain in my lungs from overexertion and the gas helped me to keep enough sense of myself to navigate. I turned right on 19th Street NW and headed north. I espied a college-age woman wearing a T-shirt and bell bottomed jeans, and I followed her. She was holding a handkerchief over her face. She unlocked the front door of a Georgian high rise near F Street. I came up right behind her and followed her inside. I had entered a college dorm. Out the front window a convoy of seven squad cars rolled by in an obvious show of force. I found it convincing.

Even inside the building, the smell of tear gas was sharp. I would be better off on a higher floor. There was a bank of elevators in the back. I stepped inside one and pushed the top button for the 8th Floor.

The air was a little better up there. The hallways were crowded with out-of-town demonstrators who had thought better of making the scene on this morning. They were sprawled everywhere with backpacks and bags of food from a local grocery. I walked over and around them to the window at the end of the hall. Two intersections were clearly visible below. Occasionally groups of five or six demonstrators would gather at one and block it. There they would stay until police showed up. Then they quickly would disperse. Presumably they reconvened on another block. Scenes such as this were repeated all over town.

The government didn't shut down. The Administration claimed that the demonstrators had the same affect on traffic as a moderate rain. This surely was a lie, but just as surely the demonstrators had failed in their goal. The war went on.

I found an open spot on the floor of the hall and settled down with my back against the wall. I became the wall. I became the building and all the people inside. I was the three couples who at that moment were making love in the building. I was the sewage flowing through pipes to treatment and to the Potomac. I was the rats who lived in the pipes. My fur itched. I was the long-haired bearded student who walked down the hall that afternoon with a pile of books under one arm as he called out cheerfully, "Back to school! The Revolution's over!"

I largely came back to myself then. I found the hall lavatory and decided to spend another night in the dormitory. The other hallway residents thinned out, but I was not alone. It was that night on the 8th floor of Mitchell Hall, ironically named after army hero Billy Mitchell, that I met my future wife.

Across the hall from me was an open door. Inside the room a half dozen students were arguing about reality and the meaning of life. Each spoke full of passion as though he or she really knew the answer and the others were being obtuse. A woman with stringy light brown hair waved me in when she saw me sitting in the hall.

"Come on in! Don't just stare at us."

I stood up and walked over. "Hi, guys, what's up?"

"Well, I'm trying to explain to these assholes that reality is like universal. You know, the whole Buddhist Nirvana thing where you become a drop of water returning to the ocean. Individuality is just an illusion where we cut ourselves off from seeing the truth," the woman said.

"Bullshit, Carolyn! We whom cutting off whomselves? Your very statement presupposes individuality!" a conservatively tressed young man objected. Presumably he understood his own question.

"Now you are being seduced by pronouns!" she responded. "Grammar is just a construct."

"I wouldn't go that far," objected a thin young man in torn jeans and green striped shirt.

"I want to know what this guy thinks," said my future wife.

"I don't know," I answered. "I haven't thought about it much."

"Think about it!" she demanded.

"Well, there is something to both points of view. You are not the whole universe, but you are an inseparable part of it."

"Cop out!" they all shouted in unison.

"What's your name?" Carolyn asked.

"Aardvark."

"Oh, like the artist?"

"That's me."

Carolyn was impressed in a way that my co-students in Syracuse were not. I was too familiar up there to be taken seriously.

"You must be rich."

"I do OK."

"I hope you give your money to the poor."

I shrugged. In truth that was something else I hadn't thought much about. I didn't even spend money on me.

Carolyn spent that night with me after insisting I get a room for us at the *Roger Smith Hotel* up on Pennsylvania Avenue.

"Doing it in the dorm is tacky," she explained. "Besides, you can afford it."

Carolyn grounded me better than anyone has before or since. Despite her willingness to give away my earnings to charity, she was the most self-centered person I ever met. Whenever I felt my consciousness bleeding away into my surroundings, I would concentrate on her. There was a black hole of need inside of her that sucked up all of my wandering attention. The furthest I could get away from myself in her presence was Carolyn herself.

Carolyn wanted a horse farm in Maryland. She wanted highly trained horses that could take her to the Palm Beach Wellington show and bring her back blue ribbons. She wanted a mansion and a swimming pool. She wanted emeralds because she liked them better than diamonds. She wanted 24 carat gold because anything less than 18 carat gave her a rash. She wanted a Porsche. She wanted a goose neck horse trailer and a heavy-duty truck to pull it. She wanted to travel Europe and stay at all the best hotels. She wanted a condominium in the US Virgin Islands. All the while she listed her wants to me, she simultaneously railed against the inequalities of capitalism, which in her opinion were unconscionable. She was perfect for me.

My friends had driven back on their own as soon as they were released from RFK, so I had to fly out of National. The police had been so overwhelmed by the numbers of arrests that they had failed to fill out individual arrest forms. Therefore charges had to be dropped against almost all of the demonstrators. Carolyn and I called each other regularly after I returned to Syracuse. Carolyn always reversed the charges.

My draft lottery number was 183. At the time it was picked it was low enough to make me a potential draftee if I lost my student deferment. That changed as the troop withdrawals from

Vietnam accelerated. In June it was announced on the news that few young men would be called up over 160. My 2S deferment was no longer necessary. I dropped out of college, bought a Porsche, and drove to Silver Spring, Maryland, where Carolyn lived with her parents. I asked Carolyn to marry me. She agreed subject to certain conditions that were, in her words, "fair to myself." These included the purchase of a "suitable" Maryland residence and ongoing support for her equestrian ambitions.

Carolyn often was fun. An example was in 1973 when I hand painted the backs of two jackets, one for each of us. The artwork was so stylized that the messages were not immediately recognizable, but if you looked closely you could see that mine read "Impeach" and hers read "Nixon." We wore them on the White House tour. We got as far as the Ballroom before a White House guard stopped us.

"You can't wear those jackets in here!"

"Why not?" Carolyn objected. "They're our jackets."

"Could you at least cover them up?"

"You're pretty good at that around here, aren't you?"

We were thrown out, of course, but it was enjoyable. The incident also made the news and that gave my sales another boost. I licensed production of those very jackets for a tidy sum.

Carolyn's incessant demands kept me sane. We bought a 900-acre estate on the Eastern Shore with a 10,000 square foot Greek Revival home, a 24-stall horse barn, and an indoor riding ring measuring 200 x 100 feet. Carolyn was disappointed because she had her heart set on something larger and closer to the city but I simply couldn't afford it. It came as a shock to her that my net worth scarcely came to more than $11,000,000 in the dollars of the day. However, as long as my art continued to sell, she could hope to trade up one day to a more respectable residence. Meanwhile, she bought a condominium in Watergate, more fashionable than ever since the scandal, and signed a long-term lease on an apartment in the East 70s in Manhattan.

Sex used to be a big risk for me. I would lose myself so much in a consciousness of mutual biology that I sometimes would turn comatose for hours. When I lost myself during the act I could feel and be blood coursing in veins, sugars absorbing through cell membranes, gametes struggling to make another human. I actually could sense amino acid molecules assembling into proteins on an RNA matrix within an individual cell. I was the proteins. I was the RNA. It is strange and somewhat disturbing that none of my partners ever called an ambulance. A few left me alone and went home. One of those was kind enough to call back to see if I was all right. "I must have done an exceptionally good job," she giggled.

Carolyn and I didn't have sex very often because she didn't much like it. She probably would have forgone lovemaking if abstinence were less contrary to her self-image and her social image as "a liver of life." Such a lack would have been hard to explain to her girlfriends and she wasn't a good liar. The woman was not a conscious hypocrite, mind you. Her most outrageous contradictions were sincerely mutually held. When we did have sex, her self-absorption with all the discomforts involved in the act kept me focused superficially on her.

The extent of her aid to my sanity can be comprehended with a description of a typical day. Such a day began at six in the morning when it was time to brew Carolyn her coffee. It wasn't right, she insisted, to awaken servants that early. Breakfast ought to be my job, not theirs.

"Don't make it weak this morning! Try measuring for a change!"

"I always use five scoops to a pot."

"You didn't yesterday. Don't argue with me, just do it!"

I prepared her coffee. She took four sugars and vanilla flavored creamer. Then I would cook her French toast, cinnamon toast, or a cheddar omelet according to her whimsy that morning. Often she would change her mind after one taste and send me back to the stove.

Afterward it was time for me to feed the horses and clean their water bowls. The stalls had self-filling waterers but some horses liked to make soup by dumping hay in them during the night, so they always needed cleaning. Then I would turn out the horses into their respective pastures. It was perfectly normal for stable workers to begin that early, but ours worked the hours of 9 to 5. The horses couldn't wait until 9 so I tended to them.

Carolyn didn't believe in exploiting foreign workers or minorities who commonly worked in stables, so she hired her old waspy schoolmates. She paid them more than twice normal wages for the job and allowed each free board for one horse. She enjoyed playing the role of generous employer at my expense. Since farm work usually runs past 5 PM, finishing up for them was my job too.

Once I was back in the house after the morning barn chores, Carolyn gave me her shopping list. On our arbitrarily chosen typical day, this included more tack and horse related equipment even though she had a large shed filled with nothing else. More show clothes also were required including two jackets at $600 each. Her newest pair of $1,000 custom boots would be ready that day and I was to pick them up as well. The list included more picture frames for the latest photographs of herself on horseback. Though I was one of the nation's most popular artists, there was none of my art on the walls of our house, but there were endless pictures and posters of Carolyn. As usual, the list also included specialty food items, on this occasion chocolate pop-tarts and vanilla frappocino. Woe betide me if I were to bring back the wrong brand.

By this time, one of her trainers arrived. Two or three of them showed up every day and helped her refine her form and technique in dressage and jumping.

"It is my dream to ride in the Olympics!" she often told me with an edge to her voice that implied I was the major obstacle to her goal.

During the day I cleaned out her car and truck, built a new display case for her ribbons and trophies, shopped for new bedspreads, and repaired two fences. Had it been a horse show day I also would have hooked up her trailer, acted as her groom, and videotaped her rides.

In the evening she had me take her latest friends out to dinner at a posh new seafood restaurant by the Bay. She insisted, as always, that I pay, so as not to embarrass her. After dinner we returned home. I fetched her juice and snacks while she watched videotapes of herself. At bedtime she was ready for a massage which lasted until she fell asleep. Sometimes this took as long as forty minutes but this was an average night and it took twenty.

Then I was allowed to sleep until six the next morning.

Naturally, my artwork production suffered, but the prices I received continued to rise into the mid-'70s. For a time, we kept our head above water although just barely.

If this existence sounds less than idyllic, remember my situation was not normal. This lifestyle was ideal for focusing my attention on my immediate surroundings. There was not much opportunity for my senses to wander beyond Carolyn's needs. I understood her nature when I married her and in large measure I got what I wanted.

Trouble started in the late 70s. My work suddenly became passé in the era of John Travolta and Donna Summer. Prices for my output plummeted when it sold at all. My income fell off precipitously. Meanwhile one of the Smythes from the pharmaceutical company Smythe and Smythe bought a 2000-acre estate several miles from us. Jane Symthe brought 20 of her prime show horses to the estate. The cheapest of these animals had been purchased for $200,000. Jane drove a Ferrari. She and her horses were headed for the Olympics.

Carolyn was livid. "I think it's disgusting that people can live like that when there is so much poverty and suffering in the world! It shouldn't be allowed. That car of hers just sucks gas. Doesn't she know there is an energy shortage?"

I made a rare objection. "But you can't survive on less than a million per year. Your truck is as bad on gas as her sports car."

"I'm pursuing a dream!" she responded as though that answered everything.

For all her disgust, Carolyn started to hang out at the Smythes. The son Kevin was a well-regarded rider on the show circuit, almost in a league with his stepmother Jane. He was already an alcoholic at age 23, but so far had suffered no legal or health consequences. He and Carolyn sometimes traveled to local shows together.

So it happened that, just at the time when my annual income fell to near zero, Carolyn's need to spend increased sharply. It would have been embarrassing to her to be left behind by the Smythes because of money concerns. She therefore began to travel with them to international horse shows with her own horses. She attended celebrity fund-raisers with Jane for left-wing causes. Mr. Smythe never accompanied Jane to these. Carolyn spent ever longer amounts of time in the District and New York. My increasing alarm at our financial situation only produced derision and anger from her.

"That is your job! When we got married you promised me said you could support me and let me keep horses!"

"Yes, but not on this scale."

"We're talking about my dream!"

In June 1979 I filed for bankruptcy. In the same month Carolyn filed for divorce. I did not answer her complaint charging me with extreme cruelty, so a default judgment for divorce was granted in the Fall. Carolyn took whatever the creditors didn't. In December of 1979 she married Kevin Smythe. They defied President Carter's ban on the 1980 Moscow Olympics and entered the equestrian events there. Their performances were unremarkable.

I was nearly destitute. I lived in a one-room apartment in Baltimore. I remained in my own self, pretty much. Poverty proved almost as effective as did a demanding spouse for focusing the mind.

Then one day I received a call from a campaign worker at the Republican National Committee. An amazing collection of people was backing Ronald Reagan for President that year. They included such unlikely folks as Civil Rights leader Ralph Abernathy and the former Democratic peace candidate Eugene McCarthy. The RNC worker once had several of my posters on his wall during his college years. On his own initiative he looked me up and asked if I would speak at the Convention. I accepted.

When my upcoming appearance at the Convention was mentioned on the news, I got a call from the ex.

"Are you entirely out of your mind? Now you're a freak-o neo-fascist! Do you know how humiliating this is for me?"

"I hadn't thought about that..."

"No, you wouldn't, you selfish bastard!"

"...but that is not a disincentive. I'm not a fascist, by the way, neo or otherwise. I'm just tired of America being pushed around. I'd like to keep more of the money I earn instead of it all being stolen in taxes. You realize there is currently a maximum marginal rate of 70%."

"You don't make any money! You don't pay any taxes. You are broke! Look what a fix you left me in after all your promises to support me! You're a loser!"

"Goodbye, Carolyn."

The RNC sent me a plane ticket and paid for my hotel. The events leading up to the Convention were so diverting that I had no trouble with my sense of self. I began to think I was cured.

I'm not surprised if you didn't hear my speech. It was after Midnight in three time zones. The Convention schedule, as usual, ran late. If you did hear me, you may have noticed that after a strong start I seemed to rush the rest of it. I used only four minutes of my allotted ten. Most people just thought I was politely trying to let the delegates get back to their hotels. The truth is that old feelings were welling up within. You wouldn't think that Republicans would remind me of Woodstock, but they did.

My political activism faltered that night. Although my consciousness began to wander again, I kept it from expanding beyond the people in the Hall. I became a right-to-life housewife from Kentucky. I became a manager of a strip mine in Montana. I became an anti-busing activist from Georgia. I became a survivalist from New Hampshire wearing a shirt with the legend "Happiness is a warm AK47." I wasn't happy with the new identities. I may have become these people, but they sure weren't me.

In November I neglected to vote. My ex and her friends, with their willingness to be very generous at the expense of others, truly had turned me off leftish politics. The Republicans themselves turned me off rightish politics. The Anderson campaign was no help to me that year. He simply combined things that bothered me about both Carter and Reagan.

My appearance on TV had one salutary effect for me personally. It reminded a large audience that I was still alive. It seems that there was a widespread misconception that I had overdosed myself into oblivion along with so many other personalities from the '60s and '70s. My phone started to ring. Enough of a niche market returned for my work that I at least was able to pay my bills.

My one big disappointment was in Wyoming. One of the

numerous post-hippie neo-yuppie Reaganites who had come into government with the new Administration offered me a chance to do some large scale temporary art in Yellowstone. It would have involved Day-Glo paint, lasers, and Old Faithful. I jumped at the chance, but it turned out that the fellow hadn't cleared the offer with his bosses. Secretary of the Interior James Watt nixed the deal the same week he canceled the *Beach Boys* for the July 4 celebration. I was, he explained, unwholesome. In my case he was right although it was hard for me to see what that had to do with anything. However, my notoriety from this cancellation beefed up my sales even more. I was able to put a down payment on a townhouse in Baltimore. I came to terms with the last of my creditors. To my amazement, *American Express* approved me for a card.

The return of modest financial security had a down side. It eased my mind enough to cause it to slip again. I found a chemical that could help: alcohol. My caution with mind-altering substances had dissuaded me from trying this earlier, but in a night of desperation I swallowed glassful after glassful of *Southern Comfort* and the stuff kept me on planet earth. I spent the next morning leaning over the toilet bowl, but it was an earthly toilet bowl.

I became a serious alcoholic for the next decade. I don't recommend this for most people, but it kept me sane. Booze took the place of Carolyn at a tiny fraction of the cost. I don't remember much else about the '80s.

My next clear memory was getting a phone call for "Mr. Aardvark" from someone named Dick Cheney in 1990. A major US build-up was in progress in the Middle East in an operation called Desert Shield. It was news to me. I hadn't kept up. Mr. Cheney remembered my appearance at the 1980 Republican Convention. He asked if I wanted to do some nose art for US aircraft stationed in the Gulf. Many of the pilots were veterans of Vietnam and were familiar with the Aardvark name. He thought they might appreciate it. It would be good for morale.

I agreed, but not out of politics. I knew nothing about the crisis at the time. I simply liked the notion of being appreciated by old fans.

I arrived in Saudi Arabia in November 1990 aboard a C5 cargo plane loaded with high-tech munitions. Somebody should have told me Saudi was a dry country. I do not refer to a shortage of water. My next few days of alcohol detoxification were terrible, but my illness kept my mind on the work in front of me.

You may have seen photographs of A10s with purple pterosaurs on their noses, others with multi-color representations of the Milky Way spiral, and still others with zoot-suited wolves. Those were mine. The pilots seemed to like them.

I settled into a routine of working in the morning, hanging out in the mess, napping in the afternoon, working some more in the evening, chatting with the soldiers, and getting a good night's sleep. I rather enjoyed it. I felt almost normal. Once again I had cause to hope I was cured. Perhaps, I thought, years of alcohol abuse had destroyed enough brain cells to stop my unscheduled trips.

I had such a good time I began to wonder if I would have liked the army. On January 16, 1991, I decided the answer was no. The previous night the first waves of F117s, F16s, F15s and cruise missiles had shattered Iraq's air defenses. As dawn broke, I stood on a runway in northern Saudi Arabia. The sky was cloudless. The sun was peeking above the eastern horizon. A hot wind blew sand in my face and some grit irritated my right eye. I watched a wing of A10s with my nose designs take off. The planes were armed with anti—tank missiles, HARM missiles, guided bombs, and 30mm cannon.

My mind left me. I felt myself soar with the aircraft. I was an A10. I felt my jets suck in air as though they were lungs. Fuel fed into them, mixed with compressed air, and exploded creating a rush of raw power. I felt out to the surface below where hundreds of pieces of artillery and heavy equipment were dug into the sand. I locked onto infrared signature of a tank. The airflow around my wings disrupted as I swooped to the right and began an attack descent. I reached out to the signature with a Maverick missile.

I was the Russian built T72 struck by the missile that was myself. I was the Iraqi tank crew who lived just long enough to understand what was happening to us. Heat seared me. Screams formed in my throats but never reached my mouths. My consciousness expanded. I was hundreds of tanks, APCs, and crews. I was hundreds of aircraft. I was thousands of 30mm shells. I was what and whom I struck.

I woke up in a hospital in Riyadh. A doctor with a heavy accent told me I had passed out at the airfield, probably from heat exhaustion. I would be sent home on the next available flight. Within an hour of reaching Baltimore I was drunk.

My health deteriorated over the next several years. I was diagnosed with Gulf War Syndrome. I didn't argue with this, even though I knew my case was special. In one respect it was not so special. I was a drunk and suffering the usual effects.

All on their own, my finances improved dramatically. The '60s had something of a revival in the '90s as the generation that had come of age then assumed the highest positions of power. The Boomers were feeling nostalgic. They started buying *Grateful Dead* concert jackets and attending movies about The Doors. They were not the only customers. There was a new generation of teenagers younger than the Boomers' own offspring and therefore not inclined to rebel against them. They bought 60s style products too. My work became very popular again. I even got contracts for TV commercials. That neo-psychedelic animated *Fresh Flowers Butter* commercial that ran all during the latter half of the '90s was mine.

Much of my restored income went to lawyers because my ex-wife sued me as soon as she realized I was commercial again. She had divorced Smythe years before and had spent her way through her multi-million dollar settlement. She argued my current success was entirely due to her assistance earlier in my career. She demanded half of everything plus a 15% agent's fee, which she insisted I had promised her. We settled out of court. Even afterwards I had enough money to be comfortable for the rest of my life provided I didn't marry another Carolyn.

I bought a nice but unimpressive home in Columbia, Maryland. There was a detached garage that I converted to a studio. Despite my health problems and my drinking I was reasonably content. I even reacquired a romantic life.

I struck up a conversation one day with a woman named Sherry who drove locally for *Federal Express*. She was at my house frequently with packages of contracts and special orders. She was in her late 30s, divorced, attractive in a tomboyish sort of way, and had a daughter just entering college. We went out. She stayed over.

The sex did not cause me mental disturbance. Unlike Carolyn who had focused my mind with the strength of her own ego, Sherry achieved the same result with friendly kindness. This was as welcome as it was unexpected. Our relationship afterwards was more than casual but less than consuming. She was a stress-free lover. I loved her in an easygoing 1960s sense. There is something to be said for nostalgia.

For her sake I cut down on my drinking. Also for her sake I did not quit entirely. I drank just enough to keep a grip on myself. She was disapproving, but tolerant.

Sherry moved in with me in the year 2000. At her urging, for the first time in 20 years I tried to pay some attention to political matters. I voted for Bush, she voted for Gore. We probably were the only mixed party couple in America who thoroughly enjoyed the election that year. We agreed on election eve that we would make love whatever the outcome, but if Bush won I would be on top and if Gore won she would be. That night and in the weeks that followed, as the counts and recounts and recounts of recounts favored first one candidate and then another we exhausted the Kama Sutra.

In 2001 Sherry was diagnosed with lung and liver cancer. She had never smoked and always had been health minded. By May she was gone.

My life since then has been gray. I am not depressed in the usual sense. It is more that I feel nothing. Not even the horrible events of late 2001 fazed me; I regretted the loss of life, of course, but I would be lying to say that the war stirred me emotionally. My emotions already had been spent.

I have not produced any art. Color means nothing to me. My unhealthy habits have caught up with me. My arteries are sclerotic. My liver is cirrhotic. My doctor calls me a walking time bomb. As a matter of survival I have had to stop drinking. This means I am quite literally losing my mind.

Last evening I walked along my quiet street. A warm breeze

refreshed my face. I smelled freshly cut grass. My consciousness leapt to the setting sun. I became hydrogen nuclei fusing into helium. I became plasma forming enormous arcs shaped by the magnetic fields which also were myself. I followed light from distant stars and became them as well. Below me I was earth's nickel iron core churning in a magma sea. With a mighty effort, I pulled myself back into my own shell. I could still smell grass. I walked home.

I read somewhere that human beings are the universe becoming aware of itself. I wonder if this is in any way true. Are my flights of consciousness real at all? Are they a connection in some sense to a greater whole or are they a self-contained insanity? Do I become that of which I am conscious? Do I leave myself behind? Is Sherry there too in any real sense? I have no answers but I know where to look for them. I have no reason to stay here. Tonight I will let go. Tonight I will be a drop of water returning to the ocean.

SOOT

Donald dreamed that he somehow missed the brake pedal. He stomped again and missed again. The Jeep Cherokee surged through the closed garage door and took out a lally column. With a dreamer's equanimity he watched the garage collapse around him. He felt himself pressed down to the seat as ceiling joists crushed the roof of his car. He worried how he was going to afford a new car. The Jeep had just been paid off the previous month. His ex-wife had gotten the Taurus, which was at her new home some 90 miles away in Weston, Massachusetts. All his bank accounts were empty.

As he slowly awoke, his first thought was how to extricate himself from the mangled vehicle. It took several seconds of coalescing consciousness for him to realize that he was not in his vehicle. He was not in his garage. He had not even bothered to garage his Jeep earlier that night. He was in bed.

Don's relief was short-lived. Something was wrong. Objects really did press on top of him and the bed was tilted at a crazy angle. Don slid an arm from under the covers and felt loose sheetrock. Straight over his head his hand encountered 2 x 4 studs. A wall had collapsed. Perhaps the whole house. With his toes he could feel 2 x 10 ceiling joists that had smashed into the edge of the mattress. Don wished his dream had been true. It would have been cheaper. He still owed his ex $50,000 on the home buyout. He hoped his insurance was up to date and that it covered whatever had happened.

He couldn't see anything. People use loosely the phrase, "so dark you can't see your hands in front of your face," but it is disconcerting when this is literally true. Presumably most of the roof perched precariously a few feet above his head.

The mattress had enough give to allow Don to slip from under the rubble and wriggle toward the headboard which, he considered, had been placed against an outside wall. If the collapse of the house had created a hole perhaps he could just crawl outside. As a sharp point of a snapped 2 x 4 stabbed into his side, he had occasion to rethink his preference for sleeping in the nude. Splinters, nails and awkwardness were the price he now paid for his comfort on other nights.

Don reached around the edge of the headboard and felt cinderblock. He was in the basement. He stopped to think about the geometry of his predicament. The headboard had been against an exterior front wall of the house. At the back of the house was a walkout basement with an exposed block foundation wall. This rear wall, he reasoned, must have shoved outward causing the first floor including his bedroom to shift off the front plate and drop to the basement.

If the house had indeed fallen rearward his best bet was to find a route directly up. The wreckage allowed enough handholds and spaces for him to work his way up. Soon one hand was over the top block of the foundation. There was only a six-inch gap at that height between the block and heavy framing. Don guessed that rafters were the obstructing lumber. The gap was much too tight to squeeze through, but there seemed to be some play in the framing. Perhaps he could push back the rafters a foot or two. Don braced his back against the foundation wall, gripped hard on two 2 x 8s, and pushed with all his strength.

A series of snaps and cracks escalated suddenly into thunder. The 2 x 8s ripped out of Don's hands as the timbers gave way in an uncontrolled collapse. Soon quiet returned except for a single noise that Don recognized as his own scream. Embarrassed, he stopped shouting and cleared his throat, which now was hoarse.

Above him, his hand felt open air. By luck he had survived again. He pulled himself over the foundation and tumbled into an English Hemlock bush. He lay there for some time without minding the minor assaults on his skin by the twigs.

Something was still odd and it said much about Don's state of mind that that a full minute passed before he noticed. He was outside, but the dark was as deep as it had been in the basement. His eyes may as well have been shut. There were no stars, no streetlights, no automobile headlights. He wondered if he was blind. The still air had a smoky taste to it. He scarcely felt motivated to leave the bush and its oddly comforting leafy smell, but he knew the situation required some action.

Once again he contemplated geometry. The Jeep Cherokee was somewhere in the driveway. The distance should be some 30 feet along the front of the house and then 10 more feet at a right angle to it. He crawled through and over the plantings to keep contact with the foundation. Irrelevantly he noted that deer had eaten most of the plantings but hadn't touched the hemlock. At last he felt driveway gravel under his palms. Turning a right angle, he crawled away from the house. Gravel and shattered glass bit into his hands and knees. He stopped after what seemed too great a distance and thought some more. Did he miss the car and crawl right by it? He resolved to go a few feet further and then double back on a parallel course. He lurched forward and banged his head sharply on steel. Don had found his Jeep.

He stood up unsteadily and reached forward. His hands grabbed a tire, which spun under his weight and tossed him back to the ground. The Jeep was upside down. More carefully, he located a door on the passenger side. It refused to open, even though Don knew he had left it unlocked. The back door was stuck too. The roof must have crushed enough to jam them. He worked his way around to the driver's side, felt for the handle, and tugged. It gave. The small ceiling bulb exploded light upward into the compartment. For a moment Don basked in it as though it were the sun.

Happy to have escaped whatever disaster had struck with his limbs and sight intact, he sat in the overturned vehicle and turned the rear view mirror up toward himself. He was surprisingly dirty but the cuts and scratches seemed minor. A tug on the headlight switch shot two highly defined shafts of light forward. The murky air almost prevented the headlights from reaching what was left of the garage. The rest of the world was as dark as ever. It was quiet too. The air probably would have felt cold had there been any breeze at all. As it was, he actually felt warm when he wasn't moving. The exception was his posterior, which was chilled by the Jeep ceiling. Only the absence of other sound allowed him to hear a muffled voice.

"Help!"

He opened the glove compartment in search of a flashlight. He always bought a new flashlight every few months and always misplaced it almost at once. Occasionally he encountered a stockpile of them in some seldom-used drawer or closet, but he never could remember where they were when he needed one.

The contents of the compartment spilled out onto the ceiling. He rummaged through the maps, candy wrappers, screwdrivers, manuals, and expired insurance documents. There was no standard flashlight, but he uncovered a mysterious set of keys. He couldn't imagine what locks they fit. The key ring had a tiny penlight for illuminating key holes. It wasn't much but it might help the caller to see him.

The voice came from the neighboring property of Fred and Judy. Their house was 600 yards away. In this rural bit of New Hampshire lake country, that was closer than average. Don kept the lighted Jeep to his back and walked toward the voice. He had to clamber over blown down pine trees. They all had fallen toward the east, which helped him maintain his orientation. He began to suspect a tornado. Perhaps a big oil depot had caught fire and added the smoke. As far as he knew, though, the largest oil tanks nearby belonged to a local home heating oil distributor. They hardly seemed enough to account for the blackness. Maybe there was a forest fire, he speculated.

"Can you see me?" he called out.

"Yes!" a woman's voice answered quite clearly now. "Turn to the left! No! To YOUR left! Straight ahead! Keep coming! That's right."

"Right?"

"Stop joking!"

Don hadn't been joking but he thought it best not to mention this. The voice sounded close. His foot caught on a limb and he pitched forward into a fallen tree. Striking a branch numbed his nose, but neither the branch nor the nose broke. The penlight in his outstretched hand illuminated the chin of the young woman pinned by the tree. She apparently thought Don's move was intentional.

"Good navigating. Are there others, or was that you hollering before?"

"Just myself."

"Look, I'm trapped under this tree, obviously. The trunk has my legs pinned and I can't quite budge it. Maybe the two of us can lift it."

"Yeah. I think I can get enough leverage near the tree top."

He was relieved to have thought of something modestly intelligent. Although reasonably bright in an academic sort of way, Don had sounded stupid in front of women often enough for the novelty to have worn off years ago. Naturally shy, his occasional efforts to be gregarious had resulted only in social blunders of varying enormity.

He worked his way toward the top of the tree and managed to get a good handhold.

"Push up when I pull. OK, now!"

Don lifted hard and felt the tree lift slightly.

"Can you move?" he asked.

"I think so. Ouch!" she yelped as she slithered out. "OK. You can let go."

A branch scraped Don's shin as the tree settled back on the ground.

"Are you hurt?" he asked.

"I don't think so."

Don sat down next to her on the grass and patted her shoulders. He felt a flimsy nightgown. She reached out to return the pat, but drew back at the touch of skin.

"Thanks," she said uncertainly.

Don was quite at a loss for words. "Do you have a name?" he ventured.

"Typically."

"Is this one of those typical times?"

"Yes."

Don tried a more direct phrasing. "What is your name?"

"What name do you like?"

This confused Don, which he presumed was the intention. He was astonished that she could speak so playfully under the circumstances. It didn't occur to him that the young woman was dealing with her own fear through a display of insouciance. Even at his best, Don was poor at social games and banter. He was far from his best tonight. He covered his fluster with a serious and literal response. Resorting to the alphabet, he picked a name starting with A.

"How about Anne?"

"I can be Anne."

"Don."

"I prefer Anne."

"No. I'm Don."

"OK Don, do you have a plan beyond sitting here in the dark? Shirtless."

Actually he did, though the plan didn't originate in the cerebral cortex. Ever since he had touched her shoulder he had been aware of a stiff sensation. Normally he would have kept this to himself so soon after an introduction. In fact, normally he would have kept such a feeling to himself long after the time was ripe to mention it. Yet tonight he let his hands wander gingerly.

It was Anne's turn to be astonished. His display of lust was untimely to say the least. It also was curiously tentative. Only this characteristic prevented a violent response on her part. She realized that Don wasn't actually dangerous and could easily be deflected. She chose not to deflect him. With the detachment of an anthropologist observing a chimpanzee, she allowed him to continue.

Don's first grope had been virtually unconscious. On the second, his conscience warned him that this behavior was inexcusable and should stop at once, but as his hands met no resistance, the less refined portions of his mind reasserted their authority. He decided to worry about manners later. While the couple made love on the grass, Don wondered if Anne was pretty. Anne wondered if Don was sane.

When they were done they sat quietly for several minutes. "Do you have any other plans?" she asked at last.

"Uh, yes," Don asked with deep embarrassment. "Maybe the two of us can rock the Jeep upright."

"We'd better hurry before the batteries wear down."

She was right. The headlights already were noticeably dimmer.

"Right. Let's go."

"Wait! Don't you want to check the house first?"

"For what?"

"Survivors," she explained patiently. "Your neighbors. My boyfriend."

Don had so adjusted to living alone since his divorce that he forgot most of the world lived otherwise.

"My boyfriend was Fred's roommate in college. We were visiting him and Judy. They're a cute couple. My boyfriend's an asshole, but we still ought to look for him. Don't mention the rape."

This description of their encounter sent a chill through Don's chest.

They walked toward the house. The penlight was almost useless. From what little they could see and feel, it was apparent when they reached the house that it was pile of rubble. Don leaned over and, remembering his own experience, shouted into the basement.

"Hello! Hello! Can you hear me?! Are you down there?"

They were answered by silence. Don began to pull at the lumber.

"Forget it, let's go," said Anne suddenly and firmly.

"But..."

"I said forget it."

Don fell twice over limbs on the walk back to the Jeep. This would have been less embarrassing had Anne the courtesy to trip just once. Rocks and twigs were painful to his feet. Anne wore sandals. Soon they stood by the vehicle. They looked at each other and then wordlessly placed their hands on the Jeep. On their first attempt to push the vehicle upright Don did not take proper account of the center of mass. The Jeep spun around 90 degrees on its roof. This was an improvement, since now the slope of the driveway could be used to advantage. He let Anne think the spin was intentional. On her part it was.

They repositioned themselves further apart and began to rock. On the sixth push the Jeep rolled on its side, perched precariously for a moment on two wheels, then landed upright with a thud. Don held his breath as it continued to roll until it lifted on the other two wheels. He breathed again when the Jeep tilted back and slammed on all fours.

"Start her up," Anne suggested.

Don looked at the key ring.

"These aren't the car keys."

Anne took note of Don's absence of pockets.

"I don't suppose you have the right ones."

Only then did Don remember he had put a spare set in a magnetic hide-a-key box when he had bought the car 3 years before. He hadn't looked for it since and had serious doubts that it had survived 50,000 miles of less than cautious driving, plus a recent tumble in the driveway. He felt beneath the rear bumper near the license plate. Rather to his surprise he found the box, which now was held in place more by crusted dirt than by magnetism. He gave it a yank.

He slipped into the driver's seat and turned the ignition. After a series of repair bills in the past year for minor items including a faulty door lock and a speedometer that simply stopped working, Don had not been complimentary about Chrysler products. When the V8 caught on the first turn and purred gently, he nevertheless resolved to buy another one.

"The door is locked," Anne said from the outside the passenger door.

"No, it's jammed. Slide in this way."

Don got out and let Anne slide over the driver's seat to the right. He climbed back in. They looked at each other for a moment.

Anne was quite pretty, despite her dishevelment and sooty face. She was twenty-something with shoulder length brown hair. He couldn't tell the color of her eyes, since in the interior light of the car they reflected red. Anne began to speak but bit her lip instead. Don realized she was reserving comment on his undress but that the silence was costing her. With some embarrassment he shut the door and for once was happy to be in the dark.

"Where to?" she asked.

"Anywhere away from here. Something terrible has happened and we have to drive out of it. South and West I think. Maybe the damage reaches all the way to the coast."

"Don't you know?"

"How would I know?"

"I mean don't you know what happened?"

"No."

Even in the dark he could feel her eyes lowering him in their estimation.

"The civil defense warning went off last night on TV because of the asteroid."

"What asteroid?"

"Astronomers picked up a dark body approaching earth yesterday. They said there was a 20% chance that it might hit."

"Rather an underestimate, I would say."

"Is that a joke?"

"Uh...yeah." Don experienced the peculiar discomfort of having an attempt at dry wit treated as idiocy. "How could that happen? Something big enough to do this much damage should have been visible months ago."

"Not really. Back in '97 a big one came within 500,000 miles of the earth. That's a near miss. No one saw it until it already had passed by."

"Why didn't NASA or the Air Force blow it up or divert it or something?"

"This isn't the movies, Don. There wasn't enough time to do anything effective. The broadcast said it already was too close to be nudged much and too big to shatter, even if we did manage to hit it with some kind of warhead."

Don heard her esteem waning with each word. This stirred his resentment. He didn't see why he should be harshly judged for missing TV last night or for being generally unversed in asteroid risks. He wasn't much of a fan of science or science fiction.

"Well, our plan is still the same. Let's drive out of the damaged area."

"This not local, Don. I went outside last night to see if I could see anything in the sky..."

"Did you?"

"No. But they said that the most likely impact was the Pacific or Asia."

"We're blacked out from something that happened on the other side of the world?"

"I guess it's not that big a world."

"I guess you're right, Anne."

"Zoe."

"What?"

"My name is Zoe."

Don's choice of names no longer rated. He hoped the new name was real so that the letter Z was coincidence rather than commentary.

If Zoe was right there was no place to go that would be much better off than where they were. Still, they had to do something to survive. They needed shelter, food, and personal defenses. Don made a decision. With his ego stung as it was, Don hoped he was acting wisely and not just posturing to regain some respect from Anne or Zoe or whatever her name was.

"OK. First thing is we had better protect ourselves. There are a lot of scumbags in the world. They're as likely to have survived as anyone. There's a gun shop in the mini-mall on 128."

"You're suggesting we loot?"

"I'll mail the owner a check. Let's pick up a few weapons and move out."

"Again, move out to where?"

"To wherever there are buildings still standing. Steel framed buildings and wind protected downtown areas probably survived. Maybe Manchester would be a good bet. There should be some emergency services, food stores, and other people.

"Other people with guns?"

"Do you have a better idea?"

"What about Wolfeboro or Laconia? Big enough without being crazy. Maybe some schools and public buildings are still there. We can escape from those places easier if the people turn out to be more dangerous than the weather, if weather is the right word for this stuff."

Don felt a breeze from her hand as Anne/Zoe gesticulated at the grimy air enveloping them.

"OK, we'll try Wolfeboro, but we'd still better go to 128 first."

"Fine."

The trip was painfully slow because of downed trees. At each blockage they managed to move, go around, or drive over the obstruction, but Don saw that a chain saw was one more piece of equipment they would need. At one point a dazed deer stood in the road. Don had to exit the Jeep and shoo it out of the way by hand. Soot collected on the windshield as they drove. The fluid and wipers smeared the glass more than they cleaned it. They encountered no other people or vehicles on the way. Eventually they neared their destination.

"The gun shop is just around this bend." At that moment the windshield exploded.

Civilized society is a soporific for the instincts. We rely on ordinary codes of conduct and forget that many people obey them only out of fear of the police. Four such citizens had beaten Don and Zoe to the gunshop. One had tried out his new shotgun on the Jeep windshield.

Zoe dove under the dash. Don, showing rather more sense than gallantry, slammed on the brake and rolled out the door. He tumbled into a drainage ditch and splashed in the icy cold water scraping his arm on the edge of a drainage pipe. He scrambled up the other side and into the brush. In order to elude detection he crawled toward the shop under cover of the brush, even though that brought him closer to the gunmen. He reasoned that the men would presume he had retreated in the direction he had come. As the water evaporated from his back he felt cold for the first time that night. Greasy black snowflakes fell lightly about.

He heard shouts and peered through the brambles toward the lights of the car. A man carrying a flashlight and a shotgun was silhouetted in the light of the open door. Another flashlight shone on the other side of the car. Two more played over the brush near where he had climbed the bank. One of those beams shifted to the road away from the shop. The Jeep door slammed shut so the interior of the vehicle was no longer visible. One of the flashlights went out too. Don wondered if he was witnessing a rape. Of course, if Zoe's choice of words was justified, he was in a weak position to moralize.

Don didn't seriously consider attempting a rescue and wasn't sure Zoe would appreciate it if he did. In the current situation, the thug with the shotgun might be a more sensible partner for getting on in the world. After all, his wife had reasoned similarly when she left him for that obscenely rich Boston investment broker. A part of him objected that this was an ungenerous view of the matter, and Don didn't like to think of himself as ungenerous. On the other hand, a more generous view would be a reason to take action now. He had no intention risking his life doing that, so he retreated into misogyny at least until the odds were better.

A distant rumble in the west could be felt before it could be heard. Shades of black shimmered in that direction and the rumble grew to a roar. The three flashlight beams froze in their positions. Don plunged through the brush, rolled back into the ditch, and crawled into the drainage pipe. Don guessed some sort of shock wave or violent storm front was approaching. A cacaphony smashed over him. Quiet returned suddenly as the air pressure dropped precipitously. He gasped for breath as his ears popped and nearly burst. His ears popped again and his lungs filled with air. He stuck his head out of the pipe. The blackness had lessened to a dark gray. High in the sky through the clouds or smoke he seemed to make out the full moon. He remembered with a start that the moon had been one quarter full the night before. The disk above was the sun.

He crawled out and peered over the top of the ditch. The Jeep was gone. So were the men and Zoe. The Jeep had been tossed at least beyond the ridge, perhaps farther. Nothing at all remained of the mini-mall but a slab of concrete and scattered bricks. No full-grown trees were left standing anywhere in sight. Had the pipe end been facing the shock wave he was sure he would have been blown out of it like a cannonball.

Had another asteroid hit? Or was this some triggered secondary effect such as a volcanic explosion? Was volcanism even possible in New England? Or was it the shock wave from last night's impact going around the world again? Don concluded that he was out of his depth. He didn't know what was going on, or what new dangers he faced. He owed his survival to accident and serendipitous stupidity. It was not wise to rely on these much longer. The best bet was to join up with someone competent. He needed help. If that meant being someone else's servant, so be it. The state motto was "Live Free or Die," but when faced with the choice he preferred to be a live lackey.

Don knew at once where to go. The gun shop owner, Hans Von Kluge, lived only a mile distant up a long private drive. Don knew him slightly from the local Rotary. For once, those boring meetings would prove useful. They certainly hadn't helped with business connections as he had hoped. Von Kluge was a survivalist and the offspring of survivalists. He lived in the family household, which had been built with a state-of-the-art bomb shelter at the time of the Cuban missile crisis in 1962. The gun club of which he was president was nearly a militia. The club held wargames once a month using paint ball ammunition. If anyone was equipped to survive disaster, Von Kluge was. Don had to hurry. The sky already was darkening again and he expected it would revert to blackness soon.

A mile is a negligible distance in a car, but barefooted after a trying day it is a very long walk indeed. Don was exhausted by the time he approached the residence — or rather the former residence. The security fencing which had surrounded the Frank Lloyd Wright style house was gone. So was the house. The Doberman whose job it was to kill intruders had somehow survived and was racing toward him at a full run.

Don was too tired to run or to fight very effectively. He accepted the prospect of being killed by a dog. The Doberman stopped short, placed his front paws on Don's chest and licked his face. Relieved at finding any human being the animal was in no mood to enforce trespass rules.

"Hello, dog."

Don was in no mood to pick any more names. He walked up to the former site of the main house with the dog at his side. It was sheared away at the foundation. Wreckage covered the back lawn and blended into the stumps of what had been pine woods. The poured concrete foundation was intact. Don descended the concrete steps to the basement with the last light from the rapidly darkening sky. The dog nearly knocked him over as it brushed by his legs. Don remembered Von Kluge boasting at a Rotary dinner about the bomb shelter underneath the lawn. Most such shelters could be entered from the basement. Don also remembered the threat to "blow away" any intruder. Don felt along the basement wall. Soon he touched the cold steel of a door.

"Von Kluge! Hans! It's me, Donald! You know, from the Rotary? Don't shoot! Please. I want to talk!"

There was no response. Don banged on the door. The door swung open with a creak.

The man who all his life had expected disaster, who actually seemed to relish the prospect, who had prepared exhaustive private defenses against marauding UN black helicopters, against bandit gangs, against civil disturbances, against class warfare, against racial warfare, and against the aftermath of nuclear war had taken no precautions against asteroids. They were not political and so they were not on his radar map. He and his family no doubt had been sleeping peacefully upstairs when the first shock wave had struck. Don wondered idly if the security system had time to sound an alarm before the house disintegrated.

Don and the dog entered the bomb shelter. He clanged the door shut in back of him and slid in place a steel bolt, the simplest but by far the best interior lock. For the first time since waking up he felt secure.

More by habit than by expectation Don reached for and found a light switch. He was pleasantly surprised by a dim light, apparently battery-powered. This was an antechamber of some kind. On the wall to the right hung four full-body protective suits. Knowing Von Kluge, he was sure they were safe against radiation, biocontamination, and chemical weapons. Overhead were infrared and ultraviolet lights which of course would help decontamination. They would require more than battery power and Don was sure Hans had provided for them. On the wall to the left were a circuit breaker and a panel with switches marked "generator." One switch was marked "start." Don flicked it and was rewarded with a mechanical growl that settled into a hum. Don reasoned that the generator was in a separate vented chamber in back of the wall so as not to contaminate breathing air. From the sound of it the machine was a diesel. This made sense. It could be fueled by the 2000-gallon home heating oil tank buried in the yard.

The Doberman sat impatiently with a "Feed me!" expression.

"OK, OK, dog. Give me a minute."

A tightly fit but unlocked door opposite the main entrance opened to a second room further out beneath the lawn. Bright fluorescents lighted promptly when he flicked the switch. The room was about 18 x 12 feet with four bunk beds, stereo, TV, VCR, videotapes that leaned heavily toward westerns and war movies, a kitchenette, and 3 more doors. The first opened to a walk-in pantry with enough canned goods to feed a family of four and a dog for a year. The second revealed a large closet that contained military-style clothing from boots to helmets plus enough weapons and ammunition to have provoked an ATF raid had the feds known about them. It also contained painting supplies and canvasses. Don hadn't known Von Kluge was an artist. The third door opened to a bathroom.

"This place would rent for $4,000 per month in Boston," Don muttered to himself.

In the bathroom was a well pump-head, a water heater that was already beginning to crackle from the flow of power, a toilet, shower, sink, and apartment size combination washer/dryer. Von Kluge didn't intend to face the apocalypse without a clean shirt.

The Doberman nudged his leg and again sat expectantly.

"OK, dog, I get the idea."

Don retrieved a can of dog food from the pantry. He found plates in the kitchenette cabinets and an electric can opener on the countertop. The dog started eating from the plate before it reached the floor. Don warmed a can of ravioli for himself while the water heater did its job in the bathroom.

The hot shower felt wonderful. Soapsuds on his skin rapidly turned sooty. Black grime spiraled down the drain. Although no injury looked serious, hardly a square inch of his body was unblemished by bruises, abrasions, or scratches. As he became cleaner, they began to sting. Some damage had been done to his feet. After toweling dry he wrapped his feet in gauze from a med kit. He retrieved underwear and a forest camouflage combat uniform from the closet and dressed for the first time that day. He felt warm, cozy and secure.

The selection of CDs for the stereo was far from his taste. Maybe he would learn to like Wagner, but he doubted it. He slipped one into the CD tray and lay back on a lower bunk. The dog jumped on top of him, but Don was too tired to argue about it. He drifted out of consciousness to the sounds of violins and mellow horns.

Don was startled awake when the dog used his stomach as a launch pad and bounded to the antechamber door. The music was louder now. Don got up and opened the door of the antechamber. Someone was banging on the outer door. Don ran to the weapons closet. He had never fired an automatic rifle, so he picked out a simple twin barreled shotgun. It was loaded.

Don approached the door and pondered what to do next. He was surprised that Von Kluge hadn't installed some sort of video security camera outside for just this situation. The man dropped a few notches in his esteem.

"Donald, are you in there?" a voice faintly sounded through the door.

"Who are you?" he called back.

"Who do you think? Zoe!"

"Are you alone?"

"Yes!"

"Wait!"

Don did not entirely trust her assurance. He turned off the lights, except for the dim battery bulb by the entrance. He quietly slipped back the steel bolt and retreated through the open door to the dark back room. He lay on the floor and leveled his aim at the outer door. He doubted anyone would see him before he could fire both barrels accurately. The Doberman stood in back of him. He apparently knew to stay in back of guns.

"OK! Come in slowly and close the door behind you!"

Zoe pushed open the door and slipped into the room. She closed the door behind her. Don still expected the gang members to burst in.

"Throw the bolt!"

The bolt slid into place. Don stood up and turned on the

main lights. By chance he stood under the light in an arrogant posture just as the climax to Rienzi blared and clashed.

"Very dramatic. I see you got the gun you wanted. And your fashion sense has improved. Slightly."

"Where are the others?"

"One of them went sailing over my head in the Jeep after I was thrown clear out the window into a ditch. I don't know about the other three. I've been trying to catch up with you."

"Why didn't you call out or something?"

"I had the wind knocked out of me! And then you just took off down the road like you were on some marathon. You might have looked for me. You might point that shotgun somewhere else too. And turn that crap down!"

"Oh. Yeah."

Don lowered the weapon and walked over to the stereo to turn down the volume. The Doberman approached Zoe and sniffed her thoroughly.

"Is he friendly?"

"Seems to be."

"What's his name?"

"Dog."

"Easy to remember."

Don took the time to look at Zoe without the distraction of an onrushing crisis. Zoe was a mess. Her clothes were scarcely more protective than Don's bare skin had been and she had lost her sandals. She surely was at least as battered as he was. She was covered in mud from the ditch although that probably saved her life. Had she been thrown by the wind into something harder, she surely wouldn't have walked away.

"Well come on in. Take a shower. I'll warm up some ravioli. Since you admire my clothes I'll get you something matching."

"Best offer I've had today."

Refreshed from a hot shower, Zoe sipped coffee. Combat camouflage was laid out for her on a bunk, but she hadn't donned it yet. Instead she wore a bathrobe that also had been in the closet. It was olive green.

"Still planning on going to Wolfboro?"

"No. I'm staying put for now. Actually, I'd like to hide the entrance better so more people don't stumble on us. We have plenty of supplies. We probably can scavenge more from other basements. There is lots of fuel in other oil tanks. Besides, I'm not feeling competent enough to face post-civilization head on."

"What do you mean?"

"I've messed up almost everything I touched. I lost my house. I lost my car. I molested you. Then I abandoned you. Twice. The only time I met anyone else I nearly got killed. My only talent is running and hiding. That worked out OK."

"That's a little harsh. You've done all right. Everyone lost his home. As for the guys you met, you're alive and they're not. You had the sense to crawl in a pipe. So you weren't Rambo. Sometimes you have to have the sense to know when you are out-gunned. That is a survival skill too. Now that you've had some practice, maybe you'll do better the next time an asteroid strikes."

"I can hardly wait."

"As for me, so you got horny. You would have backed off if I asked, wouldn't you?"

"Well, yeah. But..."

"No buts. You are right about staying here too. The snows will start getting heavy."

"It's only September."

"No sunlight. At best we'll have a really bad winter. It may be worse. This may trigger an ice age. Most folks will go south. That alone is a good reason to stay. Until things straighten out, we are safer here."

"We can scavenge the ruins for a while, I suppose, but that ice age talk doesn't sound promising. Do you think we can live in snow all the time?"

"Eskimos do it."

"I saw a T-shirt in Alaska that said something like that."

"Like what?"

"'Eskimos do it cooler.'"

"We're going to have to work on your humor."

"OK, Zoe."

"You can call me Anne if you like."

"Let's take that one letter at a time. How about Yvonne for now?"

"Betty."

"Xaviera."

As they negotiated their way through the alphabet, Don looked at the bare walls. With lots of time to kill, maybe they could do some murals with the paint supplies. Future archaeologists would need some help reconstructing the events of this time. Written records had a way of disintegrating, but shelter art could last a very long time.

He heard a rumble and his ears registered a slight decrease in air pressure as another shock wave passed overhead. It didn't cause even a ripple in his coffee. Things were going to be OK.

UNRAVEL

"Dilettante!" sneered Professor Zee, my Biology 51 professor at *George Washington University* and author of the textbook *Biology from A to Zee*.

He was angry with me for having deviated from our laboratory assignment. Instead of dissecting a frog I had assembled one. When the patchwork amphibian moved a foot the pretty young lady named Suzie who sat across from my station was as impressed as I had intended. She was not impressed in the way I had intended. She departed rapidly for the lavatory.

The professor was right about me, of course. I have some true talent, if I may say so myself, but I don't have the patience or temperament for serious science. It surprised me as much as anyone when my tinkering nearly altered the course of evolution on the planet. "Nearly" isn't the right word actually. To some degree I have altered it, but with any luck the effects will be limited and more odd than harmful. Only time will tell.

The idea for frog a la Mary Shelley had occurred to me some weeks before my professor's outburst when an article in *National Geographic* on Antarctic fauna had caught my attention. It described fish with natural antifreeze. These fish can lie trapped in ice for months. They then thaw out and swim away with no apparent harm done. This struck me as altogether marvelous.

On my own I attempted to synthesize a similar substance. My ultimate goal was to find a safe way to freeze mammals, most especially humans. There is an enormous potential value to an antifreeze formula of this sort. It would allow true suspended animation. Surgeons could take as much time as they liked on tricky operations such as transplants without risk of losing the patient during the procedure. The old sci-fi fantasy of sleeping crews on deep space missions would become a real option.

I set to work. Numerous concoctions and even more numerous lab rats later I had something promising. Four rodents were nominated to try the cocktail. I named them Dean, Sammy, Peter and Frank. I injected each of them with my latest formula and tossed all four in the freezer for a week.

The results were inconsistent. Dean was a qualified success. I removed him from the freezer, soaked him in warm water, and administered a blood transfusion. He revived. He had a disconcerting tendency to walk into walls and to follow his own tail in mindless circles, but he revived. Frank, Sammy and Peter refused to cooperate further after the deep freeze.

My brew plainly needed adjustments before it was ready for humans, but I had confidence I was on the right track. In a somewhat backwards approach to experimentation, I tried the formula on lizards and amphibians. These have, in many ways, a less delicate biology. Chemical damage therefore often is less systemic and easier to pinpoint. This would assist me in refining my antifreeze. To my surprise they weren't damaged at all. On them the antifreeze worked splendidly.

My results with lizards and amphibians inspired the experiment that annoyed Suzie and Professor Zee: I decided to freeze a frog, transplant organs from another frog, and then revive the specimen in class. It worked. The frog didn't exactly hop away, but he did show signs of life.

"See me after class, Mr. Bathory."

"Yes, sir."

Professor Zee sat behind his desk with his hands behind his head. I stood. This common classroom geography is intended to express the authority of the person behind the desk. It doesn't work.

"Mr. Bathory."

"Yes, Prof."

"Not Prof. Professor or Doctor."

"OK, Doc."

"Professor or Doctor."

"Yes, sir."

Dr. Zee sighed. He searched for words. "What kind of a name is Bathory?" he asked irrelevantly.

"Hungarian, sir."

"Do you understand Hungarian?"

"No, sir."

"Pity. Since you plainly don't understand English I had hoped we could communicate in some other language.

"Sir?"

"See if you can follow this. I'm taking the trouble to speak to you because inside your adolescent and irresponsible head lurks the larva of a very good mind. What is more, you sometimes show true innovative thinking. During the past few months in this class, despite your tendency to perform everything but the assigned tasks, you inadvertently have revealed a solid grasp of chemistry, biology, and physics. When that pretty Miss Benson asked you about Heisenberg's uncertainty principle a few weeks ago, for example, you lost her completely with your sample probability calculations for electron locations. Incidentally, you lost me too. Today's demonstration reconfirms to me that you are bored. You should be in an advanced class, not in introductory level biology. You must know that so why are you here?"

"There are more girls in this class."

"I see. Thank you for being honest. Judging by what I have witnessed, however, women are not among the many subjects you have grasped. For you, therefore, their quantity in this or any other class is not a significant number. Perhaps I should tell you that Miss Bensen didn't care about Heisenberg, Mr. Bathory; she was giving you a chance to show off because she liked you."

"Really?" I asked with interest.

"Forget it. She doesn't like you now because you showed off too much and made her feel like an idiot. She isn't likely to forgive you for that.

"Getting back to the things you do understand, do you plan to upgrade your course selections next semester to a mix more in keeping with your capabilities? Do you plan a science major?"

"No, sir. May I be honest again?"

"Please."

"I plan to get a Bachelor's degree. I don't know what kind yet. Maybe it will be a BS in biology or chemistry but maybe it will be a BA in history or English. It doesn't matter much.

"Professor Zee, I am not really trying to be a smart aleck. I'm just saying it like it is. College is fun. I enjoy all my courses immensely, except maybe the Calculus. I get my A's in it, mind you, but I actually have to work a little to get them."

"I can see how that would be a problem for you."

"Yes, sir. Otherwise school is a blast and that is how I want it to be. I am not attending college as part of a narrow career path."

"So why are you attending college — a rather expensive private one at that? Are you really here to have fun? Do you hope to broaden your mind? Do you plan to get a job or are you going to live on the street?"

"Yes to all three — I mean yes to the job rather than the street."

"I thought you just pooh-poohed the idea of a career path."

"That is not a contradiction, sir. I meant that my career would not be based on my schooling. My career, my job, will be as an investor, mostly in conservative mutual funds and federally insured CDs. My plan, you see, is to collect my inheritance as soon as possible."

"Should I warn your parents?"

"Too late. They died in an accident when I was in Eighth Grade. According to the terms of their wills, I don't get full possession of my trust fund until I am 30 unless I acquire at least a Baccalaureate from an accredited university. I don't want to wait until I'm 30. Besides, so long as I attend college and make 'reasonable progress toward a degree' the trust fund pays my tuition and pays me a monthly allowance. So basically I'm just taking whatever I enjoy that puts me on course for a degree. Any degree. The day I graduate I get full control of the whole fund. After that I plan a life of cheerful dissolution. Perhaps that sounds lazy…"

"No 'perhaps' about it."

"…but it is the truth."

"I don't doubt it. So you have no real interest in chemistry or biology or, for that matter, history or English."

"On the contrary, sir. I have an interest in them all. But I have no wish or need to be a drudge in the service of any of them."

"Well, that is a shame and a waste. You have a great potential. But it appears you have no discipline as a scientist or, from what I can see, as a human being. Everything worthwhile in life requires drudgery, Mr. Bathory. Serious scientific research is not a haphazard 'Let's try a little of this and a pinch of that.' That is at best useless and at worst dangerous. You need to ask a question properly and carefully arrange a repeatable experiment to answer that question clearly. Set up proper controls. Take proper safety precautions. Repeat everything. Have you ever done this with any of your bizarre activities? Do you even try to quantify your results? Do you keep any records at all? Are you in any sense a scientist, or are you just a dabbler?"

"I keep notes of a sort, sir. But I suppose they are not publishable in the form I have them."

"You are a dabbler. I see." He paused for nearly a full minute while staring at the ceiling. "Our discussion is over, Mr. Bathory."

Professor Zee again was right. The world is built on drudgery. Real science is narrow, plodding, tedious work. It seldom is adventurous. It rarely makes a scientist rich. Yet it is the source of the revolutions that reshape our world. I respect the process and the results. I respect the tenacity of a donkey too, but I have no desire to be one.

It happens that I myself am something of a scientific experiment, so perhaps that gives me a different perspective. I understand the perspective of the lab rat. I don't have much tenderhearted sympathy for the creature, you understand, but I do have empathy.

My father was a brilliant mathematician who inherited a small sum of money (two or three million I believe) from my stockbroker grandfather. My father turned it into more serious wealth by applying formulas for analyzing, of all things, fluid dynamics to the stock market. He credited his breakthrough insight to a review of turbulence data from a Boeing 777 wing at high angles of attack. However that may be, his investment strategy paid off handsomely in less than a decade. I suspect that he just may have been lucky with his timing. He invested during the long stock market boom of the 1990s. A monkey throwing darts at *The Wall Street Journal* could have picked out a winning portfolio in those days. My efforts to apply his formulas to the market during leaner times produced very mixed results.

My mother was a geologist. She made fairly good money too by working for a petroleum company, but she by no means was rich. What is more, she hated her job. Oil deposits meant little to her. Her real interest was volcanism. A major source of my dad's attractiveness to her was the financial independence he offered. With him paying the bills she had the free time and the resources to pursue her interests. His money wasn't all there was to it though. She had other special requirements for a husband. What kind of special requirements? The same kind my father had for a wife. That was where the experiment started.

It is fair to say that neither of my parents was socially proficient. From all accounts they were barely presentable in public. It is not surprising that by age 40 both were still single. My mother was counting the ticks of her biological clock. My dad too was in that acutely age conscious stage that men with reach at the same time as women, but with less excuse. My mom was egotistical enough to believe her personal genetic heritage was far too precious to discard. My dad felt much the same about himself. Neither wanted to dilute such marvelous genes by an admixture with those of some lesser light.

Independently, both placed ads in the *Mensa Bulletin*. Each sought a potential co-parent with superior qualities of health and intelligence. They read each other's ad and marveled at the coincidence. They exchanged e-mail and set up a time and place to meet and to exchange medical records. Each required the other to take a monitored standardized IQ test and a battery of aptitude tests. It was love at first data compilation. They married one weekend in Las Vegas and I was output one year later. They hardly looked at me again.

One may ask if their eugenics experiment was a success. Well, I am healthy enough so far. I physically take after my mom's side of the family, which definitely is the more robust. My IQ test scores are high — not phenomenally high, but in the lower regions of genius. I am very good at math by conventional standards, but not brilliant like my dad. On the other hand, I have a broader range of interests than either he or my mom. Perhaps this makes me a qualified success. However, I have personality weaknesses upon which my acquaintances often feel obliged to remark. Did I inherit the weaknesses too, or are they a consequence of the lackadaisical way I was raised? I don't have an answer to that one.

I didn't know my parents very well. I was raised by a succession of *au pair* girls from Sweden. It frankly amazes me that well-to-do women so often are willing to allow pretty 16-year-old girls into their houses. It would seem to run counter to normal human jealousies. Perhaps raising children is such an awful experience that the apparent risk to marital fidelity is worth it. In truth, the arrangements didn't damage my own parents' marriage. As far as I know, my dad never made a pass at any of the girls. He was not a charming man, of course, so even if he had, it is unlikely he would have gotten anywhere. I conclude this because I have a charm much like his and I made passes at all of them. Every single one laughed. The spectacle of a pre-pubescent boy attempting to seduce a worldly high school junior no doubt is funny. Even after my voice changed, I was amusing. I prefer to believe it still was because of my age, but I could be wrong about that. I have educed the same reaction from other young women since then.

When I was 12, my parents went on a trip to Colombia. My mother was working on a method of predicting volcanic eruptions with greater accuracy. At her request, my dad applied a variation of his turbulence formulas to data she had collected from seismic stations and from radar satellites that monitor minute topographical changes. The numbers led her to predict the imminent eruption of a volcano in Colombia. The two flew down there and climbed the mountain to examine the crater first hand. My mother's calculations were right on the money. The mountain exploded while they stood at the top. After that I lived off income from their estate.

A maternal aunt whom I had never met took me in right away. She obtained a salary from my lawyer who also was executor. I suspect there was a kickback involved, but I never investigated the matter. She then fired the current young Swede who in my opinion was beginning to look at me with a somewhat more favorable eye.

"Don't expect me to do your work for you" were my aunt's first words to me. I was to do my own shopping, prepare my own meals, do all of the household chores, and perform all of the lawn maintenance in exchange for my bedroom. I didn't mind much, even though my work always was unsatisfactory to her, because she left me pretty much alone otherwise. So long as I didn't make noise and didn't bring back guests she scarcely acknowledged me. I came and went as I pleased. Most of my meals at night were microwaved *Stouffer's* frozen dinners. They weren't bad.

My parents had left instructions that I finish prep school. The trust fund provided money for the tuition. I bought my own clothes, my own computer, my own books, and my own food with my fund allowance.

A further addition to my bank account came at the age of 18 from yet another death in the family. My maternal grandmother, whom I had never met, left me $50,000. My aunt was furious, even though she was the beneficiary the rest of the estate that totaled close to half a million. She demanded that I surrender my portion in order to compensate her for her years of care. I refused. This was very useful money to me because it was not in a trust and I was legally an adult.

I took the opportunity provided by the cash to move out of my aunt's house. She made no objection, but as I exited for the last time she muttered just loud enough for me to hear, "Ungrateful wretch."

We never spoke again, although her salary continued until I graduated college. The trust money was well guarded in locked accounts so that in the end my aunt and my attorney managed to steal only about 25% of the total. I deemed it an acceptable loss.

In the years after my talk with Professor Zee, my collegiate life unfolded according to my plan. I chose Classical Humanities, of all things, as a major. I did not continue with my antifreeze experiments. Perfecting the formula for mammals would have required too much drudgery. My pursuit of the ladies during those years was about as fruitless as the good professor predicted. I was missing some element of real attraction. I had not the looks of the pretty boy, the charm of the comedian, the swank of the musician, the physicality of the athlete, the allure of the ruffian, or the dope of the dealer. Even golddiggers left me alone because my allowance was not enough to make me appear rich, and I was cautious enough not to brag about my trust totals. On most Saturday nights I hung out with other young men and talked with them about the girls we weren't dating.

In order to get one foot out of the ivory tower, during the summer of my 20th year I acquired a license to sell real estate, which I figured was as bourgeois an occupation as was imaginable. Thus, it would be in its own way instructive. So it was. I even had a bit of a knack for it though I wasn't exactly a star. I worked in a local *Century 21* office and made commissions almost equal to my fund allowance.

Graduation day arrived. Constitution Hall is a fine classical structure a short walk from either the White House or my F Street apartment. *George Washington University* leases it from the Daughters of the American Revolution for its graduation ceremonies. There I received my diploma and, in consequence, my financial independence. I doubt any other recipient of a BA from GW in Classical Humanities that year had collected credits in particle physics, business accounting, Russian language, astronomy, Byzantine history, and pre-Colombian art, besides the usual ones in Greek drama and Roman poetry. My education wasn't focused, but it had been as enjoyable as I could make it.

I immediately returned home to Mendham, New Jersey. With a little fudge on the requirement for "two years of full time employment" as a real estate salesperson, I qualified for a broker's license.

So, I'm lazy. I can afford to be. I'm not super rich, mind you. Thirty million dollars is not as much money as it used to be, especially in this overpriced area of overpaid execs and their oversized homes. Nevertheless, interest and dividend income keeps me adequately comfortable.

I opened a one-man real estate brokerage right on Main Street. The idea appealed to me as engagingly retro in an age of chain offices, real estate franchises, and internet based virtual agencies. Besides, I enjoyed having something akin to a job without the hassle of employees or bosses. The business was useful for tax reasons, for medical insurance, and for extra income. Yet, while I dabbled in real estate and finance, I continued to read the exploits of plodding revolutionary drudges in Science magazine.

I dabbled in science in a small way on my own too. Laboratory is perhaps too strong a word for my hobby room in my converted detached garage, but I had fun there. I also had one notable success to which I alluded earlier. Although I still don't quantify my results properly, the following is a record of that success for the benefit of Professor Zee. He should know that his time and his advice weren't wasted entirely.

A dilettante has one advantage over the forest-viewing generalist or the tree-counting specialist: the leisure to pick fruit. One day a particularly ripe apple fell in my lap. An odd little man named Harvey Konovolov walked into my office looking for a rental. He was a small, unkempt, and nervous fellow who always looked as though a stranger had just shouted "Boo!" at him. There was an attempt at bravado in his choice of words, but the effect was only to underscore his timidity.

"Hello. May I help you?"

"I hope so, sir."

"No need for sirs. I'm Stephan Bathory."

"Pleased to met you Mr. Bathory."

"Stephan. Steve, if you prefer."

"OK, I'm Harvey Konovolov."

"So, Mr. Konovolov…"

"If you are Steve, I must be Harvey."

"So, Harvey. What are we looking for?"

"I'm looking for a place to live. As for you, I couldn't say."

"Uh-huh. Well, let us be more specific. Do you want an apartment or a house? How many bedrooms do you need? How much do you want to spend? You know: the usual questions."

"Are there usual answers?"

"Yes, actually, within certain broad categories."

"I want as much as possible for as little as possible."

"Not categorical enough."

"What would be enough?"

"I can't tell you. Of course, if I knew such things as whether you were single or married and had kids and how many and what ages, I probably could predict what you would want, or at least what you would accept. However, I'm not supposed to ask those questions."

"Whyever not?"

"The state legislators are concerned that the answers might influence me to select houses or neighborhoods for you in an inappropriate way."

"Don't customers tell you all that on their own?"

"Usually. Eventually. Not always. You haven't, for example. So, if you could just describe the kind of unit you need and where you would like it to be, you can keep your motives for your preferences to yourself. It is legal for me to ask what you can afford. Necessary, too. I've learned not to prejudge that one even without the prodding of the law. I've met millionaires in rags and bankrupt poseurs in tuxedos. Which may you be, Harvey?"

"I'm not wearing rags or a tuxedo."

"I'll try to overlook that."

"Has anyone ever told you that you have a flippant approach to your business that discourages trust?"

"Yes, and that is unfortunate. You'll find that I do my job quite well and that I'm rather honest."

"As opposed to being honest without qualification?"

"Oh, now that is a very unlikely degree of virtue, which is just as well since it would be socially very objectionable. Tell me, would you believe someone who told you that he was honest without qualification?"

"Hmmm... Probably not."

"Good call. Count your silverware when that man leaves your table because he is a liar on a grand scale."

"I don't have silverware. My knives and forks are stainless steel."

"Fine. Now I know how much you can afford. How many bedrooms would you prefer?"

Harvey laughed nervously.

"OK, OK. Not for the record, by the way, I'm single and have no kids. I don't need a very big place. I'm more interested in privacy, so a house would be better than an apartment. I want to spend only about $1,600 per month. I gather that limits my options around here."

"Yes, that does limit your options to something close to zero, but by sheer luck I may have something for you."

Buyers always lie about what they will spend. I added the usual 25%.

"One of my own properties at $2000 went vacant over on Schoolhouse Lane. It is a four-room cottage in back of a larger house, but because of the trees it is very private. In fact, about two acres of trees separate you from the other house. It has only one bedroom, but there is a nice fireplace in the living room. The place has a lot of charm."

"Charm? That means it is small."

"You've rented before."

The cottage was less than ten minutes from my office. As Harvey had deduced, the house was small, but it really was charming as well. There were wood paneled walls, beamed ceilings, oak plank floors and a floor to ceiling brick fireplace. The property was bordered on all sides by mature pine and spruce trees. Howard Hughes might have found the setting too public, but a recluse of any lesser order could be happy there.

Harvey liked the looks of the outside.

"It's cute. How far are we from Route 10?"

"Is that where you work?"

"Um, yes. At Nucleicorp."

"That's a biotech firm of some kind, isn't it?"

"Yes. Of some kind. I just transferred in from the company's Delaware labs."

"Manager? Technician? Scientist?"

"The last two, I guess."

"So you are a biochemist or some such thing."

"Right."

"If I may ask, is that lucrative?"

"For the company, yes. For me, not especially. That is why I am looking at a one-bedroom cottage. I manage to pay my bills, but my checking account rarely makes it above four figures and sometimes goes below two. I guess my old plan to be a millionaire by the age of 30 is in trouble."

"When will you be 30?"

"May 1st."

"Ah. Yes, that might be a tight schedule. Anyway, you are less then 20 minutes away from Route 10. Go right out of the driveway, go all the way to the stop sign, turn left on Sussex and go straight. You'll run into Route 10 in Succasunna."

"Cool."

"Let's look inside."

Harvey peered cautiously into each room as though he expected something alarming. Harvey plainly never recovered from the high school experience endured by members of his species. Hollywood movies and the gratifying success of Bill Gates notwithstanding, brainy teenage outcast nerds seldom get their revenge. They get by. Nor are the linebackers who terrorize them destined to be janitors. They often end up as corporate managers with control over the R&D budget and the nerds' paychecks. So, when I asked about his work, Harvey was pleased that someone showed genuine interest and respect. Of course, I would have pretended to pay attention even if for some reason he had recited the Republican Party Platform. That is a basic sales technique. But in this case he really piqued my curiosity.

"My job is to work with DNA."

"Toward what end? Is your work forensic or medical?"

"Pharmaceutical. I was transferred up here because of my experience with individual cells."

"Individual cells? I thought DNA usually was extracted in batches."

"Yes, that's right, but that doesn't give you much insight into what a strand actually does."

"So you find out what it actually does somehow and you use that information to develop new medicines."

"Or, in a sense, old ones. The most likely source of pharmacologically active chemicals is a living cell. Interactive evolution, you know. Many researchers collect exotic species of plants and animals and test any new compounds they find. But cells know how to make more chemicals than they actually bother to make. The coding is in the DNA."

"Do you mean that you coax cells to make chemicals that normally they don't?"

"Right. Genes have folds and markers which say, in effect, 'Start reading here and stop reading there.' The rest of the DNA strings, most of the lengths really, are unread. But it's not just gibberish. Much of it was once active in ancestral cells when the folds and markers were in different places. Evolution stuffed these sections into the inactive file so to speak. So even well-known species have a wealth of unexploited data."

"Enter Harvey."

"Right. I designed a mix of radical molecules that identify and attach to probable sites of earlier markers. They re-establish the markers and reshape the DNA strand so it transcribes its data onto RNA. The RNA in a number of steps manufactures the archaic chemicals. Naturally, there is some degradation or mutation from the original combinations, but a surprising amount of paleobiological information remains intact."

"You perform these DNA manipulations inside actual cells?" I asked.

"Yes. That is the point of my technique."

"Living cells?"

"Well, yes. They would have to be or why bother? The idea is to get them to produce the final proteins or whatever. We've transplanted some of our more interesting modified genes into *e. coli* bacteria too."

"What about larger plants or animals?"

Harvey smiled. "Genetically modify them with this method? Bring out some old biology in them?"

"Yes."

"Well, naturally I've thought of it. Who wouldn't? But it is not really practical and there are no clear benefits. That is not to say I don't work with a few cells from large organisms, but since each cell contains the entire genetic code, there is no need to work with a whole plant or animal. Besides, that would be more in the area of agriculture than pharmaceuticals. Other firms specialize in engineered crops and such."

"Leaving aside your company's specialization for the moment, why isn't it practical? Scientifically, I mean, rather than economically."

"Trying to modify a large organism almost surely would kill it, perhaps quite painfully. That would be playful at best and cruel at worst."

"Is ethics the only problem?"

"No, but perhaps you should rate ethics more highly than you seem to do. There is a technical obstacle too. Assume for the moment that what you propose would be both harmless and painless for the subject. There simply is no adequate method to do the job."

"Why not? Why wouldn't your radical molecules work as well on a bunch of cells as on one?"

"Because a multicellular organism is more than just a bunch of cells. The problem is with delivery. My modifiers are highly reactive. I insert them directly into the nuclei of single cells in order to get them to the DNA. But the fact is that they would never survive in a digestive system, or in a bloodstream, or soaked into a root. They wouldn't make it past a cell membrane on their own. They would attach to everything. Without cell by cell injection, I doubt it is possible to get significant amounts to any nuclei, even if we used quantities lethal to the organism."

"Which would defeat the purpose."

"Quite."

"Well, even on the unicellular level it all still sounds exciting. Why aren't you rich?"

"Oh there are lots of people reading and manipulating DNA with different techniques these days. I'm replaceable. My company sees no reason to overpay me."

"Do you like the cottage?"

"The cottage? Oh. Yes. It's fine. I think I'll take it. Just one question."

"Yes?"

"In whose backyard am I? Who has the main house out front?"

"Those are two questions. The answers are mine and I do."

"You live right in front?"

"Yes."

"I see. Do you have kids? Dogs?"

"No. I'm single. I have a cat."

"OK, I'll take it anyway."

"See, you're beginning to trust me already."

Biotechnology firms have been the darlings of daring venture capitalists for thirty years. By and large the money has been frittered away. Conservative investors have taken to borrowing an old joke from the fusion power industry: "The technology of the future; always has been, always will be." I am too cautious an investor to have been burned by biotech, but I keep a close watch on the industry all the same. There really is tremendous potential and there have been a handful of spectacular commercial successes, but without inside information the odds of picking a winner are better at the Meadowlands Race Track.

A week after renting the cottage to Harvey, I sat in my office with my feet up on the desk reading *Scientific American*. There were some phone calls to which I should have been attending, but they could wait an hour or two. One article was about cows that had been genetically altered to produce antibiotics in their milk. There also was an unrelated article about the increasing use of carbon nanotubes in everything from airplane wings to semiconductors. A nanotube in essence is a single large molecule, a characteristic that gives it remarkable tensile and electrical properties.

I stopped reading and for a while pondered the role of fashion in science. Oddly enough there are fads even in chemistry. Near the end of the 20th century scientists had discovered carbon molecules in the shape of soccer balls. Typically they were carbon60 or carbon70. They were named buckminsterfullerenes after Buckminster Fuller, the architect who designed the geodesic dome.

For years the hollow tiny carbon soccer balls were all the rage. Commonly known as buckyballs, they seemed to have many possible applications. They could make a lubricant superior to graphite. They could alter the electrical properties of semiconductors. Medication, it was suggested, could be encapsulated within them. An impurity added to the spheres could function as molecular zippers. The chosen impurity would attach to a specific structure at a specific site and release the medication. Perhaps because there were other methods of achieving the same ends, nothing much practical came from these ideas. There are lots of lubricants, for example, and it seems that every week some drug company heralds a new "silver bullet" medication.

Along came the discovery of nanotubes. They were sometimes called buckytubes. Suddenly everyone seemed to forget about the balls because the tubes were the happening thing. The electrical properties of nanotubes were far more interesting than those of buckyballs. Structural applications were immediately obvious.

Near the end of the buckyball fad I had played at manufacturing them in my home lab. I made excellent grease and sealant from them but I didn't develop anything that would qualify for a patent.

The production process for buckyballs is not very complicated. A carbon arc fullerene generator can be put together out of spare parts found in any mechanic's garage. Blend powdered carbon with a toluene solvent and pass the blend through an electric arc. Remove the toluene using a rotary evaporator. What is left behind is mostly C_{60} with small amounts of larger fullerenes.

If you need pure C_{60} for some reason you can separate it by liquid chromatography. Dissolve the fullerenes in toluene again and pump the stuff through a column of activated charcoal mixed with silica gel. The magenta C_{60} comes off first, followed by the red C_{70}. Collect the different color solutions separately and remove the toluene from each using the rotary evaporator again.

Given the relative simplicity of producing buckyballs, one wonders why it took so long for the molecules to be discovered in the first place. The answer must be that no one was looking for them.

As I daydreamed about all this, an idea formed in my mind. I dialed the phone.

"Hello, Harvey?"

"Yes?"

"It's Stephan."

"Hello, landlord. I've been meaning to talk to you about the water pressure."

"Never mind that now. A question for you. Those radicals you whipped up for DNA manipulations. Are they patented and, if so, by whom? What rights do you have to them?"

Harvey paused before answering. "Everything I make or discover belongs to my employer. But no, in answer to the patent question. The specific technique I use is considered proprietary. However, it is not really clear that it meets the criteria for a patent; so the company hasn't gone to the expense of trying to get one. A patent might be counterproductive anyway. Why give the competition such a detailed look into our business? Besides, I regret to say that the radical molecules you are talking about are not as valuable in a commercial way as you seem to think. There are lots of other ways to read or play with DNA.

"Why the interest? What do you have in mind?" Harvey paused again before adding with pleasantly outdated slang, "Let me point out that industrial espionage is not exactly my trip even when it is worth it."

"Not espionage. I would like to propose an experiment with some commercial possibilities. I need your help and the pay-off could be substantial. I don't see how anything that comes out of my hob... um... laboratory, or that we say comes from there, should belong to your employer. Have you got plans for tonight?"

"Nucleicorp has plans for me. They want me to work overtime. I'm on my way out the door now. I probably won't be back before midnight. Maybe another day."

"Tomorrow is Saturday. Do you have plans tomorrow?"

"Yes, actually. I was going to Philly to see my mom. I figured I'd stay overnight."

"That's the only excuse for staying over in Philly that I would believe."

"Hey, I've heard all the jokes, but I'm from Philadelphia and I like it there."

"You worry me, Harvey. Anyway, you can go visit your mom Sunday, can't you? Let's go into New York for a bite tomorrow evening."

"New York? I don't know. That is a place I don't much care for. Besides, I'd hate to kill the whole day until then," Harvey complained.

"We won't waste the whole day. We'll go in early. Catch a show or go to a blues bar or a strip club or something."

"I don't go into places like that."

"Which of those places don't you go into? Never mind. How about doing something more bucolic then? Do you like horseback riding?"

At last there was a trace of interest in his voice. "Yes, actually. I haven't been riding since I was a kid."

This news was awkward. Neither of my horses was ideal for an inexperienced rider, but I would just have to chance it.

"Great. Stop by my house around noon. We'll head out to the stable and go on a trail ride. If you're up for it we can have dinner afterward. We can talk about your rent, your security deposit, and chemical supplies. And you can tell me what you know about buckyballs."

"Buckyballs?"

My horses boarded at a stable in Long Valley, about 15 miles West of Mendham. It had been named German Valley until 1917. Apparently "long" was the best alternative adjective the locals could dream up on short notice when war was declared. Nestled on the valley plain, *River's Edge Equestrian Center* is located off of West Mill Road on the way to Califon. It is a lovely setting. True to its name, it is on the edge of the south branch of the Raritan River. On the other side of the river rise wooded hills with miles of trails. The best trail is over a buried gas pipeline. The gas company is obliged to keep the right of way passable for their own vehicles so the path is broad and the footing is good.

Harvey sat in the passenger seat of my Suburban wagon as we turned into the farm driveway. We pulled up to barn "B" and parked. The barn was painted an awful hunter green. Riders who horse show in hunter/jumper divisions are inordinately fond of this color. Most of the horse blankets, half of the T-shirts, and a plurality of the automobiles on the premises also were this shade of green.

"Very pretty," commented Harvey. "How long have you been riding?"

"Since I was a teenager. It was part of the sports program at the snotty little prep school I went to in Gladstone."

"You're a preppy?"

"Yes. Bonnie, my riding instructress back then, would be disappointed in me though. I gave up English and now use a Western saddle for trail riding. I like to believe that I am a neutral in the saddle war and that my choice is just for comfort, but maybe I'm taking subconscious revenge on her for never acknowledging my schoolboy crush."

"Ah. Is this mostly a Western stable then?"

"Gosh, no. There are 30 other boarders here. They're all English riders. Moneyed show circuit types mostly. They just barely tolerate me."

"Then why did you chose this barn?"

"For the women, to be honest."

"What women?"

"90% of regular English riders are female. I don't know why. More than a few of the remaining 10% are gay. Again, I don't know why. Anyhow, I figured that a predominately English stable gave me good odds."

"Did your gamble work out?"

"No. I should have known better. Firstly, most are offended by me."

"And you figure that is on account of your saddle?"

"What else? Secondly, it turns out the women here are too young, too old, too married, or bear too much resemblance to their horses."

"I see. Well, where are our horses?"

"In the second pasture on the right. Grab a couple of lead lines from the back of the car. You bring in that light palomino way down by the far fence. His name is Malo. I'll get the paint next to him named Pollack."

My two colorful quarter horses stood out like sore thumbs in the fields full of chestnut and bay thoroughbreds and warmbloods. The palomino had earned his name. He had an evil temperament. I knew he would allow Harvey to catch him and lead him back to the stable though. He always had high hopes of being fed there. The paint was better natured but was much more inclined to spook. I didn't want him dragging Harvey across the pasture.

The mid-afternoon summer day was warm but not oppressive. Malo pleased Harvey by walking up to him when he spotted the lead rope. Pollack made me walk the entire way across the pasture to him. Both behaved well on the walk back to the barn, except at one point where Pollack decided one fence post looked particularly frightening. He froze with eyes wide and nostrils flaring until he gathered courage and leapt past the post. The leap pulled me into the air, but I landed on my feet.

We put the horses on cross ties inside the barn and I retrieved the tack from the tack room.

Further down the barn aisle stood Kristen Van Der Weide next to one of her warmbloods. While braiding her animal's mane, Kristen repeatedly eyed our Western gear and us. She wore an expression appropriate for watching junkies vomit in a gutter. A skinny and leathery 38-year-old horse show veteran, Kristen's equestrian passion was financed by her financial consultant husband. In the evenings and on weekends he often was at her side fetching brushes, polo wraps, saddle pads, and whatever else she might demand in none too pleasant tones. It was hard to reconcile this meek subservience with his obvious success as a hard-nosed businessman.

So far Malo was being polite, but I knew it wouldn't last. He allowed Harvey to brush him and even to pick his feet, but I was concerned about the saddle.

"Do you know how to cinch a Western saddle?"

"No. The few times I've ridden I did English."

This was a break.

"OK, I'll do it. Stand by Pollack. He gets panicky if you leave him alone on the cross ties."

Harvey did as I said. During the saddling process Malo bit me on the arm and tried to cow kick me twice. Harvey was too busy petting Pollack to notice. After the usual struggle to get the snaffle through his clenched teeth, he bit me once more. Malo was ready. The paint tacked up easily.

We led the horses out to the mounting block. Twice Malo pulled Harvey off the mounting block before he could get a leg over the saddle. Finally, I held Malo in place while Harvey got on his back. This was successful only because Malo was distracted by the proximity of Pollack whom he was trying to bite by reaching around me. I hopped on the paint and we walked off to the river.

The Raritan River's southern branch is no Mississippi. At this location it was 18 feet across with a median depth of eight inches. However there were pools and hollows three feet deep or more so one needed to pick one's footing carefully.

"About buckyballs, Harvey..."

"Not now, Stephan. Is Malo OK with this?"

"Crossing water? Sure."

This was true. One of Malo's virtues was that he feared nothing. He went wherever a rider pointed him. He didn't always go at the right gait. He would bite the rider and any nearby horse at any opportunity. He kicked. Sometimes he would buck. Nevertheless, he went where he was pointed. This made him a better trail horse than most.

"Stay behind me because I know where the deep spots are," I advised.

"I presume you mean to avoid them, not go into them."

"Yes. We'll go swimming another day."

We waded into the stream. Pollack suddenly leapt three feet sideways and frightened himself again with his own splash. Malo stood placidly in the water.

"Am I supposed to do that?"

"No. My horse saw a fish. He must have thought it was the Great New Jersey River Shark."

"Is there such a thing?"

"Pollack thinks so."

We completed the crossing, and, as Pollack walked up the riverbank, Malo bounded up behind him and bit his rump. The paint jumped but didn't kick. Harvey was holding his horse too tight.

"Loosen up your reins. Believe me, he'll act better. He gets angry if you hold him tight."

"What if he runs off or tries to buck?"

"Then tighten him up. About buckyballs..."

"I can't concentrate on that now. I'm still a little nervous. Please don't use words with 'buck' in them."

"OK. Want to try a trot?"

"OK."

We picked up the pipeline trail and began a trot. Pollack shied at a squirrel, a wren, a ground hog, and a twig. Malo trotted steadily. Glancing back, I could see that Harvey was bouncing uncomfortably. I held up a hand.

"Walk. Having fun?"

"Sort of."

We approached a bridge where the Raritan doubled back on us. The bridge was only six feet wide and had a wooden deck. There were no handrails. The bridge was ten feet above the river surface. Old stone headwalls on each side of the river indicated that this was once the site of a more substantial bridge. Probably the old Rockaway Valley railroad line, torn up for scrap in World War One, had crossed here.

"I don't know about this Stephan."

"Relax. Malo has been over this bridge dozens of times."

So had Pollack, but he still stepped gingerly and hyperventilated the whole way. Malo followed quietly.

"I must admit, it is very beautiful out here."

"Yes, it is. About fullerenes…"

"Can we just relax for a while?"

"Sure."

We rode on for the better part of an hour in deep woods. Harvey gained confidence as we went. He loosened up on Malo's mouth. Both he and his horse seemed to be enjoying themselves. The over-rich fragrance of honeysuckle was intoxicating. Birds chirped noisily. I relaxed and almost dozed.

There was a sudden clatter. Two bicyclists wearing shorts, helmets, and elbow pads whizzed past us at high speed from behind. Pollack reared up twice, backed into a tree, and then jumped forward. Malo stopped cold. His ears went back. The bicycles already were out of sight around a bend in the trail but their clacking was still faintly audible.

"Harvey, better tighten up your reins now."

"Why?"

Malo dropped his head sharply, which pulled the reins out of Harvey's loose grip. The horse took off at a full gallop in pursuit of the bicycles. Harvey hung on for dear life and struggled to regain a grasp on the reins. Horse and rider disappeared around the bend up ahead.

"Oh shit."

I pushed Pollack forward into a canter. We caught up with the bikes and Malo a quarter mile ahead. One bicycle leaned against a tree. The other was on its side. One cyclist, a twenty-something man, was helping a young woman to her feet in a ditch next to the trail. Beyond them Malo stood quietly on the trail. Harvey, still in the saddle, looked shaken. The young man climbed out of the ditch and raged.

"What the hell is the matter with you?! You could have killed us! What were you trying to do, trample us? Moron! Get off that horse and I'll kick your ass! I ought to sue the shit out of you too!"

"I'm so very sorry," Harvey mumbled.

"Don't apologize, Harvey. Look guys, the horse doesn't know any better. You two do, or should. You scared Malo and made him angry. I don't blame him either. Try announcing yourselves a little better next time."

"You son of a bitch!"

"Have a nice day."

"Screw you!"

The cyclist's companion was silent but she concurred by giving us the finger.

I turned back toward the stable. Harvey followed. Malo was mellow.

"Well, that was entertaining."

"For whom?" asked Harvey in a shaky voice. There was blood on his upper lip.

"Harvey, what happened to your lip?"

Harvey wiped the blood with the back of his left hand. "Nothing. It's my nose. When we cut off the bikes Malo planted his feet and threw up his head. I smacked into it."

"See, he was taking care of you. He didn't want you to fall off so he caught you." This may have been true, but it was just as likely that he deliberately had hit Harvey in the face for less amiable reasons.

Harvey seemed to be too distressed to discuss chemistry, so the plod back to the stable was quiet. As both horses knew they were going home they were content and mannerly. Harvey seemed to relax again by the time we reached the river. It was early evening. The temperature had fallen and a mist rose off the river and the fields beyond. The effect was eerie. The horses waded through the river and quickened their pace for the remaining distance.

While we untacked our horses in the stable aisle, Susan the barn manager approached us. In appearance she was a near clone of the Van Der Weide woman.

"Are you going to Vetrolin their legs?" she asked.

"No. We walked the whole way back. They should be fine."

Susan huffed.

"I've been meaning to talk to you about something."

"Yes?"

"This is a show barn and appearance counts for a lot. It is part of the atmosphere."

"What appearance is bothering you?"

"Your tack. All that Western gear just doesn't look right in the tack room."

"Why not?"

"You know why not. This is New Jersey, not Wyoming. The US Equestrian team is only two miles from here. The Cheyenne Rodeo is two thousand miles."

"This is western New Jersey."

"Very funny."

"OK, where should I hide my tack so that it won't offend passersby?"

"There are a couple of extra racks in the feed room."

"OK. No problem."

"Aren't you putting Rainmaker on their hooves?"

"No ma'am."

Susan grimaced and walked off mumbling something to herself. I'm not sure, but I think she said, "Western assholes."

"She doesn't like you very much."

"No she doesn't."

"I'm surprised she doesn't throw you out."

"I always pay my board on time. You'd be surprised how rare that is."

"Have you thought of moving to a Western barn now that you've abandoned your quest for dates here?" asked Harvey.

"I like this location. Besides, folks in those other places laugh very cruelly at English riders. Strangely enough, I'd rather be the taunted than the taunter. In a way I feel I am an asset to this place. Normally hunter-jumpers hate jumpers for being hard on their horses. The jumpers hate hunter-jumpers because they are prissy and the judging is too subjective. Both dislike dressage riders for being too formal in their riding. The dressage people despise all the others whom they believe can't ride at all. But because I'm here they all can dislike me. I thereby promote social harmony."

"Surprisingly noble of you."

"No, I don't mean it that way. I'm neither a masochist nor a particularly kindly person."

"That hadn't been my impression of you either."

"So I can't explain my reaction really."

"I think I can. You enjoy being outsider because it makes you special. I also suspect you are not a team player. You don't enjoy taunting people because they wear a different color jersey. You prefer to taunt people out of personal malice."

"Well, that is very generous of you to put it that way, Harvey. Thank you. Anyway, we should stop back at the house and change before going into New York. We smell like our horses."

"New York? You know, I think maybe I'll pass on that. I told you I'm not fond of that place. Besides, I was up most of the night at work and this trail ride wore me out."

"No, I mean to treat you to a meal and that is all there is to it. Besides, I want to talk to you about something."

"So I gather. OK, but can't we eat around here somewhere?"

"Trust me, Harvey. You'll like where we are going."

On the drive back to Mendham, Harvey began to talk about the ride. He praised the scenery and finally found some humor in the way Malo ran the bicyclists off the trail. By the time we pulled in my driveway he had convinced himself that he had enjoyed the whole experience.

We changed in our respective neighboring homes. Harvey then walked through the woods to my driveway, climbed into my car and promptly fell asleep. He didn't wake up when I slid behind the steering wheel and slammed the door. Harvey wore a rumpled cheap gray suit. I wore a tan corduroy sport jacket. I had learned the bachelor's trick of picking clothes that resist rumpling even when tossed on the floor for several days.

Traffic was unusually light on the way to the Lincoln Tunnel, and the backup at the EZ Pass tollbooth was less than 5 minutes. Harvey snored as we traveled beneath the Hudson River. When we emerged from the tunnel, I cut across town on 40th Street. It is a rather dingy street but it is one way. This prevents the bother one has on 42nd of making a turn against oncoming traffic when going uptown.

I turned left on Third Avenue. We hit our first major jam in the 50s. We inched forward beneath the Citicorp building, a glass monolith perched alarmingly on spindly legs. Moonlight glinted off its odd slanted roof. I read once that it avoids toppling over in the wind through use of a dynamic damper. This is a large spring-loaded slab of concrete near the top floor that moves opposite to any sway and so damps it out. It seems to work. A sudden gust blew papers along the sidewalk. Harvey awoke.

"Where are we?"

"Third and 53rd."

"New York? Already?"

"Yes. Feeling refreshed?"

"Yes, actually. Wow, traffic is terrible. You must have had a lousy drive."

"I should have taken Park Avenue. I think the backup is for the 57th Street Bridge."

"Oh, we should be out of it soon then. Where are we going?"

"*The Manhattan Café*. It's on First between 63rd and 64th."

Eventually we broke through the clogged roadway and found a parking garage on 63rd Street. The hourly parking rate was four times the national minimum wage, about average for Manhattan. From the garage it was a short walk to our destination.

The *Manhattan Café* is a landmark restaurant that tries to recapture the atmosphere of the great steak houses that served robber barons more than a century ago. Heavy on woodwork and heavier still on service, it succeeds fairly well. The restaurant serves some of the best basic American fare in New York City: chops, seafood, and excellent vegetables in heaping portions. All can be washed down with selections from a solid wine list. Only an anorexic could view the table and smell the aromas without slipping into a warm sense of contentment. The experience is worth the tab on which prices also are provided in heaping portions.

There is nothing like a table piled with wonderful food to produce fellowship. I allowed alcohol and cholesterol to worked further attitude adjustments on Harvey before I sidled into the business at hand.

"How is the genome business, Harvey?"

"Pretty good, but that is not exactly what I do. We don't really try to map the entire genomes of species the way Celera does."

"Tell me, is there as much duplication of genes among species as they say? Popular magazines like to quote that we share 99% of our DNA with pygmy chimps. If that number is about right it would account for a lot."

"Yes, that is right; but it is deceptive. Most of that DNA is not expressed in either species and much of the remainder is information basic to the functioning of any eukaryotic organism. We also share a huge chunk of our DNA with turtles and a surprising percentage with houseplants. There is a lot of data packed into the differences."

"So there is a leafy turtle in each of us."

"Well, in a sense; but not literally. It's just that we share more common functions with other creatures than you might think. There is a lot of hidden ancestral information besides. Bringing that out is the whole point of my work, of course. So, Stephan, why have you been talking about buckminsterfullerenes all day?"

"I've been trying to talk about them, but without much success so far."

"Here is your chance. Pass the sour cream please."

"Sure, here. Umm... Listen, are your radicals small enough to fit inside buckyballs?"

"Inside buckyballs? I'm not sure, to tell you the truth. Possibly.

Probably. Maybe not Carbon60. But if not, maybe Carbon70 or 80. Why would you want to put them in buckyballs?"

"You said the radicals couldn't survive in the bloodstream of a large animal. The buckyballs could protect them, couldn't they?"

Harvey looked thoughtful.

"Yes, I suppose. But what would that accomplish?"

"Suppose we were to develop just the right buckyballs with just the right impurities and structure…"

"We?"

"… that could protect our radicals and could pass through cellular membranes and could attach themselves to the nuclei…"

"That's a lot of 'coulds'."

"…and could unzip themselves there and deliver the radicals to the genes of an adult wheat plant, lizard, or maybe a cow. What would we likely get?"

"A dead cow."

"Suppose it lived."

Harvey toyed with his spoon in a bowl of creamed spinach before answering.

"Well, we wouldn't get some huge Pleistocene bison if that is what you mean. An adult plant or animal already has its parts fully in place and isn't going to grow into anything radically different. Its body chemistry might change in unpredictable and probably unhealthy ways though."

"So we might get a more ancient type of bison milk out of it."

"Maybe. One in a billion shot. It is nothing to bet your life savings on." Harvey cut another slice of sirloin.

"You see where I am going with this."

"Yes. You are trying to reproduce archaic biochemistry in large plants and animals. Could you pass the sautéed onions, please?"

"Sure. More wine?"

"Uh… OK."

"What if the organisms were not adult?"

"Well, now that is a more interesting question. If they survived at all they might develop somewhat strangely."

"Joint venture? 50/50 split? The investment shouldn't be all that much and the returns could be huge."

"I can't tell if you're joking."

"Assume I'm not."

"Well, to humor you for a moment, this is very long-term research you are talking about. The investment actually would be enormous. Even if I hit on the right techniques and chemicals tomorrow we would need extensive study and follow up to do the job properly. We have to start with microbes and small plants and work up from there as we learned more about what we were doing. We don't know anything about the potential dangers. We need a lab where we safely can isolate biohazards because we could alter disease bacteria or viruses accidentally. Then there are FDA approvals for anything useful. That would take tens of millions of dollars and it is anyone's guess how many years. That's really why I work for a big company rather than work on my own. This whole scheme could take decades and huge amounts of money."

"When rules are too annoying or costly to obey, people ignore them. They jam open safety doors, they disconnect catalytic converters, they pour used motor oil down the drain, they silence warning beepers..."

"What's your point?"

"Those expensive safety precautions you mentioned are unnecessary. We can do the research well enough on the cheap. I think you are exaggerating the risk. After all, you're not whipping up anything new, just re-expressing something old. The planet survived the presence of the old genes the last time they were active."

"They were active in a different environment."

"Everything worthwhile in life requires a little risk, Mr. Konovolov. As for the FDA, we bypass them and produce in Mexico. That is what Mexico is for. If we have a good product the dollars will find us."

"What product?"

"Maybe we'll restore some hardiness to an over-domesticated food crop. Maybe we'll make a better sheep. Maybe we'll grow plants that make useful medicines naturally. Maybe we'll just patent the technique and license it to companies like Nucleicorp. Whatever. We'll know it when we have it."

"I'll have to think about it."

"I know just the place to meditate. Dessert?"

Harvey patted his stomach with both hands.

"You must be kidding."

"Here comes the selection."

The waiter rolled a tray to the table full of sugars and artery destroying fats.

"Well, maybe."

Soon Harvey was plunging his fork into a Mount Everest on a plate called "Death by Chocolate." I had a cup of coffee. I also had a hunch. If my suspicions about Harvey were correct, he might be enticed to work for me.

"Tell me about your social life, Harvey."

His answer was no surprise. "That will take no time at all. I don't have the opportunity or the money for a social life."

"Aren't there any women at work? I'm presuming you're straight."

"Yes, I'm straight; and, yes, there are women at work. Obviously you haven't kept up on harassment laws in your one-man office. Company policy..."

"...is ignored in every company office. Only unwelcome advances or remarks get guys sent to the Human Resources Manager for sensitivity training."

"Yes, but one usually doesn't know what is unwelcome ahead of time, does one? Actually, in my case I do: anything I said would be unwelcome. My success with women is about equal to yours at that stable — or elsewhere I take it. You are single and you haven't mentioned a girlfriend."

"True, I have two left feet in the mating dance, but I found a way around that — to have Prom Night without the Prom. An actor by the name of Charlie Sheen showed me the way."

"What are you talking about?"

"There is a club about a dozen blocks from here."

"This is that meditation place you mentioned?"

"Yes."

"I don't go to strip clubs, Stephan."

"It's not a strip club."

The bill arrived. Harvey gasped when he saw the total. His

right hand, which had been reaching for his wallet as part of the male ritual of fighting over the tab, froze in place.

"This is mine, Harv."

Actually it belonged to American Express for the remainder of the month.

Rather than go through the process of getting my car out of the garage, driving twelve blocks, and putting it in another garage, we hailed a cab. I miss the old Checkers that still made up a sizable part of the taxi fleets when I was a kid. The standard sedan in which we rode was cramped. The shock absorbers were shot, so potholes jarred us uncomfortably.

As always, taxi driving attracts recent immigrants. When I was young, many were from the Middle East or the Caribbean. Then for a time there were large numbers of Russians. The license on back of the front seat identified our driver as Piter Doren, apparently Afrikaner like so many others these days.

Piter let us off at the corner of First Avenue and 49th Street. The ride with tip cost as much as an average restaurant bill in Jersey. The UN was visible a few blocks from where we exited. Once considered radically modern, the architecture of the structure now looks quaint. Harvey and I walked a short distance, turned a corner, and entered a door on our left. I buzzed 4A and smiled at the security camera. A return buzz signaled the unlocking of the security door. I held the door open for Harvey and followed him into the empty foyer.

The "up" button next to the elevators required an unexpectedly hard push before it would light up. The doors to both elevators opened. We got in the one on the left. It rose in an unsteady motion.

"This is a club? This is just an apartment building."

"Trust me. You'll like it."

"That is the third time you said that to me today."

"When were the other two?"

"When we left to go horseback riding and again when you insisted on going to the Manhattan Café."

"Did you like both?"

"Well, yes."

"See?"

The elevator door slid open on the fourth floor. The black and beige hallway carpet was worn but not ragged. The off-white walls were smudged but not filthy. The hallway formed a square horseshoe around the elevator shaft. We walked around to the left and came to the steel door of 4A. My knuckles hurt slightly when I knocked. The door was opened by a tall woman of about 30 years. She had light blonde shoulder-length hair. She wore a black pullover top. Below that she proved that there are at least a few humans on earth who look good in spandex.

She put her arms around my neck and kissed me lightly on the cheek.

"Hello, Stephan! Who is your friend?" she asked in a Melbourne accent.

"Vicky, this is Harvey."

"Hello, Harvey!" Harvey managed to wave his left hand in response. Vicky smiled. "Well, come on in boys and have a seat. Would you like a drink?"

"No thanks, Vicky. You know I don't like to mix my vices."

"Quite the purist, aren't we? How about you, Harvey?"

"Um… No, but thank you."

We entered the apartment. It had a fairly typical layout for a two-bedroom urban unit. As in any squarish high-rise building, the floor plan made the most of limited exterior wall area. We sat down on an L-shape sofa in a deep and narrow room with windows at the far end. The architect had intended it as a linear living room/dining room combination. The kitchen and bath had no windows at all. They backed up to the hallway. The intended dining room in this case was used as an extension of the living room. It held two additional couches instead of a table.

I had learned from previous chats with the staff that all six other apartments on the fourth floor were leased by the same Moscow corporation that leased 4A. Each of these was an elongated studio measuring 12 feet by 24. Out of this 288 square foot space was carved a bathroom, a wall kitchenette backing up to the bath, a closet, and a multipurpose room. The leaseholder had furnished each apartment with a chair, a full size bed, and an end table.

Business that night was slow. A rather overweight and very

pale 50 year old man sat on a couch and watched the Yankees play the Blue Jays on television. Otherwise 4A was empty of customers.

"Quiet night, Vicky?"

"Yeah, you never can tell with Saturdays. They are like that sometimes. Fridays are always crowded. Wednesdays too for some reason."

"Mid-week stress."

"I suppose. Do you want a line-up or are you going to wait for Pam?"

"When will she be available?"

"I think she is done, but she likes to clean up first."

"Good. I'll wait. Hold off on the line-up for Harvey until she comes out."

After a tomcat phase when I had hired sequentially almost everyone who worked there, including Vicky, I had become attached to a young lady named Pam.

"This is what I think it is?" asked Harvey.

"What do you think it is?"

Harvey whispered in my ear just to be certain, "A brothel?"

"Congratulations. Would you care to wager your winnings on the next question?"

"I told you I didn't go to strip clubs. What made you think I would come here?"

"You did come here. You must have had some inkling. That makes me believe the idea interests you. Come on. Relax and don't embarrass yourself."

We sat back. Harvey studiously avoided eye contact with the other waiting customer. I waved at him but the fellow was too engrossed in the baseball game to notice.

After a few minutes a buxom, pretty, dark-skinned black girl in a ponytail came in the front door and approached the middle-aged man on the couch.

"Thanks for waiting, sweetie. Are you ready?"

The man nodded. She led him by the hand out the front door and down the hall to another apartment.

Harvey looked very uncomfortable. Twice he started to speak and stopped. He succeeded on the third try.

"Look, I'm not saying I'm going to do anything more than watch baseball and wait for you, but out of curiosity, what does this cost?"

"$300 per hour."

"You're kidding."

"No. Plus whatever you tip the girl. And Harvey?"

"Yes?"

"Tip the girl."

"That settles it. I don't make enough money for this."

"Tonight is on me. Just handle your own tip."

"Which is what?"

"Up to you. I usually give a C note."

"You're the one proposing to part with the most cash. Why do I feel you're hustling me?"

"Suspicious nature. Let's say I'm investing in you."

Pam entered the room. She was a petite red head with a winsome smile. She wore a red and white checkered dress that matched the tablecloth on my picnic table at home. It gave her a wholesome look.

"Stevie!" she exclaimed when she spotted me.

She ran to the couch and jumped. Her landing on my lap would have been painful had she weighed even a few pounds more. All the same, the couch moved an inch on the floor. She wrapped her arms around my neck and planted a wet one on my mouth. This abandonment of the classic "Not on the lips!" admonition was unprofessional and a clear sign of my special status on her roster of clients. I was pleased.

"I told you to call first so I can be ready for you!" she complained.

"I was playing it by ear tonight."

"Totally wrong organ."

"We have company. This is my friend Harvey."

Pam turned her head to him and smiled.

"Hello, Harvey. Just how much company is he going to be?" she asked.

"Not that much. This is his first time here." I was beginning to suspect it was his first time anywhere. "I want your help in making this special for him."

"You want me to make tonight special for him?"

"No, no. I want someone less special to me than you to make tonight special for him."

"Jealous?"

"Yes."

Strangers were one thing, but oddly enough the thought of Pam and Harvey together bothered me.

"Good. Well, there are seven girls here tonight. Don't you want to let him choose for himself?"

"No."

Harvey's mouth opened wide at my presumption. However, the traditional line-up really is not as useful as an informed recommendation. Looks truly are not everything. A difficult disposition in one's partner can spoil even businesslike sex such as this. Yet personality is something not obvious at first glance.

Pam laughed.

"OK. Paula is in back. She is quiet, but she is nice enough. The men seem to like her."

They liked her for good reason. Paula was a stunning long-haired brunette with spectacular upper body attributes. As Pam observed, she was far from a chatterbox but she was nice enough and very good at her job.

"Excellent choice."

"Vicky!" Pam called. "Send Paula out please!"

A few minutes later Paula emerged from the back room. She wore a deep blue and low cut cocktail dress from which she overflowed. The color of the dress matched her eyes. Her heels brought her height up to six feet. Straight black hair hung down around her waist. Harvey's mouth opened again.

"Hey, Paula," greeted Pam. "This is Harvey. He's a first timer."

Paula nodded at Pam and smiled acknowledgment at me. She sat down elbow to elbow with Harvey and asked him quietly, "So Harvey, what do you do?"

"Well, uh... I work for... I mean at a company in Jersey."

"Doing what?"

"Biochemist."

When this elicited no response Harvey went into greater detail. Paula kept eye contact with him, but it was hard to tell if she really was listening or was compiling a grocery-shopping list in her head. Harvey lost the thread of his monologue when Paula started rubbing his knee.

"Are you ready?" she asked.

Harvey seemed stumped by the question.

"Say yes," I prompted.

"Oh. Uh… yes."

I reached over and handed Paula an envelope with $300. She looked at me curiously, but then gave her shoulders a barely visible shrug. She took Harvey's hand and led him out the door. Harvey's face looked as though he were going to the guillotine, but he put up no resistance.

"So what is your game, Stephan?" Pam asked me with a smile.

"Game?"

"Come on. I know you. You are that generous only when you want something. What do you want from Harvey?"

"His skills. I need to get him addicted to something so that he needs money. Then he will work for me. He isn't the druggie type. Besides, he is a chemist and could make his own drugs if he wanted them. It had to be something else."

"I figured it was something like that. You think Paula will be an addiction?"

"I'm pretty sure of it."

"You are ruthless, Stephan."

"Thank you."

"That wasn't a compliment."

"Oh. I guess I've damaged your opinion of me then."

"Not in the least."

"I'm not sure what to make of that."

Pam smiled again.

"You have your quirks, if you don't mind me calling them that, but I like you Stephan. I always did. I'm not just feeding you a line either."

"Really? Not many women have felt that way. What makes me so lovable in your eyes?"

"I said nothing about love. You do have some charming qualities though. For one thing you don't have the attitude."

"The attitude?"

"Most guys who come in here have a real attitude — like they are better than us, or like they could do better than us if they wanted to. It is hard to explain. But you don't have it. You just treat me like a girlfriend."

"Ah."

I chose not to explain that this probably was because she and her co-workers were the only girlfriends I had. It wasn't possible for me to treat them differently from some other kind.

"I was convinced for a while that you were married."

"Why? I told you I was single. I gave you my business card the first time we met."

"They're all 'single,' Stephan. Besides, the card didn't have your home number."

"No, it was a business card with a business number. But the answering machine at the office gives my home number if you call after hours.

"I know."

"Did you try it?"

"Yes. Then I called the home number. You answered but I didn't know what to say so I hung up. Then I thought maybe you told the truth after all."

"Well, anyway, I'm glad that my using Harvey doesn't bother you."

"And I'm glad my opinion of you matters to you. It's hard to make what you're doing sound admirable, but, no, it doesn't bother me. Whatever your motives, you aren't doing anything terrible to him. Maybe you are doing him a favor. Harvey is a big boy and, if I know Paula, he will get value for your money. You are not deep down mean, Stephan. I doubt you would blackmail or outright defraud anyone. That's not your style. You just are willing to manipulate people by baiting them. The bait is real enough though, so that's not so bad."

"'You're pretty cute yourself.'"

"Thanks. Have you got an extra envelope in there?"

"For you? Of course."

"Besides one for me."

"Maybe. Why?"

"It's a slow night. Vicky hasn't had any customers. Why don't you take the both of us? We can make your night special too."

"You talked me into it."

I was beginning to love this girl.

Vicky led the way down the hall and opened a door with a key. Zippers unzipped and buttons unbuttoned. As soon as I had disrobed, Pam pushed me back on the bed.

"Don't move," she admonished.

I gave her no argument.

The two were an efficient double team. It cannot have been the first time they worked together. Hot towels and condoms actually flew through the air to one another.

Many people sing the songs of love, but there is something to be said for old-fashioned lust. Pam caressed my face while Vicky worked me below. This was the best arrangement as Vicky still had professional reticence about deep kissing. My initial self-consciousness at the situation at some point vanished. Replacing it was total absorption in warm flesh. I quite lost track of who was doing what. All I can say is that it was wonderful.

When, thoroughly exhausted, I grew aware of the room around me again, Pam was in my arms. Vicky was dressing. She knew that fundamentally I belonged to Pam. When not in direct competition, women can be remarkably supportive of one another in such matters.

If Harvey's experience was fractionally as good as my own that night, I knew he was hooked on Paula.

Harvey was quiet from the time we left 49th Street until we were ten miles west of the Lincoln Tunnel. He had such a look of relaxed contentment that I refrained from interrupting his mood. At last he said, "We don't need buckyballs."

"Why not?"

"We'll work with single cell embryos and seeds. I can insert my molecules directly into the nuclei and let the organisms grow."

"Yes, of course. That is the easy way, isn't it?" Since it was a way that owed little to my input, however, I worried that Harvey might shut me out of the results. It was more important than ever to have the research on my property under my control.

"I'll get started tomorrow."

"Tell me what you need and I'll set up my lab."

"No, not yet. I can do this better at work. Nothing about it will look unusual to my bosses."

Harvey was developing a sense of larceny. This encouraged me and worried me at the same time.

"I can't back this financially unless the organisms are grown on my property," I answered. "Otherwise Nucleicorp will own them."

"What kind of financial backing do you have in mind?"

"$300 per week."

"Not nearly enough."

"$400... plus expenses."

Harvey was quiet. I upped the ante.

"And you don't have to pay me rent."

"In addition to that I'll need $20,000 ... no ... $30,000 up front just in order to set things up," he demanded.

I took a breath.

"OK."

"I'll need more later. Even so, I'll still get the ball rolling at work. You simply can't duplicate the facilities available there unless you are willing to invest millions. Once things are far enough along to require less sophisticated equipment, I'll move everything to your lab. I'll give you a list of equipment and supplies to buy."

"In addition to the $30,000 I'm giving you?"

"Yes."

This was getting expensive. On the other hand, I reasoned, I had lost more in the past on a single wrong stock choice. It was worth the gamble. Within a few days, my lab filled with equipment. It began to look like a place of serious research.

I gave Harvey some breathing space. A month passed. Then another one, and there was no word from Harvey. He never was home when I called in the evening. I began to grow concerned. I called Harvey at work.

"Harv. How is the garden growing?"

"Not great. Look I can't talk about this now. I'll get back to you."

Two days later Harvey called me at my office.

"I've been putting off talking to you, Steve. I've been working on this day and night, but we are at a dead end. The embryos won't grow properly after I treat them. They divide a few times and die. The problem seems to occur just when cells should begin to differentiate. It's no good."

"Well that is disappointing."

"I'll say."

Harvey, of course, was contemplating an end to his visits to 49th Street that were made possible by my $400 per week.

I considered the matter.

"Our changes to the DNA are too extensive then. It messes up the seeds and embryos too much. What about our original plan? Treat juveniles with radicals wrapped in buckyballs. Maybe if the organism is far enough along it can tolerate some tinkering with its genes better."

"Way ahead of you. I switched to that approach as soon as it was clear that the embryo results all were bad. But I ran into a wall making those stuffed buckyballs we contemplated."

"What kind of wall?"

"Let me explain how close I came to succeeding first. I figured that making useful quantities of radical-stuffed buckyballs by traditional mechanical or chemical methods would be tedious, so right from the start I opted for a biological approach. One of Nucleicorp's teams already had a form of *e. coli* that makes modified buckyballs."

"You're kidding."

"No. It was considered a curiosity actually. It was an unplanned variation on bacteria designed to clean up oil spills. Some of the bugs mutated slightly. They just happened to separate out the carbon from the oil in a way that produces little balls that are almost Carbon60."

"Almost?"

"The molecules are not quite true fullerenes as there are sulfur impurities built into their shapes. That is good for us though because it gives us a sort of zipper for stuffing our radicals inside the balls. The bacteria are not as good at cleaning up oil as the unmutated variety, so Nucleicorp hasn't done much with them."

"But you can use them as little factories for making zippable buckyballs. Perfect!"

"There is more. My radicals are only slightly different from toxic molecules produced by some poisonous plants, so I was able to transfer these genes with a few modifications into the buckyball-making bacteria. The idea was to have them do all the work. They would manufacture my radicals and then stuff them in Carbon60 buckyballs all by themselves."

"Fabulous!"

"Not so fabulous. The radicals are highly reactive. They break down real fast inside the bacteria. The are destroyed almost as soon as they are produced. They don't survive long enough to get sealed away inside the balls. I had to find a way to speed up the process of packing the radicals into the balls."

"That's the wall?"

"Yes. The modifications needed to speed the bacteria up in this way are too extensive. My efforts just kill the bacteria out-right. My colleagues here think I'm deliberately developing a new antibiotic. It sure looks like it. All my petri dishes are full of dead bacteria."

"Keep trying. There is bound to a way around this one problem."

"I agree, but it doesn't matter because this one problem is irrelevant."

"Which is why we have been discussing it, I suppose. OK, lay it on me. What is the relevant problem?"

"Geometry. The radicals don't fit inside the buckyballs any-way. I tried to manufacture some stuffed buckyballs by mechanical methods just for experimental purposes. Carbon60 is just too small."

"Well, we had considered that possibility. We need bigger balls. Can't you coax the bacteria into making Carbon70 or 80 instead?"

"That's a whole new project and a big one."

"OK, so forget the bacteria. Let's make the bigger balls mechanically, like you tried to do with Carbon60."

"I can make a few that way, but not enough to do what we want. If we are going to make commercially useful quantities, we will need much bigger manufacturing facilities than you can afford. This whole thing is getting way too complicated. I think we should quit."

"Wait. You give up too easily. I have a thought. We can make plain old unstuffed Carbon70 easily enough, can't we?"

"Sure, that's simple."

"Well, suppose we just supply those bacteria of yours with Carbon70."

There was a trace of embarrassment in Harvey's voice as he answered, "That might work." The notion had been too simple to occur to him. "There is still the problem of getting the bacteria to survive my alterations."

"Well, let's consider that then. When you try to modify the bacteria, what kills them exactly?"

"Crudely put, poisoning. The cells die before the modifications are complete."

"Let me think about that one."

"Be my guest."

"Can I have some of the goop?"

"Goop?"

"The bacteria … and whatever stuff you use to modify them."

"Uh, yeah. All that should be pretty safe I guess. At any rate it's no more dangerous than the bacteria and chemicals in your house now."

"It sounds as though you think I need maid service."

Harvey came by my house that very evening. He delivered two corked beakers to me. He had marked one "e. coli" and one "Do Not Drink." I hadn't planned to drink either.

At this point I would like to claim a moment of personal brilliance. Unfortunately our likes often diverge from our deserts. It was more like an idle thought. Remaining in my lab refrigerator after all these years a bottle of the frog antifreeze I had made years ago in college. I hoped it hadn't degraded. I poured some into the beaker of e. coli, mixed in the chemicals from the second beaker and put the works in the refrigerator. My hope was that my antifreeze would slow the cellular metabolism of the bacteria safely in a low temperature environment. Hence the fatal poisoning might be delayed long enough to allow the repatterning of the bacterial DNA.

The next morning I opened the refrigerator and poured the beaker into petri dishes of nutrients. The dishes were allowed to warm slowly.

I walked over to Harvey's cottage the following morning before he left for work. He opened his door unshaven and half-dressed. I handed him a box containing the petri dishes.

"Here. See if these do anything."

Harvey looked at me with deep skepticism, but he answered, "OK."

The phone call came at 3:00 in the afternoon. "Stephan! What the hell did you do?"

"Did I get the little critters to make stuffed buckyballs?"

"Yes! I mean no! Sort of."

"Which is it?"

Harvey took a breath and deliberately calmed himself. "Roughly 3% of the bacteria in those dishes show the metabolic changes I was trying to induce. However, the bacteria continued to make Carbon60, which is too small for our purposes. I tried your suggestion though. I soaked them in a liquid rich in Carbon70. The molecules were absorbed just fine and the bacteria added sulfur zippers to them all by themselves. Then they inserted the Carbon70 balls with my radicals."

"It works."

"Yes. In a way it works out far better for public safety than I had hoped."

"Public safety? What do you mean?"

"Our whole idea is to mutate genes. Anything that eats bacteria loaded with Carbon70 coated radicals will have its DNA affected. That is very dangerous if it happens in an uncontrolled or unconfined way. However, without Carbon70 shells to protect them, the radicals break down long before they can cause mutations. The digestive process of any plant or animal would destroy the radicals almost at once. Since we are the ones who provide the Carbon70 protection, even if our bacteria get loose into the wild they won't be dangerous. They may encounter ordinary carbon and hydrocarbons out there, but they'll just convert the stuff into Carbon60. Carbon60 won't protect the radicals. The radicals will break down. The bacteria therefore will be safe to eat. No animals will get sick from them. The environment won't be damaged."

"Great! Then there is no need for you to worry. Let's start experimenting at home right away!"

"Slow down! We need to go one step at a time. I want to know exactly what you did."

I explained briefly and perhaps made the analytical process behind what I did sound less haphazard than it was.

"You are full of surprises, Steve. I never would have guessed you were so talented."

"Thanks. I think. Here is another idea. Let's go see the girls tonight to celebrate."

"I may learn to like you yet."

During the next few weeks we relocated Harvey's research to my laboratory. Despite our previous agreement to make the move at this stage, Harvey put up resistance. I finally got him to agree only by promising not to pester him and to stay out of the lab entirely. I was pleased to notice that the lights were on in the lab until well past midnight every night.

I kept up with Harvey's progress during our weekly drives to 49th Street. True to my promise, I didn't pester him. I simply let him tell me what he had achieved, which for a long time wasn't much. Another month went by. I was beginning to worry that Harvey never would produce any results, when at last he had something interesting to say.

"I think I'm pretty close to something big. We are moving way too fast, of course. I don't know why I let you talk me into cutting so many corners."

"It's my charming personality."

"I don't think that's it."

"Never mind that for now. What havoc are you wreaking with your buckyballs?"

"How about konovolovballs?"

"What?"

"Do you think it is presumptuous to name them after myself? With my modifications the molecules are not really true fullerenes."

"No, but try harveyballs. More euphonious."

"Konovolovballs. Harvey was a famous..."

"Yes, yes. As you wish. What about the experiments?"

"Well, I've finished the first month of trials. There definitely are changes going on in the nuclei of treated cells. Most of them die which shows the changes in genetic expression are significant."

"What happens to the rest?"

"Nothing really dramatic. There are metabolic changes. They appear sick."

"You said 'cells.' Are you still working with algae and paramecia? You have done that before. You did that back at Nucleicorp. Our whole plan was to employ the technique on larger plants and animals."

"I hadn't tried the radicals wrapped in konovolovballs at Nucleicorp. It is useful to start with single cell organisms so I can better understand the mechanisms involved. But you'll be happy to know that I've also moved ahead with more advanced animals as you asked."

"That is good news. How advanced?"

"Rotifers."

"Those microscopic predator things?"

"Well they are pretty big. You almost can see them with the naked eye."

"Haven't you heard of lab mice? Or, if you must be conservative, tadpoles?"

"Oh, we're not ready for those yet."

"Harvey, have algae or rotifers changed much in the past half billion years?"

"Not really."

"Then perhaps they are not the best subjects for uncovering archaic biochemistry. They already are archaic biochemistry."

"I explained the reasons for moving cautiously with multicellular organisms."

"Cautious is one thing, but... well, never mind. I promised not to bug you. Just move along as rapidly as you can. So, what about the modified *e. coli* and the production of your ... uh ... balls. No problems cropping up there? No unexplained die-offs or anything?"

"No. How about konnyballs? Is that better?"

"Much."

"The konnyball production is fine. The bacteria are thriving in your basement lab. So long as I supply them with Carbon70 they churn the konnyballs out ready for use. I'm careful not to contaminate surfaces with *e. coli* or pour them down the drain. As I said, I think they are safe, but all the same we should try to keep them out of the general food chain."

We parked the car on 50th and walked to 49th. There was a jauntiness to Harvey's step that was new.

Barbara was the Night Manager that evening. She opened the door for us to 4A and then wordlessly returned to the sofa. She is a strange young woman who affects a Gothic style. She was watching a rerun of Kalifornia on cable while fingering a cheek ring. We sat on another sofa.

"Are you going to let the girls know we're here?" I asked Barbara.

"They saw you on the security camera," she answered.

"Seeing Paula tonight, Harvey?" I asked.

"Uh...yeah. Who else? Thanks for introducing us. I do understand that without your financial support I'd never afford this. I hope I can pay you back out of the research. Do you still think there's money in this project? Seriously?"

"A pile."

"OK. Hi, Paula."

Paula had appeared silently at Harvey's side. She tickled his cheek and led him out the door to one of the apartments.

Pam took advantage of my distraction to sneak up in back of me in order to surprise me too. She clamped her arms around my neck.

"Stand up," she ordered.

Though choking, I staggered to my feet. Pam got her legs over the back of the sofa and wrapped them around my waist. She pointed with one hand to the door. I carried her piggy back out the front door and down the hall according to her direction. I bent to one side as she produced a key from somewhere and unlocked the door to 4E. Closing the door behind us with a spin, I hurried across the room and let her tumble over my head onto the bed.

Our lovemaking was as pleasant as usual. The girl was special. It was time for a real date. I hoped Pam would agree.

"Pam?"

"Yes, dear?"

"Would you like to have dinner with me one night?"

"We're not allowed to date the customers."

"Is that a no?"

"No. I mean yes, but don't tell anyone about it."

"Deal."

"I'm pretty busy for the next couple weeks. Some of the girls are away. I have to cover them."

"When are you free?"

Pam smiled.

"I mean when are you available?"

"How about two weeks from Friday?" she proposed.

"Date. Where shall I pick you up?"

"I'll meet you someplace."

"*Manhattan Café* on 1st?"

"Fine. Eight o'clock. How about bringing Harvey? Paula kind of likes him."

"Really? Double date. Well, OK, I guess, if Harvey is agreeable."

"He will be."

Harvey was coming along with his work, but his approach was painfully slow. I decided to accelerate the process by conducting some experiments of my own. I set up a rudimentary lab bench in the basement of my office building.

Carrying two makeshift containers and my spare key, I entered my home laboratory, located in my remodeled detached garage, while he was at Nucleicorp. Even though I had promised Harvey to stay out, after all it was my property. Surely, as owner I had the right to inspect occasionally.

There was a lot of glassware scattered about. There were microscopes, centrifuges, autoclaves, and a number of electronic black boxes that I couldn't identify. In the corner was a tank of algae under UV light. The air around it smelled like a swamp in August. I poked around some more. In a darkened area of the room I found a container the size of a beer keg. Through the glass lid I could see it was filled with a tepid soup. I figured this was the *e. coli*. I lifted the lid and scooped some into an empty glass jar labeled Cherry Peppers. I found on the bench a container of black powder that I took to be Carbon70. I spooned some of this into an empty Sanka Coffee can. I put an extra spoonful into the jar in order to give the bacteria plenty of raw material.

Upstairs in the living area of my house I placed the containers on the kitchen countertop. A few minutes later I was concerned to find my cat, Boss, drinking from the jar. I pulled him away from the jar and kept an eye on him for several hours while I worked out my own plan for experimentation. The cat seemed to suffer no ill effects from the bacteria.

The next day I stopped by a pet store and bought some supplies on my way to my office. In my office basement, I set up a couple of trials. I spooned *e. coli* from the jar into an aquarium full of tadpoles on the verge of metamorphosis. Then I sprinkled some of the bacteria on wheat germ and fed the mixture to four mice. I chose to wait two weeks for results. There was no need to be reckless.

The reactions of the adult mice at the end of two weeks were encouraging. Two became notably aggressive, and I had to separate them. One bit me while I did it. The other two mice lost so much hair that they looked almost like little opossum. Those two didn't look well. However, all four were alive. I realized that I should have used juvenile mice from the start. That was to be my next test.

The tadpoles showed spectacular results. The survivors had put on much more weight than normal. They were growing into very big frogs.

My cat began to act strangely by this time. He seemed healthy enough but he acquired a wild look to his eyes. One night he killed a goose and somehow managed to pull it through the cat door.

I chose to not yet reveal these experiments to Harvey.

On the night of our double date, Paula, Pam, Harvey and I shared a table at the *Manhattan Cafe*. Harvey talked at length about some abnormality in his algal mats which he found exciting. Paula worked her way through an enormous lobster. Pam had ordered a lobster and filet mignon with strips of bacon. While he talked, Harvey was carving the rib eye steak that covered his plate. I was the lightest eater with lamb chops larger than my hands. A Himalayan range of fried zucchini, creamed spinach, onions and potatoes occupied the remainder of the table.

As Harvey chewed on a piece of meat I took advantage of the silence to slip in some words of my own.

"How can you stay so thin with your appetite?" I asked Pam.

"The Greenspan diet."

"Hmm?"

"Monetary theory. I eat only when someone else pays."

"Good diet," observed Paula.

She glanced at Harvey. She had grown oddly agitated throughout his monologue.

"Now let me get this straight. You and Stephan here are trying to make money with algae and … what did you call them?"

"Rotifers."

"Rotifers," she intoned. "And what does Steve have to do with it?"

"We say it comes from his research or else my employer would own it. But I've told you all this."

"Who listens? So it's a scam."

Harvey was more taken aback by the blunt rhetorical question than by the statement. Nevertheless, it was to the word scam that he responded.

"Well, that's a harsh description."

"No it isn't. You are crooked enough to run a scam, but you are screwing around with algae and rotifers. Think about this for a moment. I gather you are a highly competent chemist."

"Biochemist."

"Whatever. Anyway, this supposed criminal mastermind over here has you growing mutant algae."

"I'll be ready for tadpoles soon."

"Tadpoles!"

Paula gave Harvey a surprisingly hard whack to the side of his head.

"Ow!"

"You want to make money with potions and powders, Dr. Jeckyll? What does the word Ecstasy mean to you?"

"Happiness?"

Paula put a hand to her forehead. "Let's try again. How about methamphetamine?"

"Jail?"

"Only if you get caught. Come here, genius!"

Paula grabbed Harvey by the arm, pulled him up from the table, and led him out of the room. A moment later through the window I saw them out on the sidewalk hailing a taxi.

Pam and I looked at each other. Her knife sliced into her filet. She shrugged, smiled, and said, "Well, more food for us."

I wasn't very good company for the rest of the meal. If Paula truly intended to turn Harvey into a drug lord, our partnership was over. I had no interest in jeopardizing my comfortable life by any connection to that business. I stuffed myself morosely.

Having eaten as much as I could manage, I sat back and unconsciously licked my left thumb. Pam playfully grabbed my right hand and licked the other one. It was then that I wondered how thoroughly I had washed my hands after working with the *e. coli* a few hours earlier.

Harvey moved out of my rental house the next day and told me to keep the security deposit.

Later I heard that Harvey had received a large bonus from Nucleicorp as a reward for developing a new antibiotic; he then took a leave of absence. Pam still talks to Paula. Pam tells me that he and Paula bought a townhouse in Manhattan. They seem to have no shortage of cash.

In my basement lab, Harvey kindly left of list of recommended procedures in case I wanted to pursue the konnyball work on my own. However, as already has been established, I am rather more of a dilettante than a researcher. Despite the interesting results I already had produced, I was rudderless. Without a collaborator to do the donkeywork and the methodical business of analyzing results, it was unlikely that I would come up with anything commercially valuable. I also was worried that I might somehow be connected to Harvey if he was arrested.

It was best to terminate the project. The very evening that Harvey left, I loaded the algae tubs and the *e. coli* vat on back of my GMC 2500 pickup truck. I stopped at the office lab. In a soft-hearted moment I refrained from killing the experimental animals; I put the mice and the tadpole tank in back of the truck too. I put aside a small sample of the bacteria in case the opportunity arose to team up with someone else in the future.

I drove out to *River's Edge* farm, put the truck into 4-wheel drive, and drove across an open field. I dumped the vats and tanks into the river. I let the mice run free.

It is probably worth mentioning an odd occurrence about two months after these events. Pam and I no longer meet at 49th Street. We have developed a relationship that verges on normality. We go out, and sometimes she stays over at my place.

One Saturday we went horseback riding on the trails. Pam claimed to have some experience, so I let her ride Pollack. Malo was fairly good that day. Only once when we were riding side by side did my attention drift enough for him to be able to reach over and bite Pam's leg. We reached a narrow place on trail. Pam took the lead. Suddenly Pollack stopped.

"What's the matter?"

"I don't know," she said. "He doesn't want to go."

"He probably sees a mouse. Maybe a butterfly. Don't be too gentle. Give him a kick and a squeeze."

She did. Pollack leapt forward in three bounds of at least 15 feet apiece. Pam managed to keep her seat but only barely. Pollack turned around and flared his nostrils with his head high in the air.

"What was that about?"

"I don't know, Pam. Pollack is a nervous Nellie. Sometimes he does that."

"Thanks for letting me ride him. Next time I ride the palomino. You can get bitten and then bounced all over."

"OK."

I nudged Malo's sides but he too was reluctant to move forward. I nudged again. His ears went back. Malo spun around and lashed out with both rear hooves into the brush by the side of the trail. There was a high-pitched wail as some animal flew into the air and landed further up the hill.

Curious, I dismounted, wrapped Malo's reins around a birch, and walked up the hill. There still are a handful of wildcats in New Jersey. I guessed from my brief glimpse of the animal that this was what it was. It wasn't, quite.

Malo had killed the creature outright. It was a cat of sorts weighing perhaps 30 pounds. The back legs were shorter than the front and two upper front teeth were very elongated. It was not a full-fledged Smilodon but it was a little version of something close. I guessed that as a juvenile it must have lapped up bacteria from my spilled vats. I assumed this was a one-time fluke. Without Carbon70 the bacteria were harmless.

I wanted to bring the carcass home for study, but the horses would have none of it. As soon as I began to walk back with it Pollack started to back up and seemed ready to take off. Malo looked ready to kill me. Pam wasn't happy about bringing the body with us either. I yielded to the majority and left the animal behind.

It happened that the next day the Times science section ran a small article about the unexpected abundance of buckminster-fullerenes found in the environment. They form on automobile tailpipes. They form naturally in charred wood. They are produced by the interaction of sunlight and hydrocarbons. The article treated the discovery as an interesting but insignificant bit of scientific trivia.

How much Carbon70 could my spilled bacteria encounter? Probably not much. The molecules can't be as common as all that.

So far this opinion seems borne out by the facts. The only other aftereffects of my experiments have been unnoticeable or mild. True, some oddly shaped plants have grown back by the Raritan River but they all are of species common to the area. The strange shapes may have nothing to do with genetic change. The crickets seem exceptionally loud there this year too, but it just may be a bumper year for crickets. According to the local Observer Tribune, oversized frogs have been spotted nearby. Witnesses claim to have seen frogs as big as dogs. This sounds like an exaggeration to me. Near my own home, no wildlife or pet under 15 kilograms is safe from my cat. Otherwise life goes on much as before.

Pam and I haven't been injured by whatever accidental exposure to konnyballs we may have had. True, she has developed a wild look to her eyes and has grown quite feral in some ways. I rather like it though. I have noticed no change in myself other than something that is probably just psychological. Every now and then I have an overwhelming urge to climb a tree.

AFTERGLOW

As I reflect back, I wonder if my first encounter with Angus was as accidental as it appeared at the time. Perhaps he knew of my own chemical experiments. I was mentioned in the local newspapers recently in regard to an investigation by the DEP of a little bio-hazard spillage. Nothing was proven and nothing much came of it, but Angus might have caught wind of it all the same. My name is Stephen Bathory. Yet, this story doesn't begin with me.

I need to begin with Chuck. Chuck is morbidly age conscious in the way that, to the vast amusement of their elders, people in their 30s often are. Acutely aware of his own mortality, he allows age to so dominate his thinking that he invariably gives an age estimate for anyone he mentions regardless of the relevance of the datum. He speaks much of wills and advancing years.

A few weeks ago we ate supper together in *The Old Stone Tavern*, an old stone tavern in Bernardsville, New Jersey. The aroma of old wood underlay the smell of food and drink. Washington's troops, once camped a mile away, swilled porter in this very place. Chuck's utterances that night were in character.

"That hot receptionist Sally I told you about who is about 25 spoke to my boss Serena. She is about 42 but looks pretty good anyway. Anyhow, Sally accused Tom of harassing her. You met Tom once. He is about 37. She said he complimented her on her clothes three days in a row. I think she's being way too sensitive, but actually it is OK by me if Serena fires him. I'm next in line for his job. On the other hand, she might give his job to some 22-year-old fresh out of college. She could pay him less. I already have a bunch of so-called superiors who are younger than I am."

Chuck is about 35.

Chuck complained some more about work and then moved on to matters eschatological. He listed his relatives who, he assumed, were near the end of their lives. He wondered if any of them would leave something to him. He said he hoped he could get far enough ahead of his bills to leave something behind himself when the time came.

I am not at all comfortable with the subject of death, so my response was characteristically flippant.

"I don't plan on going, Chuck, so I won't have to find a way to take it with me. I'll just keep it with me. The fact that everyone else ages and dies is no reason for me to do so. Would you jump off a bridge just because all your friends did?"

"Probably. You'd better face reality though. I'm not the only one who thinks so either. There's a guy about 32 paying his tab at the table in back of you who heard you. He smirked when you said you weren't going."

"Maybe he's not going either."

"Maybe he is on his way to jump off the George Washington Bridge."

I glanced in back of me. A single diner was leaving the table. He had dark brown hair, sideburns, neatly trimmed mustache, and masculine good looks. His clothes were eclectically unfashionable. The tie was too wide, the jacket was too long with an odd cut to the lapels, the pants were pleated and too high on the waist, and the short vest had an ugly floral pattern. The outfit looked pieced together from raids on randomly selected attic trunks. I chalked it up as a personal sartorial statement less objectionable than the currently fashionable baseball caps and baggy shorts.

Friday afternoon at 4:00 PM the phone rang in my real estate office in Mendham, an old money-soaked suburb of New York City where I and a street full of competitors struggle to sop up some of the drippings.

"Bathory Realty," I answered.

"Is this Mr. Stephan Bathory?"

"Yes, sir."

The caller identified himself as Angus MacDuff. He asked that

I stop by his house to discuss a business matter. I knew the name. MacDuff was a local rich eccentric who owned a 20-acre estate on Hardscrabble Road. He was a recluse, though his nephew was seen about town occasionally. This sounded potentially profitable, so I readily agreed.

"I'll be over right away."

The fall had come early this year because of the wet summer. Rather than sport the usual trampy colors for a couple of months, the waterlogged trees simply shed leaves that had turned directly from green to brown. The long driveway to the MacDuff house already was hidden by the autumn mat. A few leaves swirled in the wake of my car, although most were glued to the pavement by the morning drizzle.

The main house came into view. It was substantial, but by no means a mansion. The garish new palaces built in Mendham by doctors, corporate executives, and investment brokers were much larger. This home, however, had a solid look. The walls were stone. The recess of the windows showed that the stone was no mere 3.5 inch thick facing such as we use today. It was at least a foot thick. The roof was slate with long buttressed overhangs. The ground surrounding the foundation was well pitched to keep rainwater flowing away from the foundation.

Angus MacDuff answered the heavy mahogany door himself. Angus had white hair, a white beard, fluffy sideburns, and rimless glasses. Without formality, he asked me to follow him to his study. There was a trace of Scot trill to his "r" and glottal stop to his vowels. I wondered if he was aware of his resemblance to Scrooge MacDuck.

The entire first floor was tiled. The slight bounce one expects from wooden floor joists was not present. Angus smiled as he watched my feet make this test.

"The house was framed in the '20s using steel and reinforced concrete," he explained.

"That's very unusual."

"Yes it was. Is. But there was enough commercial construction going on nearby in Morristown and Madison at the time for the right tradesmen and suppliers to be easily available."

"But why?"

"Less chance of fire. Insurance companies figure that a typical house will burn down in 100 years. That sounded too risky to me."

I noticed then that the house was shy on draperies, throw rugs, and other typical flammables. The furniture mostly was leather. A peek in the kitchen informed me that the cabinets were steel, a jarringly inexpensive choice in a house of this quality.

It hardly seemed possible that Angus was old enough to have built the house in the 1920s. I assumed his remark about the risk of fire was an explanation for why he had bought this fire-resistant property. He ushered me into his study, sat behind his steel desk, and waved me toward one of the leather chairs.

As soon as I was seated, Angus peeled off the beard, removed the glasses, and ruffled his hair. Talc dust bloomed and revealed dark brown hair underneath. I recognized the younger man beneath the disguise. This was the same fellow who had eavesdropped on my conversation with Chuck at *The Old Stone Tavern*.

"They call me Robin."

"Hello Robin. I've heard people speak of you about town. You are Angus' nephew, aren't you?"

"My name is Angus."

"Uh ... OK. I'm confused. Who are you and what is with the get-up?"

"I have a story to tell. Please do not interrupt."

I assayed doors and windows for possible lines of retreat in case my encounter with this very strange person took a dangerous turn, but I also was intrigued. I waved him on.

"As a young man," he started, "I was an enthusiast for a British writer named H.G. Wells. That was a century ago."

"It feels that long ago to me too," I remarked understandingly. I had loved Wells' stories as a boy too.

"I asked you not to interrupt."

I gestured apologetically.

"As I say, that was over a hundred years ago. He had just published a bully tale called *The New Accelerator*, in which two inventors brew an elixir that accelerates the human metabolism so much that other people seem not to move at all. Falling objects seem to hang in the air. Naturally the accelerated inventors are effectively invisible to everyone else. Oh you kid, do they have a time."

Robin/Angus' inconsistent anachronisms were extremely disconcerting.

"The plot was adapted by others many times afterwards. I even saw a *Star Trek* episode based on it. Anyway, I was a chemistry student at the time and the idea grabbed me like a bull dog. After giving the matter much thought, I determined that an accelerator wasn't practical because the human body would burn itself up if pushed that hard. But the antidote, the decelerator … that was another matter.

"Think of the advantages if such a potion could be found. How much of our lives are spent waiting? We sit through boring events. We wait for maintenance workers to arrive. We wait for a check to come in the mail. We wait for the weekend and our big date. All the time our life clocks are ticking away.

"Suppose we could reset our vibes to a more glacial metronome, say at a 1/1000 scale so that an objective hour passes subjectively in a few seconds. If our bodies aged at this decelerated pace, how much life could we save? True, the subjective length of life would not change, but wouldn't its quality? All that waiting time could be reserved for the times that really matter to us.

"Chemistry was only newly a true science. Today I would know too much in the way of sound physics, chemistry, and biology to believe that such an elixir was possible. I didn't know these things then, so I just went ahead and made one. Slowing the metabolism was easy enough. The trick was to preserve the flesh from decay without poisoning the tissue to death in the process. A mixture of snake venoms and exotic plant poisons proved effective when fixed by my own blend of inorganic chemicals. I killed a great many mice before I got the formula just right."

"You mean you were able to do this at room temperature?" I asked. "Back in college I once worked with something similar for a biology class, but it only worked below freezing temperatures. Even then, when the mice were thawed out they weren't quite right in the head — the ones that survived, that is."

"Mr. Bathory, I will not warn you again about interrupting me."

"Sorry."

"The answer to your question, however, is yes. My potion worked at room temperature, but it remained dangerous. My first self-administration involved a near fatal miscalculation. I scaled my dosage up from the body weight of a mouse to pass an objective hour in slowness. I quaffed my potion and stared expectantly at the clock. It was 5:00 PM. For a while the minute hand crawled so slowly that I wondered if I had gotten the formula reversed. Suddenly the hands of the clock blurred. The hands then became visible again and stalled at 6:30. I was ecstatic at my success. Imagine my shock when I discovered that fully two days had passed. It was 6:30 on Wednesday evening instead of Monday. Body weight plainly was not the sole factor for determining dose.

"Any number of accidents could have befallen me. The candles were burned to their bases and could have ignited something in the house. Had I not been well balanced at the time the elixir took hold, I could have toppled over and injured myself. Someone could have found me, misinterpreted my state, and sent for the coroner. I resolved to take greater care in the future.

"There was a young woman. Victoria. Her mother named her not after the Queen, but after Victoria Woodhull who ran for President back in 1876 on a platform of Free Love, divorce reform, and suffrage. My Vicky cut a daring figure with ankle-length dresses and, whenever there was an audience, cigarettes.

"Like many pleasantly spoiled daughters of the day, she was an avid reader of Shaw and Wells and annoyed her rich parents by promoting their socialist views. She scandalized whomever would listen with feminist harangues on sexual freedom. She liked to play 'There'll Be a Hot Time on the Old Town Tonight' on the piano.

"Her avant-garde views did not translate into liberal behavior. In a day when far more went on in haystacks than anyone now would suspect, she virtuously left me in a dreadful sweat at the end of more evenings than I care to remember.

"Still, I loved her and wished to share my discovery with her. When I offered to extend both our lives with my elixir, however, her reaction was fierce. For reasons that are still unclear to me, Vicky contrived to find something grossly unethical in what I had done and was deeply offended by my proposal. Not that she really believed me, you understand, but it was a matter of principle. I never was clear what principle, but it was a principle of some kind. She demanded that I stop my experiments, and when I said no, she left.

"When I was older I realized that Vicky was estranged by my open refusal to stop my experiments rather than by the research itself. Had I shown fear of losing her by openly agreeing to her demands but continuing my experiments in secret, she would have forgiven me when she found out. At least I would have proven that I cared. The thing is I did care. I still do.

"Vicky married a dealer of motorcars, raised four children, and voted for Hoover in '32. But that was in the future.

"I was not put off my experiments by a broken heart. I had time, after all, for other women. Like that *Rolling Stones* number *Time is on My Side*, you know? Yet somehow, the more I used my elixir the less time I seemed to have. The potion was addictive.

"Consider this. What time is valuable enough to use up and what should be saved for later? To me nearly every moment seemed better reserved for later. I found myself saving more and more. At first it was a day or two per week. Then it was whole weeks at a time. Soon I would drop in on the world just long enough to get current with events and technology and then drop out again. The women I met saw me so infrequently that they moved on to other men and aged with remarkable speed. My men friends changed and died. I was rushing through the world on an express train.

"In the '20s I made a concerted effort to get back in synch with the rest of the world. I mostly kept the elixir on the shelf and managed to lead nearly a normal life. Fortunately, through sound investments and low expenses I had become well-to-do. You don't spend much when you get out only several weeks in a year. This house was built to my specifications in '26.

"My old acquaintances began to look at me in amazement. Often they remarked on my youthful appearance. I found it necessary to emulate aging in order to avoid suspicion. Then one day in '28 I looked in a mirror and saw some lines in my face that were not faked. This scared me back into a serious time-saving program.

"I announced travel plans to explain my frequent absences and gained an undeserved reputation as a globe trotter. This led to my accidental financial masterstroke in 1929. Remembering the Panics of '93, '07, and '20, I withdrew everything from the stock market prior to one of my 'trips.' I exchanged my bank deposits for gold and US government bonds. This was before the days when mutual funds were common investment tools, or I might have made a far worse choice. I turned on the slowness. I snapped back into synch after the Crash and found that the purchasing power of my wealth had tripled. A few years later I switched back into stocks and my fortune was made.

"In '38 I invented a new identity, a nephew of the same name. I faked my death and left everything to myself. The time has come to pull a similar stunt. This time I'll leave my estate to Robin — which is to say to me. It is much more difficult this time around because government record-keeping and general bureaucratic nosiness is much more pervasive than it was 60 years ago. I need some help to smooth things over."

Angus, for so I decided to call him, stopped talking and looked at me expectantly. I hesitated to speak out of turn again.

"Go on," I ventured at last.

"I'll arrange for some drowning at sea or some such thing where there will be no body for which to account. I'll report the accident as Robin. That way we can get a death certificate. I carry no life insurance so there will be no private investigation into the matter. However, the police might get suspicious about Robin's motives if I leave everything directly to him. I need an executor to be my buffer. Someone who has the authority to distribute the estate among my relatives as he sees fit. I've chosen you."

"Why me?"

"Because I don't trust my attorneys as far as I can spit."

"But you trust me."

"In this particular matter, yes. You can manage the estate and turn things over to Robin."

"Won't the police then get suspicious of me?"

"Not if the job is without pay and without inheritance. If you get no money there will be no reason to suspect anything untoward."

"Without meaning to sound unhelpful, if the job is without pay and without inheritance, why should I bother with it?"

Angus picked up a translucent bottle containing a shimmering blue liquid.

"The fact that everyone else ages and dies is no reason for you to do so. Would you jump off a bridge just because all your friends did?"

I sit alone in the dining room of my house on Schoolhouse Lane. It is by no means certain to me whether I have spoken with a brilliant 120-year-old chemist or a lunatic nephew of Angus MacDuff. My good sense inclines me toward the latter view. Still, I wonder if the phone will ring and a lawyer will inform me that I am executor of the MacDuff estate.

The sun has set and the room darkens rapidly. The blue liquid in the bottle on the table in front of me luminesces for at least an hour after dark.

SCUM

The shadowy Normandy Tudor lurked behind stone gates in the moonlit hills of Watchung some 40 minutes from New York City. The home had been the scene of a grisly multiple murder. This is what had attracted Rudy. The bullet holes had been easy to spackle over, but the ornate banister was so damaged by ax blows that it had to be replaced. Nondescript stains, presumably blood, remained in the marble foyer. Rudy debated replacing the tiles or leaving them for character. He had negotiated ruthlessly and bought the property for $200,000 less than its appraised value. He knew that the more shocking the violence, the better the buy. The exception to the crime discount is the site of a celebrity murder. This type of property goes up in value. Apparently folks don't mind being haunted, so long as it is by someone famous.

Rudy stretched out on the couch in what the house plans called the family room. Rudy, a family of one, preferred to call it the drawing room. He leaned over the coffee table and flicked the remote. The motorized wall screen extended and the ceiling mounted projector TV emitted beams of light. Ordinary large-screen TVs have sharper images, but Rudy enjoyed the movie house atmosphere of the projector. A bowl of taco shells and a 2-liter bottle of Cherry Coke occupied the coffee table. He drank directly out of the bottle. Also on the table was a bowl of vile-looking junk food called Scum. Rudy wasn't sure whether to drink it or use it as a dip. *Weird Occurrences*, the show of which he himself was the host, came to life on the screen. The sound from the TV speakers generated a barely noticeable echo from the undeco-rated walls of the drawing room.

[*On screen a sequence of pyramids, tarot cards, zodiacal signs, and occult symbols advance toward the viewer. Each dissolves as it fills the screen. The theme tune is a jarring full orchestra rendition of When You're Strange. An image of Rudy fades in before a legitimate star map.*]

NARRATOR: Good evening. This is Rudy Renkel hosting a special edition of Weird Occurrences, the show that explores unexplained phenomena and the dark side of human existence. This may be the half-hour that changes your view forever on whether we are alone in the cosmos. Also tonight, the producers of this show will answer charges made by a rival news organiza-tion. But first some words from our sponsors.

[*Ads follow for corn flakes, feminine hygiene products, automobiles, and Scum. A new product aimed at 10-year-olds who want to gross out their parents, Scum looks just like its name. Fungal clumps float in lemon/lime flavored slime. Ad shows parents heaving as kids happily drip goop into their mouths. Return to program.*]

NARRATOR: Some of you may have seen a skeptical Nightline episode aired a few nights ago. The topic was the UFO phenom-enon. Guests on the program suggested that fraud was rampant in UFO reporting — so rampant that no evidence should be taken at face value. The journalistic practices of this program were targeted as a particular example. *Nightline* used footage obtained without our permission that allegedly catches accom-plices and myself in the act of faking an alien encounter.

[*Narrator looks contrite.*] Tonight I will be honest with you. For years I have interviewed farmers standing in crop circles, hikers who shared beers with Bigfoot, and weekend fishermen who hooked Champ or the Loch Ness monster. The goal was your entertainment. Perhaps in the interest of good television we embellished some of these interviews with questionable footage that programs like *60 Minutes* might hesitate to run. Some view-ers may be forgiven for wondering if the ghost in last week's episode resembled a flashlight beam played over steam from a portable room humidifier, or whether the shots of Sasquatch didn't look awfully like a man running through an Oregon forest in a gorilla suit. I am revealing this to you in hope that you will recognize my sincerity on this occasion. Because the irony is, the *Nightline* episode picked an event that was real. The alien footage was not faked. Yet the very act of revealing the truth may damage my credibility. They knew that of course. And by "they" I don't mean the folks at ABC.

[*Narrator resumes deadpan expression.*] We have employed professional actors for the re-enactments, but wherever possible we have used the actual locations and dialogue.

[*Fade to a glassy black nighttime lake surface covered with mist. The leisurely putter of a 25-horse Mercury can be heard. The bow of a small skiff breaks through the mist.*]

NARRATOR [*Overdubbed*]: Crystal Lake in Gilmanton, New Hampshire, is shaped like a fist with a beckoning forefinger. Greg Thomas, a successful insurance broker from Manchester, was vacationing with his wife and children at their weekend lakefront cabin. Exhausted from a long day of family values, he sought respite with a quiet cruise alone. Unknown to Mister Thomas, as his boat entered the finger shaped cove, yours truly awaited on a nearby stretch of undeveloped shore.

[*Zoom back and bring into frame a man looking out over the lake from behind a large pine tree. For some reason an actor plays the role of Rudy Renkel. The actor does not look much like Rudy. He is better looking and even has a mustache whereas Rudy is clean shaven.*]

NARRATOR: Earlier that day I had prepared for just this opportunity. I had flattened out a circle 30 feet in diameter with a garden scythe in a scrubby area near the shoreline and sprinkled lithium on the site. Lithium is a likely element in any practical fusion engine. I set strobe lights powered by my truck battery in the middle of the circle. As the red and green bow lights of the boat approached, I suddenly remembered why the name of the lake seemed familiar. A popular teenage slasher movie was set by a fictional Crystal Lake. [*The actor smiles knowingly as though recalling this.*] Fortunately, the only wounds delivered tonight would be to Mr. Thomas's peace of mind. The time had come to spring the trap.

[*Camera perspective shifts to boat. Weirdly colored strobe lights erupt behind a row of trees at the shoreline. They are joined by a low-pitched cacophony that a practiced ear might identify as White Zombie played at extremely slow speed. The red dot of a laser flickers over the boat and passes over the chest of the boat driver. Greg's stolid interest turns to grossly overacted fear when a silhouetted being with an enormous head appears at the shore and wades into the lake. Greg guns the engine and spins the boat 180 degrees. Boat vanishes into the mist.*
Back on shore a smiling Rudy takes off a large helmet, slips a laser pointer into his pocket, and begins to pack up his F150 pickup.]

NARRATOR: The next day my cameraman and I approached the denizens of the far side of the lake in search of the owner of the boat. Told that there had been UFO sightings the night before, several of them, as usual, reported outlandish lights and sounds. All were outside the range of my bit of theater. One young man gave a detailed description of an aircraft performing impossible maneuvers. No one seemed to remember the fog last night, which obscured one's own porch light much less anything in the sky. Eventually I found a cabin with a familiar boat tied up at the dock. Much of what happened next was caught on tape. However, the following is a recreation, because when Mr. Thomas learned the content of this show, he refused to let us use the actual interview. Mr. Thomas, a guest speaker at this week's UFO congress in Houston, insists that his alien encounter was real and that my report to the contrary is part of a cover-up.

[*Camera focuses on boat. "Mercury" is plainly readable. Pan to front door of cabin where actor playing Rudy knocks on the door. A cameraman stands by him.*]

RUDY: Good morning sir. My name is Rudy Renkel. I'm investigating reports of lights in the sky last night. Did you see anything unusual?

GREG: Hi. Greg Thomas. (Expletive deleted) yeah! My wife thinks I'm nuts. Hey honey! Look who is here! It's that guy who does that show. You know, the one last week had those K2 climbers who saw Yeti!

MRS. THOMAS: Oh, give me a break.

GREG: I'm not alone. Other people saw something last night!

MRS. THOMAS: They sell liquor to anyone over 21.

GREG: (Expletive deleted.)

MRS. THOMAS: The kids can hear you Greg. It's bad enough that they think you're a lunatic. Do they have to think you're an (expletive deleted) too?

GREG: They can hear me but they can't hear you?

MRS. THOMAS: (Expletive deleted.) [Exit.]

RUDY: Excuse me, Mr. Thomas...

GREG: Greg.

RUDY: Greg. Could you tell me exactly what you saw?

GREG: Sure. Um...

NARRATOR: Mr. Thomas at this point assumed an expression with which I have become very familiar in my investigations.

GREG: [*Greg raises an eyebrow craftily.*] What's it worth to you?

RUDY: [*Addresses cameraman*] Cut it, Fred. [*Readdresses Greg with the tone of an algebra teacher explaining the binomial theorem to a thick-headed student.*] Let me explain how this works. We get the incident in a local newspaper. That's part of my job. Then we put your story on the air once, preferably with good pictures of the scene. That gives you a veneer of credibility.

GREG: Veneer? I'm telling the truth.

RUDY: Totally irrelevant. What matters is credibility. We give a "serious researcher" something to find when he or she checks out your story. A police report should be filed no later than today for the same reason. After we put you on the air, you can get on the UFO gravy train. You can write books, give lectures, attend conferences, the works. You should be paying me. But I'm willing to do this for you for free. I like you Greg. I'd like to see you get your slice of the pie. But Flying Saucer spotters and alien abductees are a dime a dozen. So, do I turn the camera back on, or do I leave and talk your neighbors instead?

MRS THOMAS [*who had listened from the next room*]: Talk to him, Greg.

GREG [*Annoyed that agreement sounds like obedience to his wife*]: OK.

RUDY: Roll it, Fred.

NARRATOR: Mr. Thomas not only cooperated but, as is usual in these cases, added flourishes to his story. He said the alien was 4 feet tall, a description which unconsciously made me lift up on my toes. He described large deer like eyes. He said that the alien had called out to him using mental telepathy and that only concern for the future of his family prevented him from joining some intergalactic love-in.

[*Cut to shoreline scene where a circle is visible in the brush. Tall pine and spruce trees are in the background. Twenty people mill about. Two police cruisers are parked by the circle and several other vehicles occupy the wood road leading to the site.*]

This is actual footage shot soon after Mr. Thomas filed his report. The police, who were in a jovial mood, plainly considered the incident to be a teenage prank of some sort. But in the quiet town of Gilmanton, it was a pleasant diversion from writing speeding tickets. At my urging a local reporter took a soil sample and had it sent to an independent lab. The traces of lithium were found and duly reported in the article. The young woman had done her homework. She explained the use of the element as a deuterium/tritium source in fusion devices.

Everything was going according to plan, but the road ahead was about to turn suddenly to the left. These shocking events after some words from our sponsors.

[*Ads follow for Scum, Ford trucks, Mercury outboard motors, and Nutrasweet. There is a repeat of the Scum commercial, which is wearing thin on entertainment value. Show returns with scene of diner. Actor playing Rudy sits in a booth.*]

NARRATOR: Yes, I was happy with the way the story was progressing, but it needed more before it was ready for prime time. It needed sex. It needed more pictorial evidence. I already had arranged for both. But while eating lunch at the Lakeview Diner in Alton Bay, a village by Lake Winnipesaukee, a tall attractive woman with shoulder-length red hair and mirrored sunglasses appeared by my table. She seemed familiar.

[*Camera slowly pans from toes to head of a beautiful woman. Inexplicably, the actress playing the red head is blonde.*]

CINDY: Hello Rudy.

RUDY: [*Cautiously*] Well hello. What brings you here?

CINDY: [Cindy picks an ice cube out of his water glass and chucks it at him.] You don't have the slightest idea who I am! [*Having waited long enough for an invitation, she simply sits down.*] Thanks, I'd love to join you. [*She removes her glasses. The actress' eyes are blue.*]

NARRATOR: Her piercing green eyes and Australian accent gave her away. She was the woman most responsible for my career. However, I played it cool.

RUDY: I remember. Cynthia. [*She glares.*] No, Cindy.

CINDY: I wonder if I make such lasting memories with all my dates. [*The actress' accent is Southeast British. There is no trace of Down Under.*]

RUDY: In fairness, you cut me off abruptly after the story aired.

CINDY: In fairness, you were a jerk. Are you one now?

RUDY: My ex thinks so.

CINDY: [*Cindy laughs.*] Mine too.

RUDY: Maybe we should have kept dating then.

CINDY: Oh, it wasn't just the show. You were too cynical for me. You know, you actually quoted Nietzsche to me. On more than one occasion.

RUDY: Lots of young men go through a Nietzsche phase. But I quoted Diogenes too.

CINDY: Oh, excuse me. I had you all wrong. But about that show, I'm still waiting for my apology.

RUDY: It was only a local broadcast. UHF.

CINDY: You misrepresented me, my coven and all our beliefs. You made our occult salon look like The Psychic Whorehouse. The way your camera focused on our knives whenever we mentioned our festivals made it look like we were into human sacrifice or something. The police took it all seriously enough to stop by and ask me questions about soliciting. They tested a blood-stain from my townhouse. Even though it tested as pig's blood, I'm lucky they didn't call the ASPCA. I told them it was just spillage from a pork roast.

RUDY: The ceremonies didn't take place at your townhouse.

CINDY: Well I'm glad you didn't tell them that or they would have raided all my friends' homes too. [*She smiles.*] The show did double our membership though.

NARRATOR: [*Overdubbed. Actors remain in frame but speak soundlessly.*] Perhaps a few viewers still remember my very first broadcast show more than 10 years ago.

An ambitious young writer, I had submitted an article to *The Washingtonian* on DC area witches. The number of women in any large city who call themselves witches is quite surprising. At the time Cindy was a self-described pagan high priestess and region-al head of a loose organization of witches with headquarters in New York. A new male witch ("warlock," I was told, is incorrect and insulting) is chosen as nominal overall "king" each year. However, aside from being pampered by the ladies, he doesn't seem to have much real authority. He evidently goes back to obscurity after his term. I've never met an ex-king. The college of regional coven leaders really runs things.

Cindy operated a salon and shop where she and her coven members gave astrological, tarot, and psychic readings. We hit it off well together during our first interview. Her photos had just the right touch of sleaze and her story made great copy. The magazine, however, rejected the article citing suspicions about the quality of my research. Perhaps, also, the article simply struck them as too tabloid.

Rather than scrap my work, I borrowed a professional video camera and worked the article into a film documentary. Cindy let us film some ceremonial naked dancing, which we blurred appropriately for broadcast. The nakedness actually was my idea, but the coven went along without objection. Cindy and I dated during the documentary production. A local TV station liked and aired the piece. Afterwards she refused to accept my calls. I suppose I did overstate the sensuality and suggest sinister goings on, but that was a ratings thing: greed rather than malice. She should have understood.

Anyway, the documentary was so popular that the station offered me a weekly spot just after Elvira. The show proved to be a hit. By the end of the year we were syndicated and I moved to New York.

[*Actors' voices become audible again.*]

RUDY: So what are you doing here? In Alton Bay, New Hampshire, of all places.

CINDY: I like the smell of pines and my car freshener wore out. What's your scam?

RUDY: Scam?

CINDY: Scheme.

RUDY: Much better. I read about some UFO sightings up here, so I came to see what I could dig up. I found something too. Over by Crystal Lake.

CINDY: I'm sure you found whatever you dropped there. Why a UFO though? Why not bring in Nessie from your Loch Ness special. How did you get that ripple effect by the way? A toy submarine?

RUDY: [*Gratified that she had followed his work*] Crystal Lake is too small to hold a monster. But there is something in the Loch.

CINDY: If you put it there. My very favorite was the Black Helicopter episode. That was great footage. I have to give you credit Rudy. You hovered there and gave that survivalist time to tape the UN markings on your chopper while his buddy unloaded a shotgun at you.

RUDY: [*Laughs.*] The SOB shot right through the floor. I understand now why the Air Cav boys in Vietnam used to sit on their helmets.

CINDY: Do you even know what is real anymore?

RUDY: I hope so.

CINDY: Do you have any ethics?

RUDY: I hope not. Nietzsche, remember?

CINDY: [*Smiles.*] That's OK. I married a man with ethics. I have no wish to repeat the experience.

RUDY: You haven't told me what are you doing here. Are you casting a spell on someone?

CINDY: Possibly. But I'm here for recreation. So recreate with me. Let's have some fun. Show off for me, Rudy. We made a good team once. Let me help. [*She leans back and lets her cleavage carry the proposal. Rudy sits speechless for several moments with his eyes fixed below her neck.*] I must have grown taller since last time.

RUDY: What? Oh. [*Rudy makes a decision.*] OK... You're on. I have a costume for you.

CINDY: Good. I like to play dress up.

NARRATOR: The viewer may question my good sense at this point, if he or she hasn't done so already. I knew or should have known that a serendipitous meeting with Cindy was ludicrously unlikely. But we all adjust our beliefs to suit our preferences. It was fun to believe a happy coincidence had reunited us hundreds of miles from our homes. Besides, though my ego is usually considered substantial, the possibility that I deliberately had been stalked by this gorgeous witch truly didn't occur to me.

RUDY: Nessie stays in Scotland. For New Hampshire we need aliens. I need another encounter to wrap up this story, and I've decided that it will happen to that couple in the corner booth. [*He waves at an all-American couple. They wave back.*]

CINDY: Grant and Tabitha over there with the $1,000 matching dorky biking outfits?

RUDY: Yes. Their names are Rolf and Tiffany, actually.

CINDY: Seriously?

RUDY: Yes. I chatted with them in the parking lot. They work for a chemical company in some surreal white-collar jobs. Personnel Network Management or something like that. [*He points out the window.*] They drive the Saab with the Massachusetts plates.

CINDY: With the Greenpeace bumper sticker and the bicycle rack?

RUDY: French bikes. Apparently no irony intended. They're up from Boston for a weekend cycling trip around the lake country. They live together, but from the way they argue they should get married soon.

CINDY: Argue about what?

RUDY: Something about how he never agrees to drive the extra distance to Vermont instead of New Hampshire, which is so working class, and how she always avoids meeting his parents.

CINDY: How would you react if I whined at you like that?

RUDY: I'd make you meet my parents.

CINDY: Sadist.

RUDY: I hope not. The Marquis' imagination was too mono-maniacal for me.

CINDY: [*Enjoying a bit of yuppie bashing*] Do they live together in Beacon Flats and watch reruns of Mad About You?

RUDY: The new North End, but they are moving to Weston because of parking for the two cars. According to them they only watch WGBH, to which they contribute, but somehow they knew who I was.

CINDY: Is the other car a Volvo?

RUDY: Beamer. Used. Their salaries haven't peaked yet.

CINDY: Great. When do we get to kill them?

RUDY: We don't.

CINDY: Are you getting ethical on me?

RUDY: Please. We need them for the interview. The girl is sexy...

CINDY: You think so?

RUDY: ...and they have a home video camera. I already primed them with stories about weird sightings and told them I would pay for any unusual footage, so they should keep it handy.

CINDY: What if what they tape isn't believable? Or is all too believable?

RUDY: Then we don't buy it.

[*Commercial break for Scum, Panasonic video cameras, Budweiser, and, yet again, Scum.*]

NARRATOR: The trap was laid by a brush-lined dirt road overlooking Crystal Lake. The blue lake stretching out below formed a beautiful backdrop. Although the climb from Mountain Road is a tough one for cyclists, the view makes the trip worthwhile, as I had been sure to tell Rolf and Tiffany. Cindy and I set up the tape deck and the multicolored halogen strobe lights.

[*Rolf and Tiffany appear in the distance. Zoom in. The girl no longer wears the biking outfit, but a pair of cut-off jeans and a skimpy blouse tied to expose the midriff. The camera does a quick close-up of Rolf's face but lingers over a full body shot of Tiffany pumping the pedals. Cut back to Cindy, who is donning an alien costume that looks like surplus from a low budget 1950s SciFi flick.*]

CINDY: This suit should be skin-tight.

RUDY: We're staging It Came From Outer Space not Barbarella.

CINDY: Who?

RUDY: Don't make me feel old. Where did you get those boots? [*Cindy is shown donning boots, each of which is shaped at the end like two large toes, rather like an ostrich foot.*]

CINDY: Oh, I used them to scare a fussy neighbor who was always complaining about having a witch next door. I should have worn them for your first special.

RUDY: I liked the naked dancers better.

CINDY: I'll bet. Here, tape me in this outfit.

RUDY: Didn't Watergate teach you anything?

CINDY: Didn't Rob Lowe teach you anything? Bad publicity sells tickets too. Anyway it's just for me.

NARRATOR: Against my better judgment, I taped Cindy including a close-up on the boots. A copy of this later appeared on *Nightline*. Meanwhile, the Bostonian bikers approached. When they had neared to 300 feet, I set off some strobe flashes and played a few bars from *White Zombie*. The couple stopped and took out their camera. We would have something to buy from them after all. The plan was working beautifully. I was then startled to see new actors in the piece.

[*Gray-skinned aliens emerge from brush and attempt to abduct couple. They are short and match the usual deer-eyed description, but they have two toed feet similar to Cindy's boots. They push at Rolf perfunctorily but grope Tiffany extensively for the camera. Both Rolf and Tiffany manage to pull themselves free and run off down the hill on foot. Cindy walks casually to the bikes. An alien picks up the cyclists' camera, which is lying on the ground and scans Cindy from her boots to her face. She curtsies. As Rudy approaches dumfounded, Cindy takes the camera and tapes him.*]

CINDY: I'll send you the original of this, but I have to make a copy first.

RUDY: [*Overwhelmed more by Cindy's actions than by the presence of aliens*] Why?

CINDY: My boys were caught on film a few miles from here. It's in the hands of ABC. We had to find a way to discredit the footage. When you showed up, we knew we could make it look like one of your scams.

RUDY: You won't get away with this. I'll put all of this on the air.

CINDY: I'm counting on it.

[*Cindy and the aliens walk into the brush. A moment later a Ford Explorer containing all of them bursts onto the dirt road and disappears in a whirlwind of dust.*]

NARRATOR: What you are about to see now is not a re-enactment, but the actual footage from the scene taken by Rolf and Tiffany's camera. It is identical to that shown on *Nightline*.

[*Shaky home video shows a dirt road. Screams accompany blurred pictures of gray torsos and two-toed feet. Glimpses of the couple themselves show both to be wearing biking outfits. The camera falls to the ground and records some sideways images of feet. It is picked up. The lens pans slowly from the two-toed boots to the face of the red-headed woman who wears them. She curtsies. The narrator is then seen approaching on foot.*]

Yes, you have just seen actual alien footage. If the peculiar circumstances of this encounter raise some doubts in your mind, remember that this is not an isolated case. One in 50 Americans, now including myself, claims to have met an alien face-to-face. This is far too many to be dismissed lightly. Are there outsiders among us? You must decide for yourself. But One in 50 of us knows the answer.

[*After the credits the Scum commercial begins to run yet again.*]

Rudy flicked off the TV and sat quietly in the dark room.

"Mind if we join you?" asked a redhead in the doorway. The reflections of large eyes shimmered in back of her about four feet off the floor.

"Obviously I need a new security system," observed Rudy.

"Oh, it's OK for common crooks. My boys electromagnetic pulsed it. Thank you so much. I couldn't have produced a better show myself. No one will believe a word you said."

"Polls show a majority of our viewers believe our reports."

"No one who matters will believe you. That one in 50 number was great. Where did you get that?"

"Polls. It was quoted by In Search Of or Unsolved Mysteries a while back. The number is real."

"Let's see, one in 50 is 5,500,000 people. Spread over, say, 20 years, that comes to 275,000 encounters per year in the US alone. You know my boys aren't doing this. The sky would be ablaze with flying saucers. All that figure shows is how many people lie. Do you know what is real anymore, Rudy?"

"I'm beginning to wonder."

Four gray-skinned beings suddenly scrambled over the couch and began to gobble Scum. One dipped taco shells, but the others used their fingers. One alien actually perched on Rudy's knee. Rudy didn't know whether to be disgusted or flattered.

"They love the stuff," Cindy laughed. "Earth foods are banned back home, so they make a fortune smuggling it. Go figure."

Rudy sighed. "I don't get the witch alien connection."

"Pure accident. Not everything is an occult conspiracy, Rudy. Coincidences really do happen. The girls and myself were conducting seances back in DC. I was channeling on Anastasia and tuned in on these guys instead. What a kick, huh?"

"Telepathy? For real?"

"Knocked my socks off. How would you like another shot at covering our organization, by the way? The witches I mean. These guys are just friends. I feel I owe you that. We're going to need a new Sun King on December 21. One year term. I think you would be just perfect."

"I don't know."

"There'll be naked dancing," she cajoled.

He was interested, although something about the proposed term seemed to him ominous. He decided.

"You're on."

Cindy smiled and toyed with her ceremonial knife.

CATERWAUL

Hiya doll. Happy you came on by. New in town? I've seen you in the next yard the past couple of days. I've been meaning to stop by, but I'm still pretty worn out. I had a tough weekend. I always dug longhairs. That orange coat is real sweet.

Me? Boss. My human named me that. It was one of the few things he got right. At times I think he might be a bit sarcastic when he says it, but humans really aren't smart enough for that, are they?

What was so tough about my weekend? Here. Jump up here on the picnic table Sweet Thing and I'll tell you about it.

First of all my life is hard even on the best of days. There's my human, Jerk. He calls himself Rich but you know how it is. You can talk plain as can be at him until you're blue in the nose and he just stares at you like he doesn't understand a word. And you know? I think he doesn't! You have to stick his nose in it by actually standing on your plate or scratching at the door before he gets the simplest message. That's why "smart human" is a total oxymoron.

Then there is my horrible roommate Succotash. Succotash. The cat is common street trash. She's no classy lady like you. Jerk rescued her from some shelter or something and now she acts like she's Queen of the Manor. Do you think Jerk consulted me about bringing this vagabond into the house? No! They just don't think, do they?

At least you'd expect Succotash to respect my seniority and pay me the dignity I'm due, but no. That cat has got a mean streak in her wider than the white one on her belly. If you so

much as brush against her she spits and swats like you were trying to molest her or something. Yuck! Just the thought of it gives
me the shivers. Sometimes she just looks at me from across the
room and growls for no reason. I try not to let it show, but that
really annoys me. Other times she huffs that superior huff of
hers. I never met a bigger snob with less cause to be one.

Anyway, things got even worse last week when a raccoon
found my cat door. I was taking a nap on the couch when the raccoon ran right by me. He rushed to the kitchen as though he
knew right where it was, and he opened up the cabinets looking
for food. Jerk came home about then and found the intruder in
the kitchen polishing off a bag of my Purina he had ripped to
shreds. Jerk got all worked up about it. After he chased the raccoon out he set to work sealing up my cat door with a piece of
Plexiglas. There was no need for that. I mean, I didn't like the
idea of the thief running in and out and eating my leftovers
either, but I could have lived with it. I tried telling Jerk that a
hundred times, but he just gave me that stupid stare and went on
with the job.

The next morning I forgot all about it and banged my nose
on the Plexiglas while trying to go out. Was that a cruel joke, his
making the seal transparent, or what? If I even suspected the
man is bright enough to lay a trap like that I'd be even angrier.
Anyhow, I had to go all the way to the bedroom, jump on the
bed, and wake up Jerk. I gave him a whole pantomime routine to
get him to follow me to the front door. Finally he got the idea
through his thick skull and let me out. He was muttering something about "5 o'clock in the morning."

I meant to go out catting for a couple of hours. I know you're
new here, but it's quite a carnival in these parts. There are rabbits and squirrels and mice and birds and moles, and trees, and
more dirt than a feline can scratch in a lifetime. It's not without
danger, though, so you have to watch your step. If you're nice to
me, I'll show you the ropes. There are dogs around here who will
snap your neck as soon as look at you. It's not just the dogs you
have to watch either. Not all the neighborhood Toms are gentle-
men like I am.

Anyhow, my day was tolerable for a while. After I worked out
a few kinks nosing through the grass and climbing some logs I

moseyed back to the old homestead to grab some beauty sleep. I had gotten only 20 hours the day before so I needed to catch up. I sauntered up to the old cat door, and there was the Plexiglas!

I walked around to the front door to yell at Jerk, but my heart sank when I noticed his car wasn't in the driveway. Wouldn't you know that Jerk was gone to wherever he goes all day? You know how humans just wander off without so much as a nevermind and then show up independent as you please hours later, as often as not without any new food at all. They are the most self-centered animals.

Have you ever seen where they catch those cans of food by the way? No? Me either. I never see any rolling around the lawn here.

Well, getting back to my story, the day was a little chilly. In fact my tail was aching from the cold. I checked out the other doors and windows hoping to find something open, but the house was sealed tighter than a can of *Nine Lives*. I hopped up on the rail of the back deck and peeked through the dining room window. There, as ugly as you please, was Succotash on the table looking back at me with a self-satisfied expression. She licked and chewed her paws theatrically. She stretched in the soporific warmth of the house and curled up for a nap with her back to me. One day when she is eating, I'm going to sneak up on the countertop and drop the electric can opener on her head.

There was nothing much to do but find a sunny spot and wait for Jerk to come home. This plan turned out to have a near fatal flaw. While scanning the back yard from the deck rail for a reasonably warm and comfortable place, I happened to spot an ugly face in the side bushes. Splotch was favoring me with an evil cocked-head appraisal. Splotch is a battle-scarred neighborhood Tom with muscles for brains. Unfortunately he also has muscles for muscles and outweighs me by at least 2 pounds. He looks like a white cat that knocked over a can of gray paint and then got kicked down the stairs. Splotch has more claw marks than Jerk's favorite piece of furniture because nothing brightens his day as much as a scrap. You stay away from him if you see him.

Oh, you know him? You think he's cute? What is wrong with you dames? You talk all the time about how you like Toms to be sweet and sensitive, and then you fall for some outlaw brute! No, don't go away. I'll be polite. What's that? You find danger attractive, huh? Well, I can be pretty dangerous myself. I certainly don't want to give the impression that I'm a coward. I'm just refined. I could take Splotch out if I wanted to, but I feel one can spend time in a more culturally rewarding way than by brawling with some thug. I'm not so insecure that I have to prove myself all the time. So when Splotch comes by I usually withdraw to the drawing room until he gets bored and wanders off in search of someone else to fight. He never followed me inside, because deep down he respects and fears me. Besides, he doesn't like Succotash. She put one of those scars in his face when he peeked in the cat door one time.

Anyhow, with my cat door shut off, withdrawal wasn't an option. Splotch was in deep water now, but I wanted to give him an opportunity to avoid getting hurt. The next half-hour I tried staring him down, but he sat and stared back steadily without so much as a twitch. He just didn't get the hint. He's almost as dumb as Jerk. Nevertheless, I knew that even his dull brain eventually would figure out that he could come up on the rail after me. So, if I was serious about the principle of nonviolence, I would have to make a run for it soon. I soon got my chance to avoid hurting Splotch. A crow made a low pass over the yard, which distracted Splotch just long enough for me to make my move. I leaped from the deck and shot for the rear woods like, if I do say so myself, a silver streak.

As I already told you, Splotch's wits need a bit of oiling but after a few seconds he comprehended the situation. He came crashing through the foliage after me with all the subtlety of a *Metallica* concert. I had a good lead though, and let's say that I was highly motivated. You have to respect me for this: I had the strength of character to flee rather than injure Splotch who, after all, is clearly mentally impaired and deserving of our sympathy.

As I ran, the sounds of pursuit grew steadily fainter and finally ceased altogether. Just to be safe I ran some more. Then I stopped to catch my breath and get my bearings. I was deeper into the woods than I ever had ventured, and I was all turned around. I staggered to my feet and trotted straight ahead hoping to spot a familiar landmark. Soon I came to a road. There is a road in front of my house. I figured this might be the same one, so I walked along the edge reckoning that I might come upon my driveway.

The asphalt vibrated and there was a sound. The distant rumble behind me escalated into a roar. Looking back, I saw what looked like a house on wheels barreling straight at me. The letters M A C K were emblazoned on the front. I dove into the nearest catch basin and hunkered down, while crashing noises passed overhead.

I had escaped the mechanical monster, but now I was in a pit. The way I entered was beyond practical leaping up distance. Worse, I was standing in cold trickling water. The water flowed out of a long dark tunnel and then went into another. I didn't like the looks of either, but I had to pick one. I chose to splash along through the tunnel downstream. Eventually the water debouched into a canyon under open sky. I scaled up one of the cliffs which must have been a good 6 feet high and found myself more lost than ever. I was cold, wet, and tired.

The time had come for some original thinking. In the distance I espied a house with an open garage door. Normally I avoid houses with strange humans. Jerk may be a jerk, but he's my jerk. You never know about the others. However, in extreme circumstances you have to be flexible. I cautiously approached. All was quiet in the garage. An old drop cloth was heaped in the corner of the garage. I was really beat, so I snuggled in and grabbed some much-needed sleep. Four or five hours later, before I had any rest at all, I was startled awake by the noise of the garage door closing. I went back to sleep.

There is not much to say about the next 2 days. Let me tell you that after a day or so in an unheated garage with out food or water the novelty wears thin.

At long last the garage door reopened and a station wagon pulled in. Out of the car piled 2 adults, 2 screaming kids and, wouldn't you know it, a golden-haired dog. The dog froze and sniffed the air repeatedly. The sheer power and strength of presence of my personality is such that dogs always are aware of me. Suddenly he bounded my way.

I anticipated what was coming, so I dove under the car and charged out the open garage door.

"Duke! Duke!" yelled one of the brats.

This Duke wasn't as dumb as Splotch. He caught on to my maneuver right away and was hot on my trail. I could hear him gaining. On the other side of the street was a tall tree with sturdy looking branches. Taking to the air was my only hope. I cleared the pavement, leaped for the trunk, and sunk my claws in the bark. I felt Duke's breath on my tail as I clambered to the heights. I climbed until the branches grew so thin that they wavered alarmingly under my weight. Far below Duke waited at the base of the tree. Soon, one of the people retrieved the dog but I was taking no chances for a while. Night arrived and the temperature dropped. The cold hurt my eyes.

The view from the treetop was marvelous. I never realized the world was so big. Well-traveled cats often tell you this, but the stories mean nothing until you see it for yourself. Why, you could walk for days in any direction before reaching the end of it. Something was nagging me about the view to the north. There was something familiar about the pattern of window lights distantly visible through the trees. Yes, it had to be. Home was in sight.

I waited a couple more hours just to be discreet and then climbed down the tree. I walked in the direction of the lights. I hiked a long time and hoped I hadn't gotten turned around again. I persevered. The moment came when I recognized familiar woods. I made a final push through the brambles. Yes, at last, I stood before my white house. I took a deep breath. I trotted up to the old door and there was that Plexiglas again. Now this was too much! Some one was going to answer for this.

Now, as you can tell, I'm not normally one to complain but enough was enough. I stomped to the front door and started hollering.

The door creaked open and a bleary-eyed Jerk looked out.

"Boss is that you?"

"Who do you think?"

"I thought you were gone for good!"

I started to tell him about it but he just gave me that stupid blank look. So I brushed past his leg and communicated in a way his limited intelligence could manage. I stood in my plate.

"Are you hungry, Boss?"

"No, I just like to stand in my plate!"

I was so hungry that I ate an entire can without much noticing what it was. But it is not as good idea to seem too appreciative to humans. They stop trying. So I demanded a refill. He complied. I ate a few bites, sneered, and gave Jerk my best "Don't let this happen again!" snort. He sighed and went back to bed grumbling something about 3 o'clock in the morning.

I jumped on the bed, crawled under the blanket, and snatched a quick 15-hour nap.

Well, that was my weekend. I figured you might understand. And I tell you, this business with the window is not over yet.

Listen, what do you say we go behind the bushes over there and wake up the humans with our screams. Hey, don't hiss! It was just a suggestion. It doesn't have to be now. Just come on back when you're in the mood. What do you mean you're never in the mood anymore? Yeah, I know about the vet. The creep stuck me with needles and Jerk just let him do it. Something happened to you there and you just don't have any interest anymore? What do you mean you might make an exception for Splotch because he is cute?

Listen, I don't need to hear this. I'm going back to the house. Jerk is home. I'll see you around.

What a waste of time. Splotch over me? She has no class at all. Well, her loss.

DEEP FRIED

CAROL: It is Tuesday night and once again this is Carol Pung hosting *Tough Cops*, the interactive real-time police docudrama where you get to speak to and direct the action of our officer of the week. All calls are routed through our on-line editor who selects questions to be transmitted to the officer.

Tonight we are in Trenton, New Jersey. For the safety of our officers, our broadcast and cable links are blacked out in Trenton at this time. Donning the camera helmet today is Officer Klaus Mendoza of the Greater Trenton Police Department.

Hello officer.

KLAUS: Hi Carol.

CAROL: Tell our subscribers what bust you have planned for us this evening.

KLAUS: Tonight after weeks of careful preparation we plan a raid on some true predators of society. In the ordinary looking suburban house you see on your screen, criminals are operating a basement bakery. We have analyzed the effluents of the air stacks and sewer lines coming out of the house and have found traces of deep fried fat, whole butter, and pure cane sugar. Pure!

And look. What really makes you sick, we are less than 500 feet from a grammar school.

It's no wonder that kids have no respect for the law when they see criminals operating almost in the open every day of the year.

CAROL: We have our first caller.

CALLER #1: Officer Mendoza, Do you really think that junk is being sold in school?

CAROL: How about that, Klaus?

KLAUS: No doubt about it Carol. Look, some kid sees his older brother sweating 40 hours a week flipping tofu and slinging watercress at McSprout's and not earning enough to move out of mom's house. He knows he can earn as much on one Danish as his brother takes home in a day. A nickel bag (that's $500 to you and me) of donuts is his brother's take home for a week. A kilo of eclairs can set him up for a month. Is it any wonder that he is willing to poison his fellow students?

And you know how this starts, Carol? Popcorn. I know I sound old-fashioned and that a lot of bleeding hearts who popped corn over candles in their dorm rooms at college think our penalties for popcorn possession are excessive. They are not. And I don't want to hear about how harmless it is or how it comes from a natural plant that George Washington grew on his farm. This is what introduces young people to junk foods and gets them psychologically dependent. We have to think about whose rights are important here. I think our kids ought to come first. Our kids have a right to grow up in a fat free world.

CALLER #2: Isn't it true that the FDA was meant originally simply to ensure the freshness and purity of food and...

KLAUS: No! That is one of the common misconceptions promoted by extremists who are so dogmatic that they are willing to sacrifice our children to their narrow-minded ideology. Safety was always the concern behind federal and state laws and agencies such as the FDA. Sure, in the massively addicted societies of the 20th century it took time to build the political support to bring many commonly used poisons under control, but safety always has been the point. And nothing is more unsafe than sugar and fat. Far more people every year die from heart disease caused by improper diet than die from all narcotics and artificial stimulants combined.

JEROME: Klaus, this is Jerome. I'm with the NYPD. I must say it bothers me to waste my time on people who are doing what they want to do. There isn't enough jail space to hold muggers and burglars and carjackers because of all the pastry chefs and binge eaters. Violent criminals, who are a real threat to other people, are let back out on the street. Our job description says "Serve and Protect." Snacking remains a victimless crime.

KLAUS: I can't believe I'm hearing this from a brother officer. Have you ever seen a family disrupted by sickness or death because of what some irresponsible parent shoved in his mouth? What about kids unable to learn because they're all hyped up from the chocolate chip cookies they sneaked at lunch? It makes me puke to hear pastry use called a victimless crime.

JEROME: What about the victims of gang violence as young people fight for distribution territories for muffins and tarts? Drive-by shootings have turned our neighborhoods into war zones. What about the financial bonanza baking has given organized crime?

KLAUS: The answer is not to give up, but to cut off the supplies at the source. The recent invasion of Jamaica has brought the sugar fields and refineries under our control. The rest of the Caribbean is promising cooperation. Cuba so far is reluctant to take on its powerful sugar lords, but the Coast Guard is making life expensive for them: the Guard intercepted more than 300 smuggling vessels off the Florida Keys last year. We are making headway.

JEROME: Isn't it also important to our kids to inherit a country where their adult freedoms will be protected?

KLAUS: I want to make something clear. As Americans, we all believe in individual rights. No one is suggesting outlawing all use of sugars or fats, nor are we trying to put legitimate manufacturers out of business. With a doctor's prescription you or any citizen may buy whatever such foodstuffs are appropriate for you. Any honest manufacturer simply must sell only to licensed distributors who have the responsibility to screen customers, check prescriptions, and keep careful records. We only want to bring the industry under sensible regulation.

SUE: Hello, this is Sue Packer from CAFE, the Coalition for A Fat-free Environment. I just want to let you know that some of us appreciate everything you are doing to help preserve traditional American family values.

KLAUS: Thanks, Sue. That's rewarding to hear.

CAROL: All right, you have heard the arguments. Now it is up to you, our subscribers, to decide whether the raid on this suspected pie den should proceed at this time. Please transmit your votes now.
[Pause as votes are electronically counted.]
OK, Klaus. The numbers are in. We have 54,348 in favor and 21,235 opposed. It looks like a go.
[Klaus exits.]
Aren't these some great action shots we are getting from the helmetcam? You can see the risk these brave officers are taking as they break through each door not knowing what may be on the other side. It's hard to believe human beings can live in a space like this. Look at the wrappers all over the herbal tea tables and the crumbs in the weave of the dingy shag carpet!
The police have one of the suspects now! He is in the bathroom trying to flush away the contents of what looks to be bags of sugar. Officer Mendoza is tasting a pinch of white powder from a 40-kilo bag. Is that what it looks like, Klaus?

KLAUS: Yes, Carol. Pure Granada White. I wouldn't even try to guess the street value of this. This is more than enough evidence to convict. Also we can seize the real estate from the landlord. Landlords should suspect any tenants who pay in cash and report them. If they don't, they are as guilty as the criminals. They surely don't deserve to profit from them.

CAROL: The police have apprehended two other suspects: an adult female and what appears to be a 10-year-old-girl. Both appear to have been destroying evidence in the basement bakery.

KLAUS: Look at this equipment, Carol. Wall ovens, stovetop burners, and a refrigerator freezer. This is a major operation. In the back you can see a storage room with special humidity controls. We have counted 18 pies, 14 cases of donuts, 16 boxes of Danishes, and at least 50 kilos of cookies — a mixed assortment of chocolate chip and coconut sprinkle. You are looking at a fortune.

CALLER #3: Why is the suspect shouting "24 cases of donuts!" as she is being handcuffed?

KLAUS: She is on a sugar high and doesn't know what she is saying. Either that or she is trying to escape punishment by slandering Greater Trenton's Finest. You can be sure our count is accurate and that the evidence will be destroyed after the trial.

But here is what really makes you sick. This couple actually had their 10-year-old daughter baking cookies! Normally the state is reluctant to break up families even when the parents are criminals, but unwholesome abuse like this calls out for humane intervention.

CAROL: This looks like another question for our subscribers. Under the direct democracy provisions of the recent Omnibus Entertainment Act, you can decide. Should this young girl be turned over to state care?

[*Pause.*]

Once again we have a yes, Klaus, by a margin of 48,632 to 27,986.

KLAUS: It's comforting to know that the common folks will make the right decision if you just give them a chance. This girl is going to need years of professional therapy to cope with what she experienced in this kitchen. At least now she'll be able to get it.

CAROL: That's all for tonight. I want to thank Officer Mendoza and our participating audience.

Join us next week when *Tough Cops* investigates an underground publishing house suspected of printing and distributing hate literature including the long banned *Huckleberry Finn.* This is Carol Pung. Good night.

SEX, DRUGS
& ROCK AND ROLL

Chapter 1
Sex

Is paid sex romantic? Variation on an old joke: it is if you do it right. How one does it right may best be explored with a mythic tale of a boy and his tart.

Do not confuse myth with fiction. There really was a Trojan War even though the actual events grew fabulous through the retelling. There quite possibly was an Aeneas though the truth of who and what he was is deeply obscured by the mist of time. There is at least a chance there was an Arthur. Accordingly, the hero in the tale that follows ought not be considered wholly an invention.

Mythic romance is an epic theme that requires a suitably pompous voice. We shall strive to achieve this. We shall forego the dactylic hexameter however. That is as difficult to write as it is to read, and the author is no Vergil or Homer. But his Odysseus had a moment in the arms of his Calypso, and of those arms and the man I sing.

Let us call our mythical hero "Andrew." He lived in a place called Chester. This was a far-flung suburb of the mythical city of Gotham, sometimes called New York, a great metropole of a mythical country known (with the degree of sardonic humor customary to that time and place) as the Land of Liberty. Our hero was in his early 20s, epigone of a well-heeled family that had made its modest fortune in commercial developments such as small strip malls and office parks. He now worked in the family business although the precise nature of his job and authority was unclear, especially to construction site workers for whom the son of the boss was by long tradition very much a joke.

In accordance with the national fashion, Andrew had received 17 years of liberal education, which, though it prevented him from properly learning the family business or any other suitable livelihood, at least taught him how to live without the independence the education itself obstructed. So, while clumsy of hammer and lease, he could quote Euripedes aptly and accurately.

Let us look in on Andrew walking the Gotham pavement.

The bright sun had affected his eyes so as to give the world a bluish hue, but it had failed to crack the bitter cold. The February wind could be felt beneath his winter coat, a red plaid hunter's jacket ordinary in his hometown of 6,000 people but conspicuous in the city. Our hero's hands pushed deep in his jacket pockets. They turned red and complained bitterly at the fingertips. Perversely, Andrew hoped the pain would continue. His hands displayed a certainty and urgency of response that somehow his mind had stopped showing.

Andrew, like many a young man, was given to uncompromising pronouncements on this or that subject. His current favorite was libertarian politics into which he had drifted because it allowed him to "be involved" without the risk of electoral victory and subsequent disillusionment. But his pronouncements were intellectual play only. They had no real emotional content for him. Had he actually been asked to join in a pledge of "our lives, our fortunes, and our sacred honor," one suspects he would have coughed and excused himself to the kitchen. Again, like many a young man, especially of the over-educated variety, he had acquired a taste for nihilism. He found the material world to be indifferent and humans to be careless when not malevolent. He no longer was able to work up much animus about it. High hopes seemed a foolish outlook on life and paranoia seemed a waste of energy. In consequence a creeping dullness spread to his positive and his negative responses alike. He generally thought this for the best.

Weekend walks through New York City relaxed our hero. He liked the city's hard edges that contrasted so with the leafy fuzziness of his own town. Today, however, he walked with an ill-

defined restlessness. He crossed Broadway and passed the Times
building at 43rd where trucks were unloading a forest of rolled
paper. He crossed 8th Avenue and walked north past the sidewalk
princesses. He was merely window-shopping. Our hero had no
objection to the ladies or their line of work. He in fact had suc-
cumbed on one occasion when he was 18 and a virgin. Having
found the episode rather more mundane than expected, he
refrained from further incursions into the demimonde. He preferred more conventional arrangements with women although
all of his dates so far had been in some regard unsatisfactory.
Still, his hormones nudged him enough that he found himself
on the Avenue.

Andrew ambled for several blocks while deliberating grimly
on the worthlessness of humankind, the paucity of pulchritude
necessary for survival on the Avenue, and the gloomy fate of the
Republic. He scarcely heard the iterations of, "Hi, you want go
out?" It was an unusually pitched voice rather than he afore-
mentioned hormones that caused him to glance left and catch
the hazel eyes of an extraordinarily attractive young woman. Her
face was curiously innocent in its expression, her hair had the
hint of red that for some reason appealed to him, and her frame
seemed a happy compromise between the delicate and the ath-
letic. She strongly reminded him of an old college favorite who
had not in fact favored him. She stood as a repudiation of his
thoughts, except perhaps those about the gloomy fate of the
Republic. This irritated him and he continued walking toward
Central Park. He imagined the admiration of the other pedestri-
ans for his strength of character. He also contemplated the role
of cowardice in his retreat, but he was able to push that thought
away quickly.

Before long, he reached the park and now was at a loss for a
goal. He searched for a bench that was unbroken and distant
from the impecunious and the peculiar. He found one and sat to
watch the traffic. Crisp white clouds moved swiftly across the sky.
The sharp taste of ozone was strangely invigorating. The cold
bench was uncomfortable through his pants.

The image of those hazel eyes and strawberry blonde hair
returned to him. "No, don't be a low life," he muttered aloud, as

a nervous man self-consciously looked his way. "Oh, I don't care what people think," he lied to himself more quietly, and to prove it he retraced his steps down 8th Avenue. After all, it is in the general direction of the Path subway terminal, he rationalized. But to avoid looking deliberate about getting a second look at the girl, he crossed to the opposite side of the street.

The girl, who had chosen the appellation "Angel," leaned against the half-empty brick building on the corner of 48th. She hadn't borrowed the name from the movie about a girl in her profession. Her name really was Angela.

She wished her feet would stop feeling the cold. She was quite successful at her job, despite an attitude considered snobbish by some of her competitors. She made no apologies for being at least a little picky. You had to trust your instincts about potential customers. Even guys in business suits sometimes were dangerous or crazy; one such lunatic had mutilated a woman in a hotel across the street the previous week. She was arrested often, but since New York courts placed prostitution in a category with spitting in the subway, there was little risk of a penalty more severe than a couple of hours in jail and a $50 fine.

Angel had few complaints with her status. It was an improvement over her early life. Angela grew up outside of Tallahassee, Florida, as one of 4 children in a poor family. Her father was a violent alcoholic gambler who wasted whatever her mother, a NATO bride from Luxembourg, earned. She often was shuffled among aunts who made no secret of the burden of her existence. At 15 she had enough, informed the appropriate aunt of her departure with sufficient impoliteness so as to raise no objection, and hitched a ride north.

Angel went to work as soon as she reached the city. At first she rationalized that it was all she could do. Today, at 23, she frankly admitted she was too lazy to do anything else. Even within the boundaries of her selectivity, some of the men were pretty disgusting, but in general the work was neither difficult nor unpleasant. Moreover, it was very lucrative. She earned thousands per week, spent freely and enjoyed a comfortable apartment near Gramercy Park.

Today business was dead. Not even the police showed much interest. She thought she had a prospect earlier with a youngish guy who must have been an out-of-towner. He wore a plaid jacket appropriate only for duck hunting. Some men show every emotion on their faces. She could read his well enough when she asked, "Would you like to go out with me?" But like so many others he walked on past. The trouble with working in public, she reflected, is that it is in public. She knew that more men would accept if they were not in full view of others. Some girls handed out business cards, but the police didn't like it and they always fell into the wrong hands. Police were usually OK if you didn't make them look too undiligent.

Angel creased her lips in annoyance as a woman about her own age gripped her husband's arm and glared at her from behind pink sunglasses. She smirked when the man apologetically shrugged his shoulders. Across the Avenue she espied a familiar plaid jacket. There really was no reason to walk down 8th Avenue twice except herself and the other girls. She smiled that he was on the other side of the street. Do men ever grow up? She waved. He discreetly waved back. The light changed to WALK and Angel crossed the street to meet him.

Andrew occasionally had the sensation of dissociation, of being an observer of the scene in which he was acting. The most dramatic such case was when he had fallen out of a tree as a child. To this day his recollection of the event is from an altitude of some 50 feet. He clearly envisages himself in the scene below. He tended not to mention these episodes in case they indicated some psychosis. One such sensation jarringly ended when the young woman spoke to him in an unsettling accent best described as Southern fried Brooklyn.

"Hi. Mah name is Ann-gel."

It was only when climbing the second flight of stairs in the *Mayfair Hotel* that he recovered enough self-possession to ask himself, "What am I doing now?"

"Did you say something, luv?"

"Nothing important."

Inextricably committed, barring an unseemly fuss (our hero could be cowardly about such things), he decided to make the best of it. This was easier than expected. Angel was talkative, had an extremely pleasant disposition, and was determinedly normal.

His limited experience with working girls had not yet shaken the Hollywood stereotype for hookers of foul language, chain-smoking, nasty cynicism, rapid aging, and streetwise hardness. Ludicrously, it was the girl who lived next door to him who fit that description better. Besides, Angel was the most attractive woman he had encountered so closely up to that time. As their winter clothes dropped, his predicament looked less and less dreadful.

Andrew found himself appreciating the simple honesty of the transaction, as compared with the unspoken contractual provisions of conventional dating: obligations, self-restrictions, services, and, yes, financial costs. So without unrefinedly indulging in details, let us say that the afternoon was spent in pleasant conversation in both the 21st and 18th century senses. He traveled home relaxed and with a distinct liking for his new acquaintance.

Such afternoons became a recurrent and refreshing feature of his life. He fretted a bit over dollars, but in truth she was less expensive than his more socially acceptable girlfriends. He quickly lost all lingering disquiet. Oddly, after 8 years in the business, Angel still displayed sensitivity about it. Let us listen in on one occasion when our hero picked the wrong moment to be playful.

"Tch...Angel, why do I like you?" he teased.

Not playful at all, she responded, "Why, am I that hard to like?"

"Well, uh …"

"Yeah, I know. 'Get yourself a NICE girl. All that bitch wants is your money.' Right?"

"Well, uh … "

"But all those little 'Priscilla Housewives' out where you live are worse prostitutes than I am. You know they take their husbands' paychecks, I mean like all of it, for cleaning up like they would anyway if they lived alone and then giving them sex once a month. The second Thursday, you know? Unless a bridge party ran late that evening in which case he'd have to wait until the following month. I'd never do that to a guy. Like, I'd never really marry him, you know? I don't take anything a guy doesn't give me up front."

"Well, uh …"

"Does my being a hooker bug you or something?"

"Well, uh …"

"Nobody cares anymore except squares [sic]!"

"Well, uh …"

"Or fags."

Although not squeamish at all about doing a double with another girl and a customer, Angel was known to be rude about male homosexuals. Perhaps this was a trade bias. Andrew did not annoy her further. He was secretly amused that she did not refute the "only after your money" quote, but simply painted it on others. He chose not to ask what she thought of women who earned more than their men. Logically that would reverse the roles. It seemed too dangerous to ask.

Despite developing a real fondness for her, Andrew was under no illusions about the nature of their relationship. Any doubts he might have had were dispelled quickly. Thus:

"Angel, would you like to catch dinner and a show?"

"Do you really want to?" she asked noncommittally.

"I asked if you would like to."

"How much were you thinking of spending?"

"I don't know. Broadway is getting expensive. A couple hundred, I guess."

"I would rather have the money please. I'll make it up to you here."

She got it. Andrew did not propose expensive activities afterwards. Yes, our hero was fond of Angel. He bought her point of view pretty much. He did not entertain illusions. Well, he did have one. Andrew was unable to see any physical flaws in Angel. Now her attributes were estimable but not, after all, Olympian. Witness:

"Do I look OK?"

"Gorgeous."

"I meant my hair."

"That too."

"Stop it! That's no help at all. You always exaggerate."

"No. You're beautiful."

"I know I'm cute. But I'm not BEAUtiful."

The distinction didn't concern Andrew. He didn't yet know it, but this was a danger sign.

Summer arrived. The Democrats convened in New York to throw parties and incidentally nominate a presidential candidate. Chronically financially strapped New York City hoped to impress present and future distributors of taxpayers' money. A possibly misguided part of the effort was a campaign to clean up 8th Avenue. Laws against prostitution previously had been almost unenforceable since neither witness was likely to testify, but the State Assembly passed a loitering law which, taken literally, would subject any stationary person to arrest who talked to more than two other people on the street. The police, of course, were expected to enforce this selectively.

Legally armed and eager to protect the morals of the convening Democrats, the city sent its 30,000 strong police force into action. The Republicans convened in Miami that year where they were left dangerously on their own recognizance, but that is outside the realm of our tale. The impact in Gotham was immediate and total.

Angel was furious. Andrew didn't care much. He long since had acquired her phone number, so he simply called ahead and arranged dates. In principle Andrew opposed the law, but it was so typical of popular acts of oppressive busybody government, many aimed at his own business, that he didn't get emotional about it. Our hero still was not getting very emotional about anything.

It would seem uncharacteristic that our hero adored Euripedes. The playwright, after all, was the ultimate gut twister. No soap opera writer since has matched the pathos of Euripedes' final Acts. His characters were fanatics. They indulged themselves in one emotion or another and so brought themselves to disaster. Witness Medea, Hippolytus, Pentheus. Like a later author's creation, all would have been better to have suffered the slings and arrows of outrageous fortune. It should have been a warning to our hero that he liked this kind of thing. It meant that romantic excesses brewed in him beneath his placid surface. They might yet boil over.

During the summer, Andrew's visits to New York decreased in frequency. Nearly the whole month of July passed during which time he was insufficiently motivated to make the journey. The construction of a four-unit mall on Route 10 occupied his daylight hours and his leisure time was filled with innocent diversions, except for once when he and his buddies drank to excess. On the day after he was reminded why he had let so much time pass since their last binge.

He hadn't given up Angel by any means, but in truth she did not have the allure she had at the beginning. New York seemed a long way to go.

On the first day of August our hero stopped at the local delicatessen. Standing outside the store was a group of the nation's future. They were in the second decade of their lives. When Andrew walked past them to his car and bent to enter it, his wallet slipped from his pocket. Of the many witnesses nary a one spake or raised a finger aside from the usual middle one. Instead, when Andrew backed away from the curb one of their number stepped off the curb and stood on the wallet as he drove away. Contained in the wallet was a card advertising Caterpillar Tractor on one side and sporting Angel's number on the other.

Having arrived home, Andrew discovered his loss and panicked. He drove back to the bologna emporium but the politicians of tomorrow had vanished. First Andrew thought of the money and his cards. Then he thought of his license. Then he thought of Angel. What was that number? Why couldn't he quite remember it? 794-6496? 674-9476? 674-7496? The ones he tried were wrong. Maybe a digit was not just transposed but altogether wrong. Maybe two were wrong. That put the possible combinations in the thousands.

It may seem odd that our hero did not know where our heroine lived, but it is not odd at all. Andrew, after all, was a good customer but he was still just a customer. Angel liked to keep her home and business separate. Consequently, they always met in modest hotels for their liaisons.

Andrew allowed momentary free rein to a sense of romantic loss. It was surprisingly powerful. It lasted until the solution occurred to him of simply looking her up during business hours. He reprimanded himself for having enjoyed the loss overmuch.

A few days later, our hero launched his reconnaissance mission into New York. The time and place were right, but Angel was not in sight. Neither were her competitors. Enforcement of the loitering law had faltered after the Democrats left town, but sporadic animation by the police still had an effect. He decided to try later. After a taxi ride and an extended browse through *Barnes and Noble* on 18th he returned to 48th. Angel was not there, but someone else was taking the risk.

"Hi. You want to go out?"

"No. I'm looking for Angel. Blondish. Works this block."

"Why ya lookin'?"

"A friend."

"Uh-huh. Yeah, I know her. She don't work here no more. Cops were hasslin' her, ya know? Can't I do somethin' for ya?"

"No. Know where I can find her?"

"How should I know? Try Lex. Or one of the parlors. Why, ain't I good enough or somethin'?"

Refraining from the obvious response, our hero mumbled a thanks and walked eastward. En route to Lexington Avenue, Andrew grasped the serious prospect of never finding her at all. From this moment his illicit mistress grew in his estimation and seized his heart. True to his fears, she was not on Lexington. He asked one of the street's workers if she had heard of her.

"No. I'd know her if she was here in the daytime. Try at night or real early, like 3 or 4. I don't know what else to tell you. Maybe one of the parlors."

Not prepared to investigate scientifically the city's several hundred brothels, our hero felt his hopes dashed. In his mind Angel became Apollo's Daphne, Cupid's Pysche. Exquisite loss! Andrew was charmed by the violence of the emotion and he cut the reins he briefly had relaxed the night he lost his wallet. He would search for her, of course, but it would be in vain. Visions came to him of Candide and Cunegonde, Tom Jones and Sofia, Pepe le Pew and the cat. He indulged in the bittersweet taste of resolution in the face of doom, a taste that makes us feel noble. His life acquired a 19th century romantic sense it had been denied previously.

By a remarkable coincidence, WOR-TV ran *Walk on the Wild Side* that night. In the movie, the hero tries to find Hallie, a lost lover who is working in a New Orleans brothel, so he hitches a ride from Texas in a truck with Jane Fonda and... well, there is no need to recount the entire plot. Suffice it to say that our hero hopelessly identified with the story and sank ever deeper into the swamp of his emotions. It troubled him briefly that Angel didn't make a convincing Hallie but then in the movie neither did Anne Baxter.

Every weekend for a month our hero forayed into the city without result. A full month then passed before our hero returned again. The fires of longing had abated slightly, but to his satisfaction flickered still. He had arrived in town not to continue his quest, however, but to seek out the Lionel Casson translation of *The Selected Satires of Lucian.* Lucian was lighthearted, cynical, and enjoyable. Andrew still loved the classics, but had lost some of his taste for his former favorite playwright. The asperity of Euripedes' final acts bothered him of late.

Yet, he was in town, and making an effort to find his love was a dramatic necessity in his own personal theater. So, after leaving the bookstore, he went on with the show. He took the A train to 42nd and walked up 8th Avenue.

Andrew was lost in thought and paid little attention to the girls on the Avenue. His eyes focused on his feet as he rushed to make up for the lost time the detour on 8th was costing him.

"Well hi there stranger!"

Andrew looked up into the hazel eyes of the woman over whom he nearly had stumbled. Our hero could think of nothing adequate to say. He settled for, "Angel, do you know how hard you are to find?"

"I imagine. I was in California. Backpacking in the Sierras. I needed a break, Andrew."

"California." Only by luck did I not repeat the whole sentence.

"Why? Did you miss me?"

"Oh. Sure. Maybe a little."

Our hero rejoiced in rediscovery. But during his recent agonies he had acquired a more critical eye. Angel was right: she was only cute. There still was something warm and comfortable in the partaking of familiar pleasures, but his emotions lacked the edge they had in her absence. She was still likable, but she seemed overtly grasping to an extent that dismayed him. In the most intimate of circumstances, our hero stifled a yawn. He looked forward to the afternoon's end so he could finish the 3rd volume of Gibbon's *Decline and Fall of the Roman Empire*.

Before they departed, Andrew obtained Angel's phone number, placed copies in different pockets, and urged that future dates be at her own apartment. Angel hesitated at that suggestion, but then shrugged and agreed. They kissed goodbye. Andrew ran to catch the train to Hoboken.

The Path train pulled into Hoboken with 1 minute and 46 seconds to spare for the 4:30 Dover connection. Andrew sprinted from one to the other. The trains were operated by New Jersey Transit, but Erie-Lackawanna signs still decorated much of the infrastructure. Sparkling new diesels and cars had replaced the ancient electric carriages that Andrew remembered from his boyhood.

Andrew found an empty seat near a window. An autumn chill was in the air but the car was unheated. He watched as the familiar yards slipped past and gave way to heavy industry. A spotty carpet of brown leaves rustled across the asphalt in the oil yards. Our hero closed his eyes and marveled how it was better to have loved and lost than to have loved and found.

"EAST ORANGE!" the conductor bellowed.

"How long does it take to get to Millburn?" asked a nervous woman passenger.

"Not long," the conductor answered cryptically. Though he made the run four times per day, he sounded unsure. Perhaps it seemed different to him each time. In his mind, as he clipped her ticket, Old 97 hurtled toward its fateful bend.

Chapter 2
Drugs

Brandon was drunk and subject to sudden mood swings, but as the entire restaurant sang *Happy Birthday* he accepted the tribute with ebrious aplomb.

"Are you going to blow out that candle or just let it wax your cake?" asked Marvin. Marvin also was drunk. The primary effect was to exaggerate his native lack of tact.

"What? Oh." Brandon's eyes focused slowly on the cake in front of him as his two old grammar school friends looked on. He successfully blew out the candle, even though the main force of his puff was off target. "Thanks for the birthday party guys. I can't believe I'm the big Three-Oh."

Arnold stole from Oscar Wilde, "You look weeks younger." Arnold, as usual, was sober. The single glass of wine that had accompanied his dinner qualified as a bender for him.

"Fuck you. I like this place. *Le Beouf a la Mode.* I actually can pronounce it better drunk."

"The name had me worried. What flavor ice cream goes with braised beef?"

"Pistachio. So what's the plan guys? It's only 10 o'clock. It's still my birthday for two more hours."

"I guess we drink some more," proposed Marvin. "I don't think we'll have to walk far in Manhattan to find a bar."

"I drink in bars every night."

"And the man is still single."

"Asshole! I'm not a total pig farmer, you know. I like to go to the Met and MoMA and shit."

"Well, the museum guards might object to us wandering the halls at 10 PM...

"...leaving aside the coprous behavior," added Arnold.

"...and they don't sell beer there. Shoot pool? Movie?"

"Bullshit to both of you."

"We could go to a bar with some scenery," suggested Arnold. "*Spikes* is on 44th."

"A strip club?"

"Yeah."

"You're such an uptight asshole about booze and drugs, but at least you like sluts. It relieves me that you have one vice."

Arnold shrugged. The waitress, however, tabled the check with rather more force than was necessary. Neither Brandon nor Marvin noticed. Arnold covered the bill and overtipped her.

Arnold had married soon after college when his girlfriend Andrea announced she was pregnant. She miscarried thirty days after the wedding. For a few months the experience made them closer, but without children to bind them together, their diversity of interests tugged them apart again. The marriage staggered on for another two years. It ended in a divorce that was about as amicable as one can expect in such circumstances.

Arnold's marriage had left him more conservative and domestic than his old friends. He lived out on the Island in a Cape Cod with a leafy yard and a gas-fired barbecue. He drank little and avoided drugs altogether. He drove a Chevy Lumina. His marriage had left him gun-shy about relationships; so shortly afterward he began to frequent clubs of the sort that appealed to his heterosexual urges without presenting a major risk of serious romantic involvement. In an odd sort of way, this too demonstrated restraint.

Brandon and Marvin both had moved to the city after college. They lived separately, but spent much of their free time together. Monthly parking rates in Manhattan are higher than apartment rents almost anywhere else, so neither owned a car. Despite the higher salaries in the city, the higher cost of living prevented either from saving any money. They both continued to carouse as heartily as they had in college. Although they teased Arnold for his lifestyle, they often enjoyed spending weekends in his house. When Arnold visited one of them, they also enjoyed letting Arnold chauffeur them around town in his Chevrolet. Even though taxis and the subway were more practical transport, in his car they could smoke, act up, and, though Arnold grumbled about it, drink beer.

On the drive from the restaurant to 44th, Brandon lit up a joint and shared it with Marvin. Saturday night traffic is light in New York outside of the theater district and the Village. Arnold was able to find a parking place on the street less than a block from *Spikes*.

At the entrance of Spikes a spectacled young woman collected $5 cover charges. "Hi, Arnie. You can go right in but I have to charge your friends."

"They know you here by name? They let you in for free?" Marvin asked, as he paid for himself and Brandon.

Arnold shrugged. They entered the club. It was a dingy space painted in black and lit with black light. Smudged mirrors on the walls and in back of the stage imperfectly reflected the dancing girls.

"Buy your first drinks at the bar," ordered a curvy bartender, who overflowed a skimpy black uniform. "Then you can take them to the tables in the back. Hi, Arnie."

Marvin eyed Arnold for a moment and then bought two beers. He handed one to Brandon. Arnold ordered a Coke.

The air was rank with smoke and cheap perfume. The huge speakers blared music. The different DJs who worked the club had distinctive styles. The one working that night tended heavily toward heavy metal and alternative rock. He tolerated little of the lighter pop sounds that recently had made headway in the charts and none of rap.

The three celebrants took in the scene. They assessed girls on stage, the girls on the floor, and the other customers in the bar. Brandon's mood turned suddenly surly. He scowled, swigged from the beer bottle, and pounded it on the table.

"What's with you?" asked Marvin.

"Look at all these people here. They lead such totally worthless lives."

"I don't think they look at it that way, Brandon. Just enjoy the scenery. The girls on stage are hot tonight. If you like one, Arnie and I will spring for a table dance for you. Like happy birthday, man."

"These girls don't give a shit about me. All they want is my bucks."

"So? All you want from them is beaver."

"Actually it would be nice to like know someone."

"So you want one of these women here to love you for yourself. Tonight. I think you're kind of expecting too much, buddy boy."

"Besides, they say to be careful what you wish for. My experience is that they are right," advised Arnold.

"Just because you fucked up your marriage doesn't mean everybody does."

"Arnie!"

Arnold stood up as his named was called. A tawny haired dancer in a purple microdress literally jumped on him. She threw her arms around his neck and wrapped her legs around his waist until the manager gave her a warning stare.

"Arnold's been holding out on us," laughed Marvin. "Who is the human overcoat?"

"Cindy, this is Marvin and Brandon. It's Brandon's birthday."

"Happy birthday."

"Thanks, Cindy. You two go out or something?" asked Brandon who now was suddenly sentimental. The slur to his speech noticeably thickened.

"Shush! We're not supposed to date customers."

"But you do?"

"Thanks so much for bragging about me, Arnold."

Arnold hadn't bragged because, paradoxically, he was proud of her and valued her. He had wanted to keep knowledge of his relationship with Cindy as his own private property for a while longer. He had kept this treasure secret for two months.

Cindy unexpectedly had accepted an offer for dinner that Arnold had made quite casually a couple of months earlier after she had finished her fourth lap dance for him. Since then, they had seen a Broadway show together and had gone horseback riding in Central Park. They enjoyed each other's company but neither took the dates seriously. Arnold did not appear wealthy enough to Cindy for her to consider him for anything permanent, and he made a point of not mentioning to her his substantial trust fund or the several valuable income properties owned by his parents. Managing these properties, in fact, was his job. On the other side, Arnold recognized that Cindy enjoyed being wild. He didn't feel able to handle her for more than several hours per week.

"I haven't been on a date in months," Brandon stated sullenly.

"That's your own fucking fault. In this town women are everywhere. Cunts like you too, Brandon," said Marvin with poorly disguised jealousy. He totally missed Cindy's folded arms objection to his noun selection. "They always ask me about you. You have that clean cut boyish prep school look. Fraudulent advertising in my opinion."

"Fuck you. Besides, Arnie's the trust fund preppie. The women I like run away from me like rabbits."

Cindy gave Arnold a brief sidelong glance.

The Night Manager Barbara walked by. There still are beatniks in the new millennium and Barbara is one. She dresses in black, wears shoulder-length black hair, and uses no make up, but she manages to be pretty anyway. She is a nihilist, though it is doubtful she knows what that means.

Brandon pointed her out. "That one for instance. I like her better than these tarted-up strippers."

"Your friends are charming, Arnold."

Cindy's antiphasis was lost on both of them.

"Buy Barbara a drink," she suggested to Brandon with a sigh. "She'll talk to you. Most guys don't pay attention to her."

Brandon frowned as though solving a quadratic equation. After a few moments he summoned up ethyl courage and walked over to Barbara at the bar. He tapped her on the shoulder.

"Do you mind if I talk to you?"

Barbara shook her head. Without prompting, the bartender put a drink in front of her. From the steam, it appeared to be simply hot coffee.

"That's the dog boy!" exclaimed Marvin to Cindy.

"What?"

"We call Brandon the dog boy."

"Why?"

"I don't know."

"I see." Cindy was accustomed to this sort of irrelevancy from drunken patrons.

They watched Brandon from a distance. He stood and spoke animatedly, while Barbara sat on her barstool and sipped coffee. None of their conversation could be heard at the table over the loud music and general noise. Brandon's hands waved expressively. Barbara remained expressionless whenever she responded to him.

After a few minutes of this, Brandon stomped back to the table. His sullen mood had been replaced by a murderous one.

"So when are you two going to do the dirty?" asked Marvin.

"Fuck off."

"Wasn't Barbara nice to you?" asked Cindy with more than a touch of *Schadenfreude.*

"That shit face! I kind of opened up to her, you know? I told her that there really was romance in the world. I told her I believed that true love was really possible and I'd like to find it someday."

"My. How did she respond to that?" queried Cindy.

"She said she didn't believe a word of it. That life is shit. That I was living a total fantasy and I'd never find love because nobody does. She all but called me an idiot. It really pissed me off."

"Don't worry about it. She is kind of a dark person."

"That was rather an amazing thing to say to her," commented Arnold. "I'm surprised she wasn't totally speechless."

"Yeah, well, you're all bitter from your divorce bullshit. You probably agree with her. Maybe you should move in with her."

"I'm not sure I want to move in with anybody ever again. As for agreeing with her, I am rather fond of La Rochefoucauld's line that people would never fall in love if they hadn't read anything about it."

"Fuck you too."

"Barbara probably has her reasons for feeling the way she does," said Cindy.

"No, Cindy, she's a real asshole. I'm going to go back and tell her off."

"No, Brandon. Calm down. She's the manager. You'll get thrown out."

"I'm not going to do anything to get thrown out. I'm just going to tell her to fuck off!"

"That will get you thrown out." Cindy started to pet Brandon on the back.

"No, listen. I'm just going to say to her, 'You are wrong. You are a total asshole. Go fuck yourself!' I'm going to tell her right now." He rose unsteadily to his feet. Cindy grabbed Brandon by the shirt and pulled him to his seat.

"No! Do you want me to dance for you?" Suddenly feeling awkward in front of Arnold, she changed tack. "Vanessa! Come over here and dance for Brandon. It's his birthday. Arnie here is paying."

Cindy stood up and pulled Vanessa over in front of Brandon. A conventionally pretty bleached blonde, Vanessa stripped her top and wiggled between Brandon's legs. His agitation subsided.

"You see, Arnold? Men calm right down with boobies in their faces. This is what I have to deal with every evening. It's why I find you relaxing. You don't need therapy from me every minute."

"I like the therapy though."

"I noticed."

By the time Vanessa was done, Brandon had forgotten Barbara. Brandon squinted at Arnold as though to clear the image. "I've been drinking too much. I'm all fucked up. Hey Cindy. You have any coke?"

"Shhhh! Don't even talk about that. It's automatic unemployment. The city hassles the shit out of these bars over that crap."

It says something about Arnold that he wondered what the problem was with Coca-Cola. He looked at his own drink.

"They love to pull liquor licenses over drugs," Cindy continued. "The owner throws a tantrum if he sees any. I'd be out on my ass."

"You have some though? I'll pay you for it."

"Shush! No, and I can't call my connection from here."

"I'll go see my dealer then. I'll be back."

Cindy shrugged her shoulders. "OK."

"Hey Arnie, you can stay here. Just give me the keys and I'll go."

"No! Arnold, don't give him the keys! He'll kill somebody."

"I wasn't planning on it."

"Fine. Fuck all of you. I'll go by myself."

"You should go with him, Arnie. He shouldn't be wandering drunk and alone like that," advised Cindy.

"Me? I've never been involved in any of his buys."

"So don't be involved. Just go with him."

"Yeah, Arnold. Don't be such a pansy-ass," chimed Brandon. "Let's go."

Marvin chose to stay behind. Arnold promised to return to Spikes as soon as Brandon was done.

"You'd better," Cindy told him. "I'm not done with you yet."

Out on the street Arnold hailed a cab. The two climbed in.

"Onward, Abdul!" shouted Brandon. The cab driver took them uptown, north of where they had eaten earlier that night.

The walk-up apartment they sought was on 1ˢᵗ Avenue in the East 80s. The neighborhood was fairly posh, but the building was old. A pool parlor occupied the first floor. Brandon repeatedly pressed the buzzer by the door that faced the sidewalk. An irritated voice on the scratchy speaker asked "What?"

"Brandon! Blow!"

"Shut your mouth Brandon! This is my neighborhood. Come on up."

A buzzer sounded and the lock clicked open. Brandon pushed the door open so that it banged hard against the wall. He took the steps two at a time, even though his balance threatened to return him to the entrance at an even faster rate. He successfully reached the top and charged down the short hallway. Without pausing to knock, he turned the knob of the door at the end of the hall. The door was unlocked. Brandon slammed it open.

"Hey, you fucker, take it easy! You bust the plaster and I have to pay for it!" called out a voice inside.

Brandon strode in. Arnold walked in behind him.

The studio apartment was long and narrow with a single window at the far end. A full sized mattress was on the floor in the center of the room. An unconscious dark skinned young woman lay curled up on it with her shoulders exposed above the blanket. There were no signs of any clothes on her. A table and couch occupied the space between the mattress and the window. On the table was a pharmacist's scale. Next to the table stood a trim black man in his 20s with a shaven head, white shirt, and crisply creased pants.

"Hey, Harvey, this is my friend Arnold," Brandon announced. "He's cool."

"Hello, Arnold." Harvey extended his hand with the businesslike formality of a bank officer reviewing a candidate for a loan. To Brandon he was familiarly abrupt.

"What do you want, shit-head?"

Brandon wrapped an arm around his shoulder and turned to Arnold. "Harvey is a cool dude. He is a black man and a white guy."

"Cut the crap, Brandon! Excuse the mess and my looks, Arnold. I've had a busy day." Harvey actually looked quite well-groomed. The apartment was another matter.

"You're talking to a bachelor."

"Divorced," corrected Brandon.

"A reborn bachelor," conceded Arnold. "Everything looks neat to me."

"Excuse my looks too," Brandon interposed. "I forgot the white sheets I usually wear when lynching up brothers."

"Hey! Hey!" Harvey shoved off Brandon's arm. "I'm in no mood for your stupid bullshit tonight! Tell me what you want and get the fuck out!"

Brandon was unfazed by Harvey's very real anger. "Blow!"

"Keep your voice down."

"BLOW!"

"Chill out!"

"And something for Arnold. Some crank maybe." Brandon dropped cash on the table.

"No thanks. I don't do that. Or coke."

"Hey, that's cool, man," responded Harvey. "I respect that. I envy it actually."

"The dude doesn't even drink. Maybe like a glass of wine at dinner. Sometimes. Just hangs out in the burbs and watches the Disney channel and listens to Pat Boone albums or something. Haven't you even tried this shit, Arnie?"

"Nope."

"I've never even seen the asswipe take a hit from a joint," Brandon told Harvey.

"Back in college I smoked some pot when a very pretty girl offered it to me," Arnold explained. "I inhaled it, too. But she turned out not to like me, so I didn't bother with the stuff again. Once when I had insomnia I tried depressants. Too depressing."

"But you never tried snow?"

"No."

"Why not? Why not now? I'll spring for it. Come on. Don't be an uptight pansy asshole."

Arnie laughed. "*Deja vu*! We're back in the schoolyard again."

"Hey, leave him alone, man! He's brighter than we are."

"It always struck me as a bit too hard core. Either I'd like it or I wouldn't. Either way it'd be bad for me."

Brandon pulled back slightly from his frenetic state. "OK,

actually that makes some kind of sense, but you're still an uptight pantywaist."

Brandon pulled all of the cash out of his wallet and dropped it on the table.

Harvey went to work. He deposited a small amount of coke on one end of the scale until it balanced a metric weight on the other side. He then scraped the coke off the scale into a mortar bowl. A much larger pile of clumpy white powder lay on a sheet of wax paper next to the scale on the tabletop.

"I'll grind this stuff up."

"More."

"That's it, Brandon."

"More!"

"Pay me more!"

"That's all the money I've got, Tall, Dark and Ugly. More! Look, I'm your best customer."

"Don't say that! I hate that word, man! You're my friend, dig?"

"'Dig?' Now the man is Maynard G. Krebs. Well, if I'm your friend, friends don't have to ask." Brandon leaned over the table and reached with thumb and finger for the powder on the wax paper.

Harvey grabbed the back of Brandon's neck and yanked him away from the table. "I'm going to break your neck man!"

"More!"

Brandon ducked down and escaped the grip on his neck. He shouldered Harvey hard in the stomach. They fell together onto the couch. None of this disturbed the sleeping woman on the mattress.

"That's it you crazy motherfucker!" Harvey elbowed Brandon off of him. "Get the fuck off of me and get the fuck out!"

"More!"

"All right! Here. Here's more!" Harvey got up and added a small scoop to Brandon's pile in the mortar. He poured the lot into a plastic bag and threw it at Brandon. "Now get the fuck out before I kill you."

Arnold was astounded. The death threat he well could understand given Brandon's antics, but the extra scoop of coke was a mind blower.

"Hey, Arnold," said Harvey with forced calm. "Good to meet you. Sorry about all this bullshit. Brandon's really all right. He's not a bad guy when he's sober. He just gets wild and out of control when he's high."

Arnold realized Harvey was actually apologizing to him for Brandon's behavior. He apparently did think of Brandon as his friend. Why Harvey bothered was not entirely clear. Not for the first time this evening, Arnold wondered why he himself bothered. "I noticed."

In the back of the cab on the ride back to midtown Brandon rolled a dollar bill and snorted directly from the small plastic bag. The driver ignored him.

"How did you become friends with Harvey?"

"I was in *Hogs and Heffer's* downtown a couple years ago and got drunk. I wanted blow, but I couldn't score in there because it was too loud for anyone to hear me. So I went to a sleazy bar around the corner that was less crowded. I bought a drink and said loudly at the bar, 'What I really could use tonight is some blow!' and went to the bathroom. I figured someone would follow me there. Harvey did. He's all right. He stayed at my place for a couple months."

"Really? Why?"

"His mother threw him out. He needed a place."

"His mother threw him out?"

"Tossed his shit right out the window onto the sidewalk. She was pissed at the drugs, I guess."

"You never told me anyone was living with you."

"What? I was supposed to call up all my friends and say, 'Hey! I've got a coke dealer in my apartment!' Shit! You would have been the only one not bugging me for blow at all hours of the night, and you would have told people who would bug me."

Street parking was now full. After circling the block twice, Arnold gave up and parked in a 24-hour parking garage. They walked back to Spikes where Marvin waited.

"Where the fuck were you guys? It's almost 3 in the morning."

"We went to see a big black man with fleece as white as snow."

"Quiet with remarks like that, Brandon. This isn't Idaho. Not everyone is going to think you are ironically amusing."

"Fuck 'em."

Despite her earlier caution, Cindy was attracted by the presence of cocaine. She leaned over the table. "I'm off work in a little while. Chill out for the rest of the evening and we'll go to an after hours club."

The four climbed into Arnold's car. The air inside was hot and humid. Arnold turned on the air conditioner full blast. Bars in New York close at 4 AM. This causes a sudden surge in traffic. In the parking garage, the Lumina inched slowly toward the exit, which was jammed by cars entering and leaving. Cindy sat up front with Arnold. The other two were in back.

"Jews! Jews!" shouted Brandon at the other drivers.

Marvin smacked his palm against Brandon's head. "What do you think I am, you fucking Nazi asshole?!"

Brandon leaned in toward Marvin's face. "Jews! Jews!"

As soon as the car reached the street, Brandon dug the bag out of his pocket and helped himself to another snort through a rolled up dollar bill. Marvin took the bill from him and sniffed from the bag as well. Brandon held the bag forward. Cindy dipped into the contents with a long fingernail and lifted a small quantity to her nose.

The after hours club was located on a dingy commercial stretch of 30th street in Chelsea. Cindy was allowed in for free. Her three escorts each paid a $10 cover charge. Establishments of this type are illegal. They typically feature gambling and open drug use. Ever since a fire killed 80 people in one such club due to inadequate fire exits, the police have raided them frequently. This one plainly was once a large restaurant. The decrepit, but once fashionable, decor was stained by water leaks. Two very large bouncers flanked the bar. The patrons included aspiring musicians with their girlfriend financiers, bikers and their girlfriend financiers, drug dealers and their customers, compulsive gamblers, suburbanites on a lark, those strange men who wear conservative business suits and gray pony tails, and legitimate nightclub employees whose workday ended at 4:00 AM.

Cindy ordered Smirnoff and lit up her dope in a porcelain pipe. The mixture of pot, cocaine, and vodka induced paranoia in her rather than the mellowness of pot alone. "This place is hot tonight. It's gonna get raided. I can tell. It's too crowded."

An overweight, but muscular man wearing stained denim, a two-day beard growth, and a matching accumulation of body odor brushed Brandon's arm on his way to the gaming tables. He scowled over his shoulder with obvious disappointment when the bump did not provoke an assault.

"It's not the cops I'm worried about," said Brandon who was just short enough and weak enough to be self-conscious. "A lot of these guys just come in here for a fight."

"I start some fights myself," Cindy bragged. "The bouncers watch my ass."

"I'll bet they do. They'd watch our asses get stomped. Men are much more likely than women to be targets."

"Except one kind."

"Actually, a few sources claim that more men are raped each year than women," stated Arnold with more of his usual pedantry. "About 400,000 by some estimates. But 90% or so of the rapes happen in prison, and we don't care much what happens to prisoners."

"That's true," said Brandon. "I don't care what happens to them. Screw 'em."

"Yuck. The thought of men fucking each other is disgusting," spat Cindy.

"I thought you were bisexual."

"Do you like women, Arnie?"

"Yes."

"So I agree with you. Don't get all PC on me."

"OK. And I agree with you that a raid is worse than a fight. You usually can walk away from a fight. The slammer has locks."

This evoked a moment of chemically enhanced protectiveness from Cindy. "Everyone remember that the game plan is to protect Arnold. He is just humoring us here. He shouldn't be hauled in with us. If you're not doing anything illegal in these places the cops just let you go. So we don't know him." She laughed. "Actually the cops once let me go when I had a packet of coke hidden in my mouth. Shit, I paid 100 bucks for it. I wasn't about to throw it away. Hey!"

Cindy jumped up and hugged a light-skinned black man. He glanced at her table companions, whispered and left. She then looked around the room and approached a muscular white man with a ponytail. The scene repeated. Cindy returned to the table annoyed.

"No one will sell me any blow. They say some narcs are in here tonight. Some dudes at the bar have been asking for blow."

"The dealers probably think we're the narcs."

"No, they trust me. This place is hot tonight."

"Let's go back to my place", offered Brandon. "I have enough to share."

"Deal."

As they climbed into their car, three police cruisers and a wagon entered 30th street. "Shit, that was close," Cindy observed.

After a stop at a 24-hour deli to buy a case of beer, they drove south past City Hall. There was a parking space on John Street less than a block from Brandon's apartment. Brandon lived on the fourth floor of one of the rare residential buildings in the financial district.

Once in the apartment, Brandon chopped the white powder even finer using a razor on a hand mirror. He held out the mirror in his left hand and proffered a straw with his right.

"No. I don't like using other people's straws," Cindy said. "May I?" Without waiting for a response, she picked up the bag, still more than half full, and dipped her long fingernail directly into it. She shoveled to her nose.

Brandon snorted the line he had cut on the mirror with his straw. Cindy dipped into the bag again and extended a digit to Marvin. He inhaled deeply.

"I love this shit!" he declared.

At irregular intervals thereafter, Cindy supplied her own nose and Marvin's. They and Brandon also resorted frequently to the case of Budweiser from the deli. Arnold found a Cherry Coke in the refrigerator.

"There's caffeine in that you junkie!" shouted Brandon.

"So I hear."

"Arnold is disgusted with his fucked-up friends," laughed Cindy. Actually Arnold was rather enjoying their frolics, although he already placed a higher value than before on his quiet life in the suburbs.

"I don't know what he gets from us sometimes," said Brandon as though Arnold were not in the room.

"We rely on Arnold," observed Cindy, "but he knows we're his friends. He may not be able to rely on any one of us at all times, but he knows somebody here will be straight enough to be there for him."

"That Barbara really pissed me off."

"She's a black witch. You stay away from her!" She had forgotten her earlier advice to buy Barbara a drink. "Those people destroy everyone around them. They ruin their own karma and their future lives for some stupid worldly gains."

"We all sacrifice things for worldly gains," said Arnold. "But living without those gains is a sacrifice too. So you make your choice, heads or tails."

"I'm a tail man," said Marvin.

"I like head," countered Brandon.

"Giving it or getting it?"

"Fuck you."

Cindy ignored them both. "But it is not an equal choice, Arnie. Karma."

"No such animal."

"You really believe that?"

"Yes."

"Then why aren't you out raping and pillaging?"

"Being an ass in real life is consequence enough to be a deterrent."

"Ass?" repeated Marvin. "Why Arnie, you nearly cussed."

"I agree with Cindy," said Brandon. "That white light shit is no joke. Once I snorted some heroin that must have been purer than I figured."

"Usual street purity is 3%, isn't it?" asked Arnold who had read this arcane datum in a leader of The Economist.

"Who the fuck knows? Anyway, it nearly took me out. I woke up the next day on the bathroom floor, but before passing out I distinctly remember seeing a bright light.

"Were you staring at the ceiling fixture?"

"You are such a fucking asshole sometimes, Arnold."

"I think Cindy is right too," said Marvin although his agreement was influenced more by his appreciation of Cindy's curves than of her arguments.

Cindy, Brandon, and Marvin were high enough to believe their discussion had reached new depths of profundity. Though sober, Arnold caught some of the attitude.

"Look, this doesn't have anything to do with witchcraft or karma or waving chickens over the head."

"I never said anything about chickens," interrupted Cindy.

"There is something to be said for trying to be decent for its own sake. It helps the self-image. Do you really want to go around thinking of yourself as a mean-spirited asshole?"

"What a wild man! He has graduated from ass to asshole! Have you got self-image problems, Arnie?" asked Brandon. To the room at large he added, "He's got hang-ups, doesn't he?"

"That's why you should get fucked up with us," advised Cindy. "It doesn't hurt anyone else and it doesn't 'ruin your life'. That's up to you. It makes you feel better for a while. We all need to feel better for a while sometimes. I've had tough times, you know, Arnold. Like I've been raped. Twice. Try that on your self-image. So you shouldn't try to take away my pleasures."

"Who said anything about that? I didn't tell you to stop. But I choose to live my life without being high. That's my choice. Other people can do what they like. I'm all for legalization."

"I'm not," grunted Brandon.

"Wait a minute. You're the one stuffing cocaine up your nose and you want to outlaw drugs."

"Yeah, I'm telling you man, you can't trust people. If they could buy this shit, they'd be fucked up all the time. Cab drivers, elevator operators..."

"They can buy this stuff. You buy this stuff. Besides they can buy booze legally. Is that better? And most people aren't drunk all the time."

"It'd be worse, man."

"I agree with Brandon. Except for pot. That should be legal," Cindy affirmed as she refilled her fingernail.

"Why, Cindy? You can get high on pot too."

"Yeah, but it's a mellow buzz."

"OK, you don't mind cabdrivers with a mellow buzz. But there are costs to keeping other drugs illegal too. It turns neighborhoods into war zones, overloads prisons, turns ordinary people like you into criminals, undermines civil liberties…"

Marvin laughed. "Still trying to save the world. Shouldn't you have outgrown that back under George the First?"

"Washington? I'm not that old."

"You know who I mean, shit-head!"

"Yes, but no, I shouldn't have outgrown it. A lot of the damage done by drugs has to do with the criminal environment created by the law. May I guess, Cindy, that those rapists offered you cocaine?"

An offended Cindy answered, "Can we spell 'Blaming the Victim?'"

"I'm not blaming you. If someone steals your car the thief is always to blame regardless of where you parked it, but some parking spots are safer than others. I'm just saying that not many rapes happen in liquor stores where you can buy booze openly."

"You're wrong, man," insisted Brandon. "I'm telling you. People would be all fucked up everywhere. Nothing would ever get done because work really sucks. You wouldn't know about that."

"I work."

"Right. Managing mom and dad's properties and exploiting the proletariat. On a real job you want to be high."

"So you can handle drugs, on the job or off, and that's OK, but all those other people need to be locked up if they try to do the same." Arnold was struck by a minor insight. "Or do you think you can't handle it? If it were easier to get, you would be high more often. Maybe all the time. I think you have pretty easy access now, Brandon."

"Fuck you."

"Mind if I use the facilities?"

"You mean the toilet? Why even ask, Arnold? I don't want you to pee on the floor."

"Thanks."

Arnold closed the door to the bathroom behind him.

"Arnie's got money?" Cindy asked.

"His walls are papered with it," answered Marvin.

"No shit?"

Marvin walked to refrigerator to get another beer.

Cindy reached over to Brandon, who sat next to her on the couch, and grabbed his crotch. She squeezed. "We think a lot alike, head man. If you ever want to share a bag, come and see me." She released Brandon when Arnold exited the bathroom.

"Look guys," said Marvin "it's 8 o'clock in the morning and I need some sleep. Give me a ride home?"

"I don't want to leave yet," said Cindy to Arnold. She walked over to Arnold's chair, sat on his lap, put her arms around his neck, and kissed him deeply. Arnold knew this was just a ploy on her part to prevent the evening from ending, but he was happy to be persuaded.

"Guys. Guys! Do I need a bucket of water? Like I really need to go home."

"So go! Take a fucking cab!" Cindy shouted.

"I'm broke. I blew my wad in that clip joint where you work."

"Then take the subway! I'll give you a couple bucks!" She put her hand to her forehead and calmed down. "Shit! Never mind. It is late. Early. Whatever. OK. Take him home, Arnold. I'll stay and talk with Brandon. You don't mind, do you? I won't fuck him."

"You're a free woman."

"I know. But you don't think I'd try to hose your friend, do you?"

"No, I believe you."

Brandon had followed this exchange with an intense expression. "Actually I need to get some sleep too and we're out of blow. So thanks guys. It's been fun. See you later."

"That's the thing about this shit," said Marvin. "You can have a flour sack full and it won't be enough. You'll keep doing it until it's gone."

"Let me call my dealer," Cindy offered. "I'll buy some more. I really don't want to leave. Besides, I owe him $20."

"Thanks guys, but no. I don't mean to be impolite, but like get the fuck out."

"Brandon thinks you'll be jealous, Arnie. Tell him it's OK."

"Really, guys. Out!"

"How embarrassing. I'm actually being thrown out of Brandon's apartment! Do you know how many guys try to get me into their apartments? No one ever has tossed me out. Say something, Arnold. He's just worried about you."

"The man has a right to go to bed sometime."

Cindy hit Arnold on the arm, but she dropped the argument. She grabbed her bag and followed Arnold to the door.

A few minutes later Arnold's car headed north. The sun shone brightly in the clear morning. Traffic was slow due to a bicycle rally. The car approached Murray Street. "Turn here so I can buy some blow!" Cindy demanded.

"The street is blocked off because of the bikes."

"Then pull over. I'll walk."

There were no legal parking spaces, so Arnold pulled up to the corner and stayed at the wheel with the engine running. Cindy got out and walked down the block. She navigated pretty well considering her dazed state of mind. She moved out of sight. Arnold and Marvin waited what seemed too long a time.

"Do you want to sit behind the wheel while I go find her?" Arnold asked.

"Uh. I shouldn't even be sitting behind the wheel fucked up like this."

"OK. Then would you go see where she is?"

"Just leave the bitch. I need to get home."

"I don't think that would be very polite. I suspect she would take it personally."

"Shit! All right; I'll be right back." Marvin exited and walked down Murray Street.

Arnold waited. Several minutes later Marvin and Cindy hurried toward the car together.

"Pull out!" Cindy ordered as she jumped in and slammed the door.

Marvin slammed the back door and shouted, "Go!"

Arnold pulled out into traffic.

"That was a long walk just for a piss," Cindy said.

"What?"

"My dealer wasn't there. Or maybe he was getting laid and didn't want to answer. I saw his girlfriend's car outside. But I needed to go, so I went between two cars."

"Yeah. I was all bloated up too" Marvin added, "so I did the same thing when she was done. Then some guy ran out of a store yelling 'Hey! Hey!' That's why we told you to take off. We were about to be busted for pissing."

"You'll have to remember to tell that story at the family dinner table next Thanksgiving."

"Fuck you. You know, Arnie," Marvin explained, "Brandon didn't kick Cindy out because he was worried you'd be jealous. He ordered her out after she said she wouldn't fuck him."

"Thanks. I have a working familiarity with the male mind."

"You assholes! Hey, you were at Brandon's dealer before," remembered Cindy. "Let's go there."

"Cindy, it's 8:30 in the morning. Isn't it time to call it quits?"

"I'm buying some coke. Are you going to be a friend and help, or am I going uptown alone?"

"OK, OK. You shouldn't be wandering the streets alone in your condition. Maybe Harvey is still awake."

"Of course he is. You're the nine to fiver. For night people the evening doesn't end until noon."

Arnold dropped off Marvin on West 44th. He noticed that the street, though part of Hell's Kitchen, was continuing to improve. It even bordered on being attractive. Arnold pulled back into traffic and worked his way cross-town to the East Side.

Arnold found a parking space on 1st Avenue. He walked with Cindy to Harvey's building. Arnold buzzed. He was surprised when the lock buzzed open without any queries over the intercom. They climbed the stairs and approached the open door at the end of the hall.

"Come in!" a strange voice invited.

They entered. Three clean cut white men stood next to Harvey in the area by the window. One wore a black raincoat even though the sky was clear and the day was warm. The mattress on the floor was empty. The men waited for the new arrivals to say something. Cindy nearly did so, but Arnold quieted her with an admonitory tug on her arm.

Finally, Harvey spoke. "Maybe now is not a good time. Come back later man." Arnold and Cindy retreated.

Back in the car, Arnold slammed the door. The interior of the car was already hot from the sun so he opened the window. "Those were cops. They were waiting for us to ask for drugs. You nearly got us arrested."

"Lighten up. We're out of it. Let's go up to 110th. I know some dudes on the street there."

"No, that's it. We're done. We're going home."

"I don't want to go home."

"I do! I'll drop you off at your place."

"I'll just go out again."

"Suit yourself."

"You're the asshole who snitched on Harvey?" asked a voice by the open window. The man's face was above the level of the door window.

"What? No. I just got here."

"Right. That's why they let you go."

Arnold slumped onto Cindy when the bullet entered his chest.

Cindy shouted out the window at the vanishing gunman. "I need some blow!"

Chapter 3
Rock and Roll

Heather Field readied herself for the last set. Her real name was Heather File but she felt that Field was earthier, greener, and more memorable. As she sat on the stool, she viewed herself in the mirror behind the bar. She decided that she looked good. Men had hit on her often enough that night, as on all nights, to reinforce her opinion.

Still, she knew that anyone could see she was no kid. Heather was 34 and admitted to 27. Even the latter was dangerously old when it came to negotiating with record companies. They preferred to sign new artists on their 18th birthdays. She remembered the first time she had spoken to a major label rep and realized he was younger than she was.

Heather was able to survive in New York City without a day job thanks to her mother who had died a decade earlier. When her mother realized her health was failing, she had purchased the one-room condominium on Bedford Street in the West Village for her daughter. She also left Heather with a respectable sum of money. Heather already had spent most of it subsidizing her musical career.

Heather downed her first shot of the evening. Within minutes she could feel the warmth spread out from her gullet and into her arteries. A familiar feeling accompanied the glow. Something evil was about. Heather enjoyed the sense of importance this knowledge gave her. She knew that few other people shared her special sense.

When drunk enough, Heather could see the vampires inside people. These were not movie vampires with all the nonsense about bats and mirrors. These were the real ones who inhabited people whose souls were dark enough to admit them into their bodies. It was no wonder that, by and large, they went unnoticed. When sober, even Heather doubted their existence.

Heather had a drinking problem, or at least other people thought she did, but she didn't let it interfere with work. Her self-imposed rule was no booze until the last set. The other band members drank steadily throughout the night. They also slipped out to the parking lot between sets to mellow out with some weed.

The club was a dive called the *Midnight Café* in Budd Lake, NJ. Heather thought this was an inappropriate name for a bar that shut up shop at only one o'clock in the morning. Working Jersey was a pain, but there simply were not enough paying clubs in the city to keep the band working steadily. She was thrilled finally to have gotten a gig at *The Bitter End* on Bleecker in the Village the previous week, but it had been early on a Wednesday. Prime time was definitely any hour after nine on Friday or Saturday.

The unimaginatively but satisfyingly named *Heather Field Band* played "Rockin' Blues." On any given night the band consisted of herself on vocals and electric piano plus three other musicians. Although she sometimes hired strangers to fill out the band at the last minute, there were three guitarists, two drummers, and four bass players on whom she preferred to call. All of them lived hand-to-mouth, so any one of them would abandon her for a higher paying gig on an hour's notice, even if she had booked the time weeks in advance. She didn't like the disloyalty, but she understood it and expected it. For this reason she was concerned about the inadequate back-up supply of drummers. She was down to two because a third, once her favorite, went on a working trip through Europe the previous year and never came back.

There were tons of musicians in New York, of course, but she liked to rehearse at least a little with them before hitting the stage, even such a tiny stage as the one she was playing that night. She hated working with a total stranger cold to her material.

Tonight the drummer was one of her regulars, a peculiar young woman named Krista. Heather had mixed feelings about working with another woman. On the plus side it was easier to communicate with her than with the men, and she was an added novelty for the band in an industry that still was very heavy on the testosterone. In the negative column, what Krista had to communicate wasn't always pleasant, and there was no doubt that she took some of the shine off Heather as the star of the band.

Tonight Mike was on bass. He was competent and loud. The man was overweight, age 30, and sported a thick beard. He lived in his mother's basement in Westchester.

Harlan was on lead guitar. He was short, good-looking, and 20. He had excellent control of his instrument and played in an idiosyncratic style. This was far from enough to guarantee him a future in his profession. New York was full of guitarists who were original, excellent, and broke. There always was an identifiable edge to the band's sound when Harlan played with it. The irony that he was the sole black member of this self-styled Blues group was not lost on him. Harlan lived in Alphabet City with his girlfriend, a bartender from New Zealand. She, like most significant others of musicians, paid most of the bills.

Heather swallowed a second shot of whiskey at a gulp and ordered another. She glanced over at the table where Arthur sat. Arthur was a roadie, though she hadn't thought of him that way until this moment.

Arthur was once a musician of sorts himself. He never played professionally. Rather, he had studied classical trombone as a teenager. At the time, he had written a number of arrangements that had impressed his teachers. He planned to choose music as a major in college until his father heard about it and refused to help with the tuition. His father, a well-meaning but domineering man, loudly regretted ever having paid for music lessons in the first place. He said the lessons had been the idea of Arthur's mother. He made it clear that Arthur needed to pursue a more marketable skill in order to expect any support. It was for his own good. Arthur had bent to his father's will.

Rather to his own surprise, while studying at Rutgers Arthur found that he had a knack for programming. In a way, a computer program was analogous to a musical arrangement. He graduated with a degree in Computer Science just in time for the PC explosion. He was immediately employable and made a good, if unremarkable, living ever since graduation. Unfortunately, he hadn't been clever enough in a business sense to put any of his earnings into Microsoft, AMD, or Compaq when a small sum still could have turned into a small fortune. He was middle-class and expected to remain so his entire life.

When young, Arthur had made ignorance of popular music a point of personal pride. Among his tapes and CDs, Mahler's works played by the Chicago Symphony were the closest to being hit recordings. His taste, his attitude, and his major course of study isolated him in college. His social life was dismal and it didn't improve much after graduation. Before he knew it he was single and pushing 40. He had never partied on a Spring Break road trip. He never had lost in love, nor won either. He never had been to a major rock concert. Arthur believed he had missed something in life, and there was some justice to his opinion. The first time he heard Heather sing in a tiny bar on 9th Avenue in NYC he decided to find it while he still had time.

Arthur's first meeting with Heather was on his birthday. Some of his male co-workers had taken him out on the town as a present. They had led him in and out of several blues bars. Heather that night was playing in a small one on 9th Avenue where the primary clientele was lesbian. The sound of Heather's band drew Arthur and his friends in from the street. When his friends realized the environment in the bar offered them little hope of romantic satisfaction, they decided to move on to *The Pink Pussycat.* Arthur declined to accompany them there, so they proceeded without him. Arthur approached Heather rather shyly between the third and the last sets and tried to discuss music with her. He mentioned that there were a lot of little clubs in New Jersey where he lived.

"I don't have a car," she explained. "One of my drummers had a van, but he went to Europe and I don't know what the hell he did with it. A couple other guys have subcompacts, but they can barely fit themselves and their own instruments into them. So, I can't play Jersey anymore."

"I have an SUV," Arthur offered.

Heather looked at him closely. She didn't see a vampire inside. That wasn't proof, of course. For one thing, she had drunk only two shots. For another, some vampires were good at hiding even when she was inebriated. She decided to trust him anyway. She reached into her purse.

"Here's a demo tape. If you can get me some gigs out there, you can drive me to them."

She gave Arthur her phone number. The next day, when sober, Heather regretted her generosity, but it turned out to be profitable. Arthur called her after a few days. He actually had gone from bar to bar in Jersey and managed to line up several gigs for her band. Ever since then, he had driven her and often another musician or two to New Jersey clubs. He always stayed through all the sets and then drove her back. He was a reliable designated driver who scarcely drank. Heather never saw him even mildly drunk.

Arthur was a normal enough male to have made passes at her, but Heather would have none of it. She wasn't above teasing him. She rather enjoyed it actually, but in the end she always would put him off without clearly shutting the door for the future.

Men had taken advantage of her often enough. The last loser with whom she had lived was a worse alcoholic than she was herself. She had given him a place to live, food to eat, and gas for his bike. He thanked her by beating her to within an inch of her life. For the past year she had persisted in a sporadic affair with a married man. He never had hit her, but in his own way he treated her badly. It was definitely her turn to abuse a man. Besides, she felt she was doing Arthur a favor just by letting him hang out with her and her friends. She was part of New York's artistic bohemian crowd. She hoped he appreciated it.

Heather sometimes changed clothes between sets if the mood struck her, but this night she chose to stay with the fringed black leather in which she had started. She kept a few outfits stored in Arthur's car, just in case.

Heather belted down one more shot and walked back to the stage. The rest of the band slowly took their places.

Arthur's table was right next to the women's restroom door. It was an uncomfortable place, but it was where Heather had asked him to sit. Arthur recorded the sets on a cheap tape recorder so Heather could evaluate the performances later. The table where he sat was the best place to pick up the sound properly without being drowned out by bar noise. Several women had given him strange looks, however, as they walked by. One even grimaced and chided him in passing, "You like hanging out by the ladies bathroom?" He didn't.

Heather covered several classic blues numbers including a powerful version of *Unchain My Heart.* Her voice had a marvelous range. It could be sweet and smooth. It could be ragged and dirty. People often compared her to Janis Joplin, but that wasn't accurate. She was as strong in her voice as Janis had been, but the style really was all her own.

Arthur, as always, was impressed. Whatever her quirks as a human being, Heather had real talent. He was aware, however, that Heather's sound was passé. Blues-based rock and roll had a following and always would. As demotic music went, it was good, meaty, solid stuff. The surviving old bands still sold albums. Yet, for new groups it hadn't been truly commercial for a generation. One might have better luck trying to revive disco. In his opinion, an opinion he never shared with Heather, *The Heather Field Band* was destined to play in bars and nowhere else. All the same, he found his experience with Heather rewarding on some level and there was a chance he was wrong about the market. He hoped so.

Heather, as usual, finished with an original number. It was mischievously intended to diminish the chances of her band-members with any boozy floozy in the bar. They never complained about it. It probably didn't make much difference.

"This is a song called *Subterranean Groupie Blues.*"

He sure looked foxy up on the stage
With his shag, his guitar and all
And as he winked at me I thought
He might be fun to ball

One week later he moved in my place
We had burst his waterbed's seams
His amps filled up my living room
But who cared we were such a marvelous team

A rocknroll dream

Every night with the other band chicks
I sat and watched him play
We snorted smoked and tripped all night
And then we slept all day

But it got to be a drag
Oh yeah babe
Our love began to sag

He never even wakes up till noon
And then he rehearses all day
Claims he has no time to sweep the floor
But he'll sure find the time to smoke a jay

The drummer and keyboard man lounge around
Watching football on my tv
Eating my food smoking my dope
And they want me to silk screen their shirts for free

And when the band goes off on tour
He wants me home and true
But every time I pick up the phone
A female voice asks who are you

He dedicates his songs to me
Up there on that microphone
Think that's a blast, well later on
He'll be too tired to get it on

Things are going a little too far
When I take a backseat to a fuckin guitar

I'd rather not have an old man at all
Or one that's really uptight
Than to be a band man's girl
And to sit around horny all night

After the set, Heather collected $400 from the manager. She gave Mike, Harlan, and Krista $75 each. She never had offered anything to Arthur and he never had asked. Before leaving the bar Heather bought a bottle of *Jack Daniel's*.

In the dark parking lot, Krista, Arthur and Harlan loaded up the car. Mike drove home in his own Escort. Arthur's Chevy Blazer barely was large enough for the drums, amps, piano, guitar, and passengers. Harlan sat in the back seat with the equipment that overflowed the cargo area. Arthur got behind the wheel. Krista slid in next to him. Heather sat next to her. Arthur could see nothing through the rear view mirror and the girls blocked the right outside mirror. He backed up carefully while looking out the left window. There were no thuds or bumps. He changed gears to Drive and exited the parking lot.

As they rolled east on Route 46, Arthur made conversation. "You know, a body was found in the reeds down in Stirling. Remember that place we played that backed up to the swamp?"

"Man or woman?" Krista asked.

"Man. It was a local guy. They didn't find him for weeks, even though his car was in the lot. He lived alone and worked at a gas station. The station owner didn't report him missing because those guys often come and go. It took a while before anyone noticed he was gone."

"What happened to him?"

"They said he was stabbed."

"Yeah, well you know what can happen when guys get drunk in bars," said Harlan. "They get into fights about stupid shit."

"That's pretty much what the cops said too."

"Have you booked us into other deadly spots?" asked Krista.

"Actually some guy was killed in Randolph near a club we played too. But that wasn't on the grounds. It was right around the corner in his own apartment."

"That doesn't count," said Harlan. "I didn't know there were so many crazy asses out here though. Everyone says New York is bad."

"There are vampires everywhere," said Heather. She unscrewed the top of the *Jack Daniel's* and took a swig.

"You'll have to point one out to me sometime."

"Maybe you're one."

"Uh-huh."

"I have to talk to you about your playing," she continued.

"Have you got a problem with it?" Harlan asked defensively.

"Yeah. This is a blues band."

"So?"

"You don't play blues."

"What the fuck do you mean I don't play blues? What do I play?"

"I don't know, but it's not blues. And please don't talk to me that way."

"What is your definition of blues?"

"Blues notes are flattened third, fifth, and seventh notes of the major scale."

"Oh, that's bullshit, lady. I don't care what you learned in a textbook. Blues doesn't come from textbooks. Blues is about what you feel and how you make that sound. If you get too formal about it, you miss the whole point. If you're right, you don't sing the blues yourself."

"Yes, I do."

"No you don't. And that's OK because it sounds good. Why would you want to sound like anybody else?"

"I don't want to argue with you about it. I'm just looking for a particular sound. We need to rehearse some more to get it, that's all. What do you think, Arthur?"

Arthur was on the spot. He didn't want to offend Heather by disagreeing with her, but neither did he want to lose her respect by agreeing to absolutely anything she said. The question was outside his particular training. He decided simply to express his taste.

"I like the sound of your band when Harlan plays."

"You don't know shit about it," she responded.

It was nearly 2:30 before they reached the Village.

"It's still early. Why don't you guys come up for a while?" Heather offered.

"Just drop me off across town," Harlan said.

"Oh, don't be so sensitive. Come on up."

"Maybe for a while."

Arthur found a parking space on Grove, less than a block from Heather's apartment building. Each of the four grabbed some of Heather's equipment. The walk was pleasant. It was a warm night.

The four clambered up both flights of stairs to 2B, Heather's apartment. Walk-up apartments in New York often are numbered in European fashion in the hope that innumerate tenants won't notice the extra flight.

Sufficient alcohol also can affect one's step count. Heather once told Arthur she had visited the apartment of a vampire. As soon as she had perceived the nature of her host, she had fled. The apartment that had been one flight up had become eight flights back down. She offered this variable geometry as proof of paranormal phenomena. "I just barely got out of there," she said.

As Arthur more than once had helped her up steps that made only tenuous contact with her consciousness, Heather's testimony lacked credibility. While a skeptic by nature himself, he nevertheless found Heather's mysticism entertaining.

Apartment 2B measured 10 feet by 20, including the bathroom and kitchenette. A TV tilted precariously on plastic egg crates that bent under the weight. A boom box perched on top of the TV. A frameless futon mattress that could fold into something resembling a couch presently was open and topped with rumpled sheets and blankets. A small chair backed up to the window. A Baldwin upright Model 248 piano stood next to the futon.

All surfaces except the piano top and the piano bench were strewn with clothes, empty beer bottles, empty whiskey bottles, cat toys, CDs, used paper plates, cosmetics and other objects. A black cat was curled up on a jacket on the floor.

Heather settled down amid the clothes on the open mattress. She drank deeply from the bottle of *Jack Daniel's* and passed the bottle to Harlan. He shrugged, swigged and passed the bottle back. He sat in the chair. Papers audibly crunched as he did so. Krista raided the refrigerator. She cracked open a Budweiser and handed one to Arthur. Heather knew it would last him all evening. Arthur sat on the bench. Krista plopped down next to Heather.

Heather became more superstitious by Arthur's standards as she became more intoxicated. When sober Heather would entertain something close to a naturalistic world view. She was not close such a view tonight. The last time Arthur had seen Heather this drunk, she had asked him if he were a vampire after her soul. It was a serious question.

"Thanks for the ride, Arthur. Why did you talk about those killing victims? Did you stab them?"

"No. I just worry about you sometimes. You walk out of bars sometimes at 4 in the morning. A lot of the guys in those places are hot for you."

"Thank you. You don't think that maybe they like my music? The only reason anyone would stay in a bar with me is because he wants to fuck me?"

"You're welcome. Yeah, I'm sure they do like your music, but they're still hot for you. Obviously some of them are dangerous."

"That's why we want you there, tough guy," teased Krista. "Notice he doesn't give a shit if anyone comes after me with a knife. He just worries about the songbird. Or ain't I hot enough to arouse that kind of passion?"

"Sure you are," said Harlan gallantly. "I frequently feel like killing you."

"Flatterer."

Krista pulled a joint from a shirt pocket and lit up. She passed it to Harlan. He took a hit and offered it to Heather. She shook her head and swigged *Jack Daniel's*. Arthur declined with a hand signal. Harlan handed the joint back to Krista.

"Well at least that's one thing you two have in common," said Harlan referring to the non-smokers. "Probably the only thing. I'm amazed that you get along."

"Arthur has some motive I haven't figured out yet. It worries me sometimes," said Heather.

"Maybe he's in love," suggested Krista.

"Are you in love, Arthur?" Heather asked.

"I'm not sure I know what the word means."

"That is an evasion."

"Maybe, but I still don't know what the word means."

"Haven't you ever had your heart broken? Or broken somebody else's? The second is worse, by the way."

"No and no. The second is worse for whom?"

"For yourself. The only affair I feel really bad about is the one where I chased the guy away. He wasn't my first but he was an early one. He was a loser, but he was a sweetheart, you know?"

"I know," said Krista.

Heather swallowed more whiskey and stood up. "Get off the bench, Arthur. I have to sit there. Sit down next to Krista. This is my *Mean Woman Song*.

> burned out baby
> hitching around
> mountains and deserts
> bringing him down
>
> didn't wanna travel
> nothing else to do
> sweet souled man
> just wanted to be true
>
> living in a sleeping bag
> instead of my warm bed
> no loving to remember
> just mean things I said
>
> wish I had a tv screen
> to follow where he's been

wish I had a time machine
I'd love him again

if I were the sunshine
I'd dance before his eyes
If I were the ocean
I'd rock him as he cries

I burned out my baby
I sent him away
he hitched to the West Coast
he wanted to stay

A pounding resounded from the other side of the wall in back of the piano. Krista and Harlan pounded back.

"So you feel guilty when you break hearts?" asked Arthur.

"No, just that one. You can't expect me to regret mistreating all the guys who love me. I can handle guilt for only one. He's it. Fuck the others."

"Right on, sister," toasted Krista.

Krista drained her bottle and went for another beer. She brought one back for Harlan too. She lit a second joint and shared that with him too.

Harlan noticed Krista's muscled arms. "Those drums make you strong, don't they?"

"Uh-huh, but it's not just the drums. I work out a lot. I'm a good trainer too."

She poked Harlan's belly. He was not fat but he wasn't athletically trim either. "Let me train you, Harlan baby. You listen to Mama Kris; we'll bust that belly and work up a wealth of health. Eat what I tell you, and work out like I say and you'll be chiseled bitch bait in no time. The hookers will be all over you."

Heather always found people who attempted to affect an urban style of banter to be silly, unless they actually were American urban natives. As a native of Beirut, Lebanon, Krista passed beyond silly and approached surreal. She brought to Heather's mind a bar in Hawaii where she had witnessed

Japanese tourists learning to line dance.

"How much fat are you planning to take out of my wallet?" Harlan asked.

"Fat is bad. Look what I can do for you. Drink my six pack, Harlan." Krista pulled up her blouse to reveal a firmly muscled stomach. "We'll be bouncing quarters off you in no time. Another hit?"

"Sure."

Heather caressed her bottle and swallowed yet again. "I'm beginning to get buzzed," she said.

"I believe that," agreed Arthur. "The last time I saw you this way you asked me if I were a vampire."

"What did you answer?"

"No."

"If you were, you wouldn't say."

"Ah."

"I'm not going there with you."

"Ah."

"Don't be so smug, you jerk! There is more to the world than you think there is. There are vampires. There are ghosts too, Arthur. I've seen them. You would see the them too if you would just open your mind."

Arthur's skepticism was a trait that actively annoyed Heather. She would have preferred him to claim he was a ghoul in disguise.

"I come originally from Virginia and that is bloody ground," she continued. "Ghosts are everywhere there. One time I was driving home in the rain at night and there was this black woman walking along the road. Other people saw her too on other nights. I asked. I stopped to give her a ride, opened the door, and she was gone."

"Let's review this. An old black woman walking alone at night in the South. A pickup truck screeches to a halt. You would be gone too."

"Not funny."

"It wasn't intended to be."

Heather gave Harlan a look for assistance.

"I'm not touching that one," he said.

Heather tried again. "Another time, my friends and I were partying in this house we were renting. It was haunted. I saw a face form on the wall with a derby hat. All my friends saw it too when I showed them. You can ask them. They started screaming and everything. They'll tell you."

"Partying on what? Never mind. It doesn't matter. With a willingness to believe, you can see pretty much whatever you like. And maybe whatever you fear too. I can see an image on the wall right now if I want to. Sober."

"Arthur, you are so closed-minded! It's the one thing that really worries me about you."

Arthur nearly joked that he thought vampirism was the one thing that really worried her about him, but he thought better of it.

"There is an argument that mystics are the ones who are closed-minded," he told her. "They refuse to accept the evidence about how the world works in favor of wishful or fearful thinking."

"There are powers and energies in this world beyond what you can touch with your fingers, Arthur. I'm going to teach you that."

"I've had to fight too hard for my sanity to play with fantasies," he answered.

"How do you mean?"

Arthur hesitated before admitting to a weakness. He decided to proceed. "You see, about 10 years ago a tandem truckload of phobias ran over me. It's taken me a long time to work them out. Anyway, the irrational now leaves a very sour taste in my mouth. That's probably part of the reason I don't drink much too."

"What happened 10 years ago?"

"It was in New Orleans. A cousin was getting married down there. It was the morning after drinking myself into a stupor. That was one of my rare episodes of crapulence, you understand. I had them occasionally in my twenties."

"Crapulence? I'm not sure what that means, but I think I like it," said Heather throatily.

"I'm sure you do. Anyway, while crossing one of those 10 foot wide streets in the French Quarter on a traffic free morning, a cop waved me over and began to write me a jaywalking ticket."

"I always knew you were a criminal at heart."

"I was feeling cruddy and dehydrated and hung over and I was standing in the sun. Suddenly everything went gray and I fainted on the sidewalk."

"That's because you saw him as a parental authority figure and you always were so hung up about pleasing your father," Heather analyzed.

"Whether that's right or wrong, how can you think about it so intelligently and then carry on about vampires and ghosts?"

"That's why you should take me seriously. I'm not stupid."

Arthur refrained from answering "just crazy." He went on with his story. "Anyway, I woke up staring at the sky. The cop asked, 'Are you OK?' I said, 'Yeah.' He said, 'Sign here.'

"Something about that simple experience shook me," he went on. "You know, for years afterwards I couldn't shake the feeling that I was on the verge of fainting. That can be a bit disconcerting when driving a car, or standing in line, or whatever. This one irrational fear led to others and soon to full-blown anxiety attacks. You know how it feels when a deer suddenly jumps in front of your car?"

"Yeah, I feel that way when I realize I'm talking to a vampire."

"Right. I felt that way 24 hours a day."

"You should have seen a shrink."

"That turned out not to be necessary. If you keep hitting your hand with a hammer, eventually your hand goes numb. My phobias wore themselves out. Suppose I did faint at the wheel? The worst that could happen is that I die in a crash. Eventually, I started feeling as well as thinking, 'So what?' Then I got better. But it left me antagonistic to irrational notions."

"My notions are not irrational. I can prove it."

"How?"

"Do you believe in crystal power?"

"No."

"I can prove that one right now."

Heather pulled out a crystal that hung on a chain around her neck. She walked over to Harlan.

"Hold up your hand, Harlan."

She waved the crystal from side to side in front of Harlan's palm.

"Do you feel heat as the point of the crystal passes in front of your hand?"

"Yeah, I do kind of," said Harlan honestly.

She turned and did the same to Krista.

"You Krista?"

"Shit yeah."

Here. Try it, Arthur ... Do you feel it?"

Arthur hesitated before answering, "No. I'm more aware of what my palm is feeling as I see the crystal pass in front. So I sense a tingle. But the source of that is me, not the crystal. I don't feel any actual heat from the crystal."

"You are just being stubborn."

"Close your eyes," suggested Arthur. "Hold up your palm, and let me wave the crystal at you. You tell me by the heat alone when the crystal is in front of your hand,"

Heather closed her eyes as Arthur removed the necklace from her. He waved the stone in front of her upraised palm.

"Speak up when you think the point is in front of your palm."

"OK. Now... now... now... now... now... now." She opened her eyes. "How'd I do?" she asked.

"Mixed bag," Harlan answered.

Heather had been right twice and wrong four times, a purely random result.

"That's because of your negative energy. It works better when you aren't so hostile."

Heather shifted the subject to metaphysics. Her opinions were very *Star Wars*. "I'm not a Christian, but there is a lot of truth in Christianity. There is a lot of truth in Buddhism. I believe in two gods. There is a god of dark as well as a god of light. The dark side is very powerful and people are attracted to it because they get what they want in this life. But reincarnation is a fact and you evolve toward the light only by associating with the light. Most people are on the fence. They are not real good and not real bad, but sooner or later you have to choose which side you are on. The people who choose the light have a very hard time of it. They take a lot of abuse. But don't take revenge on people. You have to understand and accept they will treat you badly some-times."

Arthur chose this moment for his favorite though far from original aphorism, "Let no good deed go unpunished."

Heather aimed an appalled stare at him. "Statements like that are why I stay up nights thinking about you. You know, I dismiss a lot of this stuff when I'm sober," she said turning to Arthur, "but when I'm high I'm in touch with the way things are. I think that maybe you are very dangerous. What side of the fence are you on?"

"I don't accept your cosmology. There is no dark side. There is no light side. There is no fence."

"You say that because maybe you've already chosen the dark side."

"Ah."

"Vampires are very seductive. People allow them into themselves willingly because they bring you great pleasure. But it is hard to get them out again. They consume you until they become you. Usually death is the best escape for anyone not totally lost. Are you a vampire?"

"I don't believe in vampires.

"Are you a vampire?"

"You have seen me in the daytime."

"That doesn't matter. Vampires are not like in the movies. They are after human souls."

"No such thing."

"You don't think you have a soul?"

"No."

"I have one. A good one. I know I've really screwed up my life, Arthur. I drink too much and I don't always talk nicely, but I don't hurt other people. Not in a real way. The only person I ever hurt was me. My karma is pure. That attracts witches and vampires to me. But I'm strong and my strength scares them.

"There is this one vampire at a lesbian bar on 9th where I book sometimes. She avoids me because she knows I can turn her evil back on her. They can't have me if I don't give myself to them willingly. That is why I'm not afraid of them though I prefer to hang out with good people like Krista and Harlan.

"It isn't just the vampires either. The other night I was walking home with Susan who is a black witch. It was a chilly night and I was shivering. She turned to me and said, 'You don't have to be cold, Heather.' She was tempting me to cast a spell to warm myself up! I can do that. But that is the stupid, shallow sort of thing that black witches do. They use their powers selfishly and poison their souls. I'm not going there. I told her that."

There were elements of this story that Arthur believed. A surprising number of New York women, especially among those who work in bars and nightclubs, call themselves witches. There is a whole pagan feminist philosophy associated with this identification. There is a far larger number of women who at least like to believe in witchcraft.

Arthur recalled meeting Susan. She was a bartender at Gulps, a bar in Murray Hill catering to well-heeled Generation Xers pretending to be working class. He had watched Heather play there one night. In the same club Heather had pointed out to him a vampire waitress named Vanessa. Quite popular with the male customers at Gulps, she dressed in black, dyed her hair black, whitened her skin with make-up, and had her cuspids capped with vampirish points. She obviously enjoyed playing the part and may even have taken it seriously to some degree. The extent to which these people were self-delusional was a matter on which the opinions of Arthur and Heather differed.

Heather sighed and sipped more whiskey. "I'm sorry, Arthur. You always have been nice to me and generous to me. I shouldn't accuse you of something like that. You are a good person. But your karma is at risk. You have to learn that there are ghosts. There are witches. There are vampires. There are demons. Have you ever started awake and had to catch your breath? That was a demon holding you down. There is evil in the world and it has real power and force. Do you believe in evil?"

"Evil is whatever fashionable philosophers say it is."

"That is so wrong and so dangerous to yourself. Will you believe your own ears? Will you believe your own eyes?"

"I usually do."

"Talk to a ghost. Do it now. Speak to a dead relative. Just open your mind. You'll hear an answer."

Arthur parodied Svengali, "That would just be Arthur talking to himself."

"No, it wouldn't!" she insisted with exasperation. "I am going to conjure up demons. It will damage my karma but I can spare it. I have enough good that I won't be destroyed."

"Time out!" shouted Krista. "Don't do that, honey."

"It's all right. I can protect you. I'll protect Harlan too."

"I appreciate that," Harlan thanked her dryly.

"Still, Heather, let's pass on that one," said Arthur.

"Why not, if you don't believe? You will believe when I'm done, though. They will swirl around you and bite your legs! You'll see things that will scare you shitless! I have to do this to save you, Arthur."

Krista waved a forefinger. "Uh …"

"Don't worry. I'll put a shield around you and Harlan. You won't even see them clearly, but Arthur will."

"No. Drop it, Heather."

"Why, Arthur?"

"Because I know what is going to happen. I won't see anything. Then you'll resent me because you'll think you damaged your karma pointlessly. Worse yet, you'll think I lied."

"You'll see something and you'll be too scared to lie," she said while beginning to pick candles off the shelves. "Sit on the bench."

"I said don't do that!" demanded Arthur. Nonetheless, he obediently sat on the bench.

Heather ignored him. She cleared a space on the floor, arranged a pattern of candles, turned off the lights, and struck a match.

Krista's eyes were firmly shut. Harlan was fascinated by the bizarre scene.

Heather sat with her eyes shut amid the burning candles. She opened her eyes slowly and a look of horror came over her face.

"They're hovering over you! Saliva is dripping down your shoulder! Don't tell me you don't feel that thing clawing at your leg! What do you see? Tell me!"

Arthur sat placidly on the piano bench.

"Not much in this light," he answered calmly. "I see you. I see the shadows cast by flickering candles. There is no one else here but the four of us. Five, actually. The cat's eyes are reflecting in the corner."

Heather could see enough of Arthur's expression to tell he was evaluating her sanity.

"They're gone. The demons are gone. I'm not crazy, Arthur. They were here in this room. You would have seen them if you just let yourself!" There was desperation in her voice.

"Could somebody turn on the light?" asked an unnerved Harlan. He sincerely wasn't sure what he had seen in the shadowy darkness. His logic told him Heather was crazy. He had not clearly witnessed anything to negate that opinion, but all the same there was a part of him that wasn't sure. Besides, it was disturbing enough if craziness was all there was to it.

Heather somberly stood up and flicked the wall switch. She bent down and blew out the candles.

"I didn't see anything because I didn't look," said Krista. "I didn't want to see any of those things. She tottered to her feet. "Well, on that note I've got to run. My baby-sitter is on overtime."

Krista raised her right hand. Heather raised hers sullenly. Krista slapped Heather five.

Harlan got up too. "Yeah, it's been interesting buds, but my lady will be pissed if I don't show up soon." He looked at Krista unsure whether she had been joking. She never had mentioned a child, but she could be perfectly serious. "Baby-sitter?"

Krista smiled and nodded.

"OK, I'll drop you guys off," said Arthur.

"Wait," offered Heather. "I'll go with you."

Heather picked up her oversized leather bag. She put the half-empty *Jack Daniel's* into it.

The four returned to the car. Arthur drove first to Krista's building in the East Village. She propped open the front door to the building and ferried her drums inside. She declined help. On the last trip she called over her shoulder, "Chill, babies."

They proceeded to Alphabet City. At Harlan's building on Avenue B, Heather asked, "You're doing the gig next week on West 81st, right?"

"Yeah, if I learn to play the blues by then. Are you OK being left alone with a dangerous dark sider?" he asked with a smile.

Heather shrugged.

The door slammed shut behind them. Heather stared at Arthur.

"Let's go to your place. I think tonight's the night."

"We're closer to your place."

"Don't be so eager. Your place."

Heather was quiet on the hour drive outside the city. She wouldn't respond to Arthur's attempts to start conversation. Occasionally she would drink from her bottle.

Arthur pulled into his driveway and parked in back of the house. His home and grounds were small, but the yard was fenced and private. He leaned over and kissed her. She allowed this for a few moments before pushing him away.

"Inside," she ordered.

Heather exited the car with her bag strap over her shoulder and walked to the back door. Arthur hurriedly followed her. He fumbled with the keys at the door and opened it for her.

Arthur followed Heather through the kitchen, the dining room, and the the living room. She shed clothes as she walked. By the time she stood next to the bed in the master bedroom she was naked except for her necklace, watch, and bag. She dropped the bag on the bed.

More out of disorientation than shyness or clumsiness, Arthur was still clothed. She pushed him backward onto the bed and straddled him.

"I'm going to save you, Arthur. That's my job." There were tears in her eyes.

Heather stroked Arthur's head with her left hand. She firmly planted an open-mouthed kiss on him. With her right hand she lifted the sharpened stake she had pulled from her handbag and plunged it into his chest.

She was tired of ruining so many clothes from the blood spatters. She first had tried this trick when she killed that vampire not far from here in Randolph. After a quick shower she would be ready to leave.

Heather knew the Dover train station was only a few blocks from Arthur's house. She would retrieve her spare clothes from the back of the SUV and then head back to the city in a couple of hours. This was Saturday morning. It was doubtful that anyone would find Arthur before Monday. It was even more doubtful anyone on the train would pay enough attention to her to identify her.

Her band would need a new driver. She hoped the next one wouldn't be a vampire.

OVERLOOK

The Children's Neighborhood Association (CNA) originally had been set up with adult supervision. It was a lesson in democracy at Patrick Henry Grammar School. The lesson had been proposed at a teachers' meeting by an enthusiastic young fourth grade teacher in her first year on the job. At first the idea met with some resistance, but as soon as assurances were made that the project would require no overtime from the staff, a majority quickly formed behind it. The intention was to create a representative body for the youngsters other than the usual student council which, subject as it was to peremptory veto and dismissal by the school principal, often seemed to be a lesson in a different kind of governance altogether.

Members of grades 1-6 were elected as representatives to a charter convention for the CNA. With some guidance from a teacher of history and geography for the fifth and sixth grades, the conventioneers issued a charter that committed the CNA to "promote the general welfare, happiness, and interests of the children in the community." The emphasis was on the common good. An organizational structure was developed that for each grade provided an elected governor and two representatives to the general assembly. The assembly would choose a president from among its own membership in parliamentary fashion. Although the organization paralleled the grade structure of the grammar school, the charter made clear that the CNA was separate from, and independent of, the school system.

At this point the teachers involved in the project congratulated themselves on the success of this particular civics lesson. They scarcely gave the CNA another thought.

By and large, the association members on the Overlook Drive cul-de-sac welcomed the intervention. The standoff was technically a local matter but the wider repercussions for the community were clear.

Wendy, the Governor of Division 2, a group of youngsters roughly co-equal with the second grade was the recognized regional leader of the 7-year-olds. She had called on Barbara, this year's Assembly President for assistance when a dispute arose and spread beyond the boundaries of her division.

Barbara's style was reflective and cautious, but she could be hard as nails when the situation demanded it. She had arrived on the scene to find three Division 2 enforcers, the entire force, staked out around a tent. The fort-like tent stood in a clearing in the partly wooded yard. Two 7-year-olds named Carol and Vicky were holed up inside. The enforcers carried eggs for ammo. In order to stabilize the situation, Barbara order four federal enforcers armed with slingshots to join them. Bobby, the senior Division 2 enforcer, was relieved to turn over command of the siege to the feds, all of whom were boys around the age of 10. Had Bobby recognized the responsibility that went with his job when first it was offered, Bobby would have refused it. Already he had removed the sheriff's badge that had been the gift of his mother a few weeks earlier; he didn't want anyone to mistake it for a symbol of authority.

Although many clamored for an immediate assault, Barbara insisted on a review of the events that had brought them to this pass. Barbara hoped the dispute could be resolved peacefully. She remembered Carol and Vicky from months ago when she had made a political goodwill tour of the Divisions shortly after her elevation to the Presidency. They had just been kids then, but they had seemed cheerful and innocent.

Barbara set up a command post at the playground equipment that occupied one corner of the yard. She assembled witnesses quickly and proceeded with the interviews. She wished she could question Carol and Vicky as well, but they ignored her invitations.

Barbara called on Wendy first. "The witness may approach the swing. You are the Governor of Division 2?"

"Yes, of course I am. I'm the one who phoned you."

"Yes, I know. I'm just being clear for the record."

"What record?"

This was a pertinent question. "April, get a pencil and a pad of paper out of my backpack there. Keep notes."

"Notes," April groused while rummaging through the pack. "This is worse than school."

"Wendy, can you explain how Carol and Vicky came into conflict with the rest of the Overlook Drive Division 2 community?"

"Conflict was not the right word at first," said Wendy. "It really was just an administrative matter. Carol and Vicky came to our attention in early August. It was Carol's birthday and she had received a dollhouse as a present."

"What does that have to do with all this?" Barbara asked.

"The doll house came as a kit. It was a big elaborate model. She was excited and, according to reports, she started along with her friend Vicky to put it together that very afternoon. One of the girls at her party complained."

"Which one?"

"Colette."

Barbara grimaced. She knew Colette as a spiteful, envious whiner. "Go on."

"As I said, she complained. She left the party and showed up at my door. So that afternoon I issued a stop order to Carol until the neighboring kids had a chance to review her plans. Carol laughed at me. She stopped laughing when she saw I was serious. 'But she's just jealous,' Carol kept insisting. But Colette's motive was beside the point because she was right. If there is an issue that affects the happiness of the community, the proper procedure is to apply for a permit. Carol told me I wasn't invited to the party and asked me to leave. I went, but Vicky stayed. I strongly suspected that they were ignoring the order."

"Well, that was inappropriate, but I can understand Carol's annoyance," said Barbara who was trying to keep an open mind.

"Perhaps, but that was not responsible civic behavior on her part, so I had no choice but to take further action. I didn't want to act unilaterally, so I notified the Division Council."

"That's Freddie and Julie?"

"Right. They are very public-spirited and were elected last June by a big majority. They promised to defend the interests of every 7-year-old in the community."

"Unfortunately, that is not possible as your current problem demonstrates. Their interests conflict," Barbara observed.

"What is best for most is best for all. Anyway, they called an emergency meeting. The Council issued a warrant and sent Bobby…"

"Bobby?"

"The senior enforcer. They sent Bobby over to bring in the girls for questioning."

"How did they react to that?"

"Well, they were pretty exasperated. Carol kept insisting 'This is my room. I have the right to do what I want!' Bobby explained that no one was denying them the right to their own room, except when what they do in their room impacts on everyone else. They are, after all, part of a larger community. In the end Carol and Vicky went along with him. They appeared before myself and the Council, which then scheduled them in for a Friday meeting."

"Why wait until Friday?"

"We needed time to notify formally the neighborhood kids so everyone had a chance to be heard."

"OK. So the next Friday did Carol submit her proposal for a dollhouse?"

"Yes."

"Wasn't it a pretty cut and dried approval process? Bedrooms generally are zoned for residential dollhouses."

"There were other issues. Maybe one of the council members can explain that."

"Are they here?"

"Yes. This is Freddie."

"How about it Freddie?"

"I don't recall all the details," mused Freddie. "We had a lot of business that afternoon. There was the matter of the Andersons' sandbox. We were not satisfied with their soil erosion plan. And the major item on the agenda was Jack's permit application for maneuvers with his toy soldiers. He…"

"Stick to the doll house."

"OK. First we opened the discussion to the public. We had a big turnout from the immediate neighbors on Overlook Drive. The general feeling was against the proposal. Most kids felt that the density of dollhouses already was too high in the neighborhood. Judy, who lives next door to Carol, said she built her own dollhouse because of the rural nature of the community and thought it wasn't right to have that disturbed. If dollhouses were everywhere it would change the whole character of the place. She accused Carol of greed. She pointed out the disturbance to her own lifestyle of kids walking by her home on the way to Carol's house to play.

There was some validity to Judy's argument, so we ordered Carol to do a traffic impact study and held over the application until the next Friday.

"At the next meeting the impact study showed a definite increase in traffic, which we felt needed to be addressed. So, we limited the occupation of the proposed dwelling to a single family of dolls. Surprisingly, this hadn't previously been part of our regulations."

"Isn't that an ex post facto law?"

"No, although Carol made that very argument. We have the authority to change the rules as we see fit prior to approval. Of course, we wanted to be fair, so we told her she had a right to appeal the decision, though of course construction would have to be suspended pending the outcome."

"Appeal to whom?"

"To judges whom we would appoint. We could have arranged a hearing for her before the end of the year. She decided not to wait and accepted the condition on single family usage.

"Then questions were raised about the design of the dollhouse which had some contemporary features. This is a colonial neighborhood and Amy from the Historical Society demanded that the house be modified to fit in with the character of the community. The application was held over again until architectural changes could be designed and presented."

"Did Carol modify the design?"

"Yes, she agreed at the next meeting to add a wraparound porch in order to alter the style to that of a colonial farmhouse.

We then issued an inspection schedule so that we could be sure the work was done properly. Carol complained about the red tape and the delays caused by the inspector being available only on Saturday, but it was unreasonable for her to expect the inspector to be at her beck and call for a matter of her own personal gain. We also required that she deposit a package of double-stuffed Oreo cookies and an 8 pack of Parmalat with the Council to cover inspection costs."

"Was the house approved then?"

"Yes, subject to appropriate conditions. As you say, we had few grounds for actually denying the permit, but we still were determined to mitigate the detrimental effects of the new construction. Arnie of the Parks Commission recommended that open space be dedicated to local kids. 'In my own room?' asked Carol incredulously, as though she were not a member of a wider community.

"'It's a trade-off,' Arnie explained to her. You are asking us for something, so we are asking for something back.'

"We took up Arnie's suggestion and ordered the dedication of 20% of the floor space in Carol's room as open space for the community.

"Susie then requested off-site improvements because of the effect on her as indicated by the traffic study. So Carol was ordered to mark out a bicycle lane in the street with sidewalk chalk. She also was required to donate a box of chalk to the Council for future maintenance."

"Did Carol comply?"

"Yes. So far, so good, really. Carol hadn't shown much civic responsibility, but she did the barest amount of what was required of her. She should have been more forthcoming. After all, we were just looking out for the public interest, including hers."

"OK, if she complied with all that, why are my enforcers surrounding a tent?"

"The showdown actually began when two of the neighbors who were enjoying the open space in Carol's room noticed that she and Vicky were using the house in a manner other than its approved single family designation. This violated the terms of the permit. They lodged a complaint with the Council and we ordered Bobby to investigate."

"What happened then?"

"Carol and Vicky behaved in a totally criminal fashion. They ordered Bobby out of their room, even though his warrant was in full order. Threatening an officer is a serious offense, of course, so Bobby got hold of his junior partner and then he deputized Harry..."

"Harry? The overgrown bully who shakes kids down for lunch money?"

"Yes. It was good to see him behaving in a useful way. Together they prepared to return in force. When they did the situation had changed. Carol and Vicky had left the room altogether and apparently took the dollhouse with them."

"Order Bobby here."

"Bobby was retrieved from his stakeout position.

"Bobby, what happened when you came looking for Carol and Vicky with your posse?"

"They were gone from the house. We found them outside. They set up that tent on their back lawn and, we suspected, built the dollhouse inside."

"You suspected?"

"Yes they refused to honor a warrant to inspect."

"Carol has an older brother, doesn't she?"

"Yes, he's at camp."

"Then the lawn is outside of Division 2 jurisdiction because it is shared with another Division."

"Yes. That's what they were counting on. That's why we called in the feds."

"What are the grounds for federal involvement?"

"Environmental. The earth is all our responsibility so that was the grounds for the warrant."

"Explain."

"The tent occupies a habitat for box turtles, garter snakes, and other species crucial to the sustainability of the lifestyle of all CNA members. We all have a right to see that Carol uses her yard responsibly."

"I see. Is that the whole story?"

"No. We started hearing some very ugly rumors about goings on in the tent. Vicky was spotted entering the tent with candles."

"It's dark in there, isn't it?"

"Perhaps. But we believe they are being used in weird cult activities with the dolls. Remember, Vicky's younger sister is in Division 1 and may have seen this. We suspect the dolls are being abused. The 1ˢᵗ Divisioners in this neighborhood have to be protected against this kind of corruption. They, after all, are the 2ⁿᵈ Divisioners of the future.

"Not only that, but Carol almost certainly stockpiled arms. We saw her and Vicky carry balloons and a pitcher of water into the tent, so the threat of water bombs is real. We believe they have at least one pump-action water rifle as well. There is no record of either of them applying for a permit to own one. They refused to honor a warrant to search for weapons."

"All right. I've heard enough."

The crowd gathered to hear Barbara's decision.

"Personally, I think the Governor and the Council had a heavy hand in this matter. A kinder, gentler approach could have avoided this distasteful scene. Yet, technically the Council was within its rights and Carol is in the wrong. Vicky, of course, is an accessory. Still, I would insist that we reach a settlement without recourse to violence, except for the ongoing abuse of dolls. Bobby's argument about the 1ˢᵗ Divisioners is a telling one. The transjurisdictional nature of that interaction makes this a federal matter. I cannot rule on the environmental question until we complete an impact study. This should be at Carol's expense."

"So Wendy was right to call in the feds. I say hit them fast and hard!" opined an eager Colette.

"I make that decision. We first give them one more chance to surrender. Bobby, they know you and trust you to some extent. Explain to them the situation one more time."

Bobby took a deep breath and proceeded to do his duty. Leaving his eggs and his back-up water pistol behind, Bobby approached the opening of the tent. As the intensity of the moment heightened his senses, he was acutely aware of the smell of freshly cut grass. The sun was low enough in the sky to tinge toward red, but he could feel its heat on his face. The interior of the tent was not visible from where he stood, but he knew he was being watched from the other side of the flaps. He stopped his advance when he heard Carol and Vicky exchange muffled remarks. He called out to them.

"Carol! Vicky! Please come out. We don't want anyone getting hurt over this. Let's try to reach a settlement. Barbara is willing to work with you, maybe she can get you better terms. You are surrounded. You have to leave sometime."

"So do you!" answered a voice from the tent.

"Is Vicky's sister in there with you? We demand to see the dolls so we can be sure you are not abusing them or corrupting young people."

A water balloon flew out of the tent and caught Bobby in the chest. He staggered back as the water splattered in his eyes.

"I'm hit!"

"One of our enforcers has been hit!" yelled Harry who often exclaimed the obvious.

"All right," said Barbara sadly. "We cannot allow contempt for law and order. Send in the troops."

"It's about time!" shouted Harry as he launched a well-aimed egg through the flaps of the tent.

The barrage opened up from all sides. The monitors closed in slowly. Federal slingshots sent several eggs to their targets. One must have hit a candle inside the tent because a wisp of smoke emerged.

The commotion in the back yard had roused the adults in the house. When Carol's mother spotted the smoke from the tent she ran into the back yard in near hysterics.

"Hey! What do you kids think you're doing?!" Seizing a garden hose she ran to the tent, and called out, "Carol! Vicky! Get out of there!"

The two rushed out and stood by her. She stuck the hose into the tent and sprayed the dollhouse. The smoke had come from the makeshift cardboard wraparound porch on the dollhouse. It had ignited from an overturned taper.

"What are you maniacs? Are you a bunch of animals?!" she shouted at the kids. "Where have you kids learned your sense of responsibility? Don't you have any respect for the rights of others?" She singled out Barbara, "You, Barbara! I can't believe you of all people would organize this gang attack on two of your own schoolmates playing in their own yard. You are older than they are and you should know better! What gives you the right? Carol, get in the house! Vicky, go on home."

She addressed the abashed posse once more. "I'd punish every one of you myself if I were not in a hurry to get to a town meeting. All of your parents will be there, and believe me they all will hear about this!"

On the drive to the town hall Carol's mom was still shocked.

"Can you believe those kids?" she asked her husband.

"There are so many outside influences these days it is hard to teach kids any values," he answered. "They watch TV and I'll bet they spend hours on the internet. Who knows what they see there?

"That's why this meeting is so important. The Babsons want to build that monstrosity of a house on their empty lot at the end of the street."

"I wouldn't have moved here if I had known that the neighborhood would be over-developed that way," she grumbled.

"And they are strange people," he added. "Some kind of cultists or something. We can't allow them in our neighborhood. It's a bad influence on the kids. Maybe we should check into the way they are raising their own kids."

LANAMITE

Fingers snapped in front of my nose. I became conscious of a quiet but firm voice.

"Hey, Lana. Bimboski."

I had been clutching the stage pole and staring blankly for some minutes while thinking about elementary particles, other dimensions, and exotic nuclear structures. A wild plan formed in my mind.

"What are you spacing out on?" the voice continued. "If I want mannequins I'll buy them."

"Bimboskaya," I corrected. The manager Barbara shook her head as I resumed my gyrations in the club with the charming name *Route 69*. That route had taken me a long way from the nuclear testing grounds in Siberia, all the way from nuclear engineer to go-go dancer. It wasn't quite the career path I had in mind back at Leningrad University.

In the days of the Cold War basic Soviet strategy was to maintain massive conventional superiority to the Allies. At the same time, we needed to deter the Allies from countering us with tactical nuclear weapons. Official nuclear policy therefore was all or nothing. We hoped to scare the Allies out of using nukes in any conflict by threatening a full-scale counterstrike if even one nuke was used anywhere at any time. That way our bigger conventional forces would be free to win.

The Allies were uncooperative. Despite our posture, NATO relied heavily on relatively cheap tactical nuclear weapons that could destroy our superior numbers. The Americans, with uncharacteristic candor, actually invented the phrase "More bang per buck" to justify the strategy. In the 1970s the Americans developed a neutron bomb which would kill people without otherwise damaging the target. It was ideal for a European war.

Strangely enough, all the saber rattling worked out OK. Each side's posturing scared the other side just enough to maintain the peace.

In the 1980s a dangerous shift began. The vaunted Western technological edge, which was previously little more than a boast, suddenly became real and rapidly widened. Smart bombs, self-guided missiles, high accuracy artillery, and vastly improved battlefield command and control placed our numerical superiority at risk, even in a wholly conventional war. It was time to deploy better tactical nuclear weapons of our own in order to counter the threat.

I graduated from Leningrad University in 1987 at the age of 18. One year later, I hung my doctorate on the wall in Moscow. Other prodigies have done better, but my talents were obvious enough to win me a position in Novosibirsk at the equivalent of America's Lawrence Livermore laboratories.

My first assignment was the neutron bomb project. After one week I offered my own set of working plans to the rest of the team. They scarcely bothered to change it. It was simple really. A neutron bomb is just a stepped hydrogen bomb with a modified tamper. A lithium wrap around a fission trigger provides a source of neutrons and heavy hydrogen. The hydrogen isotopes then fuse to produce more neutrons. A few fancy tweaks to a standard SS20 warhead were enough. They gave me a medal for that. In 1990 the USSR disintegrated, but the weapons were still useful to Moscow. A Rus by any other name...

So why was I, decorated doctor of physics, shaking my shapely posterior in the face of a garage mechanic in a smoke-filled bar on the east side of Manhattan? Nuclear weaponeers in Russia are now paid less than chambermaids at the Moscow Hilton. I have no talent for cleaning rooms. So, with the help of a VIP whom I'd rather not name in the Russian government, I obtained a new identity and US permanent residency. He played a sophomoric prank. My passport reads Svetlana Korolevna Groznaya. No one in the US ever so much as has raised an eyebrow about that. He must have known they wouldn't.

Money was tight at first, but I soon found a room in a walk-up Manhattan apartment owned by a prissy Wall Street Broker named Yvonne. This was after the '87 crash and before the '92 boom in the stock market, so she needed some extra cash. I might have hesitated had I known that her slovenly boyfriend Maurice would move in with her too. He didn't provide any cash. Maurice called himself a musician, but his major occupation was spending Yvonne's money on dope. Occasionally he croaked bad poetry to her. She loved him. Probably she still does.

Don't get me wrong, I quite like some men both in and out of bed, but, even at best, living with one is scarcely less objectionable than living with a chimp. Maurice was far from best.

I needed to find a job quickly in order to pay Yvonne. I had another expense too. This was storage. I managed to ship out of Russia some very special treasures. My friend got them into the US for me under a diplomatic seal. He didn't ask about the contents. He probably thought it best not to know. He was right. The treasures are packed in old crates in an ordinary warehouse in Jersey City. From the outside, they don't look interesting enough to steal.

There was one place where an attractive young woman could earn a decent income, while still staying within the law. I walked in the door and spoke to the manager. From beneath her several strata of makeup and explosion of platinum and purple hair, the diminutive, soft-spoken, but scary Barbara regarded me quietly for a couple minutes at the strip bar *Route 69*. Then she hired me on the spot. The club offered high pay, flexible schedules, and the opportunity to speak Russian. I was not the only expatriate in the club.

So *Route 69* is where my secret history begins. Very soon it will not be a secret. Caesar was wise to have written his own history. I choose to follow his example. He is better regarded than if Cicero and the partisans of Brutus had written it all. Am I being vainglorious? You decide.

The customers in the club were a jumble of ages, classes, and types. None of them came to drink, because no alcohol was served here. That was because this was a nude bar. Evidently the legislators in Albany actually sat down and thought about the matter. They concluded that watching a nude woman while drinking was too much for a man to handle, and so they made doing both at once illegal. They figured men can handle alcohol while watching a woman wearing a string bikini, however. Since the drinking age is 21, the odd result is that 18-year-old men may enter a club to see nude women, but must wait until they are 21 to see them clothed.

Aside from enjoying the scenery, most customers just want some attention from a pretty woman. Earning commissions on drinks proved absurdly simple. Advice to the neophyte: just affect interest in whatever they say, and they keep buying. They talked to me about the strangest things. Those who admitted to being married complained about their wives, of course. Others talked about football, as though I would know or care anything about it. Still others talked about drugs, as though I would know or care anything about it. In fairness many girls did care about drugs, so this sometimes was successful as a pickup routine. A few customers would talk about art, literature, politics, or science. Second advice to the neophyte: don't argue about politics no matter how tempting. The more idiotic a customer's views are in this matter, the more passionately he holds them.

One night a literary sort named Henry spoke to me about gravity, believe it or not. Perhaps it was his way of showing off. He was a high school physics teacher, so seeing me was a major financial commitment for him. I tried to give him his money's worth. Henry was one of the sort who didn't especially want me to play dumb so I answered at his level. His level was quite rudimentary, so the conversation wasn't much of a strain for me. We discussed such issues as whether a cosmological constant existed and, if so, how its value would affect the fate of the universe. We discussed the disadvantages of living in a deep gravity well. We discussed asteroid mining, which has been a staple of science fiction for nearly a century. We decided on this last one that too much effort was needed to get things into space and back down again, so retrieving the fabulous mineral wealth floating out there would not ever be feasible with standard rocket technology. I doubt our conclusion was a news flash for NASA. Before spending his last dollar and leaving, Henry remarked ironically that something really had to be done about gravity and that he planned to take it up with his good friend Professor Cavor that very weekend.

He probably didn't expect me to catch that reference so I let it slide. As a socialist, HG Wells in the USSR was sufficiently PC, as they say here, to be available. You may remember that in *First Men in the Moon* a Professor Cavor invents 'cavorite," a substance which blocks gravity. He then builds a sphere covered with it. By opening panels on the side of the sphere facing the moon, he literally falls from the earth to the moon. Wells made a few logical errors and threw energy conservation out the window, but it was a clever and fun tale.

It was during my next set on stage, after my discussion with Henry, that my mind wandered to thoughts about the properties that a gravity blocker would need to have. This led to more thoughts of the cosmological constant which, if real, is a kind of anti-gravity. Could the relative values of these forces, or at least the way they are expressed, be changed in some way?

At the labs in Russia my last assignment was the element 114 project. This needs a brief explanation. Broadly speaking, heavier atoms are less stable than lighter ones. The general trend of half-lives of the elements beyond uranium, element 92, is to grow shorter and shorter. However, atomic number is not all there is to it; so, there are exceptions. The ratio of neutrons to protons, the shape of the nucleus, and whether the nucleon total is an odd or even number are factors in the longevity of an atom too. An even isotope, U238 for example, typically is more stable than an odd one such as U233 or U235. The upshot is that some heavy isotopes are long-lasting. Theory suggests that there should be an island of stability for some isotopes of atomic number 114. What such a material would be like is anybody's guess. It would not, of course, block gravity.

New heavy elements are manufactured by slamming together lighter atoms. Under the right conditions they stick with some bits flying off. So far the manufacture of new elements has stalled around element 112 which has a half-life of 0.005 seconds. The reason for the limitation is that the force necessary to make a nucleus this size imparts so much energy that the new nucleus spins itself rapidly into a barbell shape and then splits again into lower elements. Using current particle accelerator techniques, the pieces are too energetic to assemble at all beyond 112. The conditions may be right inside a collapsing star to assemble a variety of heavy elements, but on earth those are hard conditions to recreate.

My approach back in Russia exploited an exotic theory about multidimensional extensions of elementary particles. Multiple dimensions are not by themselves an exotic notion: they are basic to unified field theories. The idea is that all but the three commonly observed spatial dimensions are collapsed so that motion within them is significant only for quantum particles. The novel aspect of my approach was the redirection of energy in these other directions as a path toward assembling 114.

As I stood on the dance platform at *Route 69* the application to gravity of this approach suddenly hit me like a bucket of water in the face. If heavy elements could be warped in a pandimensional field, the expression of gravity and the cosmological constant might be reversed. It might even be achieved with something less exotic than 114 — maybe plain old plutonium would do, though it would have to be doped with a few higher elements in order to hold the field together.

I was reawakened by Barbara's snapping fingers. As I continued with my set, I noticed sitting by the stage a nerd in horn-rims named Neville. On a previous occasion he had pummeled me with a description of his Weather Bureau job parallel programming Crays. This was just the computing tool I needed. I bent down and waved at him between my legs. The blonde hair of my head brushed the floor. He shyly waved back and cautiously stuffed a dollar in my garter. After the last dance of my set, I stepped off the platform and stood in front of the nerd while pulling on my microdress.

"Hello, Neville. What do you say you buy me a drink?"

We chatted. Before the end of the week he gave me the data I needed. I have no idea what he thought my request. Probably he didn't really care so long as I was sweet to him. I hope Neville didn't get into too much trouble for diverting computer time to my application.

The next problem was locating or generating the proper field. It happens that the hole in an operating tokamak doughnut is just the right place. A tokamak, of course, is a large twisted torus inside of which protons and deuterium nuclei race around. Kept out of contact with the walls of the container by a magnetic field, the plasma heats up to 100,000,000 degrees C at which point thermonuclear fusion occurs. So far the machines consume more power than they produce, unless they are charged with dangerous tritium. Sustained fusion events are measured in seconds. Nevertheless there are those who think this may be a practical power source someday. Maybe. I was interested only in a pandimensional field generated during fusion by the peculiar geometry of the machine. Unfortunately, these are not common devices and they are not easy to access. Much of the work done with them is classified. A recently mothballed machine existed nearby at Princeton University, but I could hardly just walk into the laboratory and turn it on with the flick of a switch. Still, there might be some way.

I picked up some weekend gigs at a bikini bar near Princeton. I figured there were bound to be grad students and professors hanging out there. There were too. Most turned out to be economists, historians, and literature specialists. At last I hit the jackpot with Eddie, a timid young man from a well-heeled family working on his Physics thesis. He took a shine to me. He was amazed to learn that I was better grounded in his subject than he was.

I convinced Eddie to alter his thesis to include a discussion of plasma flow. Eddie had to be given a good reason so I explained to him that I had worked with tokamaks, a Soviet invention, back home and had been on the verge of a major breakthrough in fusion power. This was true, as it happens, but commercial electric power wasn't the goal. I told him if he let me help his thesis could win him fame and fortune. I told Eddie I needed a few hours with decent equipment and I would share with him any patents relating to fusion-based electric power generation. So I will. There won't be any. By themselves these temptations may not have swayed Eddie. You can figure out which ones did. Paying up was OK. I rather like corrupting young men.

The next step was convincing the University to let us fire up the machine for Eddie's thesis related experiment. I met with Eddie's wealthy father in private and told him of possible financial rewards from this research. He agreed to reimburse the University for the costs of using the equipment. I then met with a key professor, also in private, who agreed to allow the experiment provided the cost was covered. I rather like corrupting older men too.

In the midst of America's culture of casual lewdness, a shocking percentage of both men and women lead lives of erotic and social deprivation. It is easy to manipulate them cruelly. I am not a sociologist, however, I and don't analyze such things. Those who do, as far as I can see, mostly just wrap their own prejudices and politics in polysyllabic jargon. One thing I like about hard science is that no one argues the politics of leverage or the ethics of refraction. I am aware of the war of the sexes (which has at least four sides). The issues matter to those whose welfare depends on the tide of battle. I am outside that system and therefore outside any related system of ethics. I have my own system. If my plans worked out, I would soon have my own solar system.

In the meantime, I rented a little house with a large barn about an hour away from Princeton in Spring Lake, a small town by the Jersey shore. The owner wisely was reluctant to rent the space to me because of my sparse credit history, but she eventually relented. She will be paid well in the end. The barn will be a valuable tourist attraction.

Over the next few weeks on the wooden floor of the barn my lanasphere took shape. The lanasphere was just a hollow ball with a motorized hinged jaw. Its only job was to grab and hold a rock. I finished it the day before the scheduled tokamak test. A chilly, wet New Jersey autumn wind blew through the ill-fitted sideboards of the barn. The homey smell of straw and horse dung permeated the building, even though it had been empty for years. Renting a property and building a sphere had stretched my finances to their very limit, but these were a key to my future success. Another key already was en route from Russia.

I had worried that security at the tokamak would be tight enough to cause serious problems. Hardly. Eddie accepted delivery of my crate from the warehouse earlier in the day. No one questioned its designation as spare parts or prevented it from being wheeled into the lab. At midnight, several hours preceding our scheduled event I walked arm-in-arm with Eddie past the cursory glance of a sleepy university guard. We didn't even have to use our prepared explanation that we were running last minute tests on the equipment. Eddie seemed to think we would go ahead with the approved experiment the next day too.

My sheaves of calculations from the Cray ultimately were based on educated guesswork about the nature of multidimensional space. I thought I was right. If not, Princeton, New Jersey, would cease to be a prestigious address in just a few minutes. Eddie and I charged the tokamak with all of my bootleg tritium. Set in the middle of the torus was my other treasure from my old battered crate. Eddie should have questioned me more about this. Were he less love struck he would have. The spherical object was an unusual fission bomb. At its core was a near critical mass of plutonium 239 with interior layers of iron 56, niobium 92, and a few other carefully selected elements. The original idea back home had been to detonate it in a prepared underground chamber where any fleeting presence of element 114 or higher created in the implosion could be detected. The survivability of the next few minutes depended on whether I was right about redirecting the energy of the explosion out of three-dimensional space by creating the right mix of elements in the right field. The detonation had to be timed precisely with the fusion event in the tokamak, which would last only about a second.

"Eddie, perhaps you had better duck behind something."

"Why?"

"Just do it, galubka."

I hit the floor just as a blinding white light engulfed us both. Objects whistled overhead. For a moment I thought I miscalculated. Then it was quiet. I tried to see through the fuzzy blueness similar to what one sees when a flashbulb goes off in the face. The atomic blast had snuffed itself out as planned or I would be vapor; but a small shock wave had escaped before the new spatial geometry took shape. This is what destroyed the lab. My vision returning, I saw moonlight streaming in where a wall had been blown out of the building. We would have visitors very soon.

I pulled a toppled desk off of Eddie and dragged him to his feet.

"Hurry! Get up!"

He looked about the lab in horror.

"What..." he barely gasped.

A silvery sphere was smack against the ceiling. I crawled up some wreckage, peeled off my blouse and netted the sphere with it. My weight was scarcely enough to pull the object to the floor. A gas line, intended to serve laboratory equipment now buried by rubble, protruded from the wall. I kicked it repeatedly until it began to hiss. I could hear shouting and distant sirens.

"Come on, Eddie! The chekists are coming!"

"I'll get 20 to life!"

"Don't worry about that. Just move!"

Eddie shook off his stupor and led us out the back exit at a run. I stuffed the sphere into the back of his car and we accelerated toward Route 571. We pulled into the driveway of my Spring Lake house at 5:00 am. A startled deer bounded out in front of the headlight beams. I grabbed the sphere, still wrapped in my blouse, and held on tightly until we entered the house. I then let it rest on the ceiling.

"What is that thing? Why does it float?"

"Would you believe me if I said helium?"

Eddie looked at me with long overdue suspicion.

"Maybe I'd better believe that," he sighed after a pause. He followed this wisdom with the asinine suggestion, "I think we should turn ourselves in."

"You don't want to do that," I said while scratching the nape of his neck. I didn't want to have to kill him. Moments later, he again was willing to do what I told him.

The next day *The Star Ledger* headline read: "EXPLOSION ROCKS PHYSICS LAB AT PRINCETON. NO CASUALTIES. DAMAGE ESTIMATED IN MILLIONS. FIRE OFFICIALS SUSPECT GAS LEAK." The body of the article stated that the guard on duty, who was dazed by the explosion, could not confirm if anyone was in the building at the time. He said he was too shaken to remember who had entered or left at precisely what times. There was no sign of anyone in the wreckage.

We were home free.

"When you go back, act shocked and disappointed I advised Eddie."

"I don't know if I can do that."

"Would you prefer 20 to life?"

"On second thought, I can do that."

"Good."

Lanamite is true anti-gravity. It accelerates out of gravity wells at precisely the same rate normal matter, even normal antimatter, accelerates into them. My silvery sphere strives to leap from the earth's surface at 9.8 meters per second squared. Since I have only 54 antikilograms of the stuff, it is an easy matter to keep it from flying away. But here is the strange part: it also blocks gravity. If I use a rope to tie a 2-kilogram rock to a 1-kilogram block of lanamite, the rock will hold the lanamite down. Yet, if I batter that same block of lanamite to the thickness of metal foil and wrap it around that very same rock, gravitational interaction between the rock and the earth stops. The enveloped rock will accelerate away from the earth just the same as the lanamite would by itself. Although I had predicted this effect, it bothers me. The interior rock, when released, attains an energy of position and a kinetic energy it does not appear to have earned. Energy conservation should forbid this. There are no free lunches.

Perhaps there is an analogy. An ordinary spacecraft can use the gravity of a planet to slingshot itself to a higher velocity without cost to itself. There is of course a cost. It is borne by the planet, which slows down, by an amount precisely equal in energy to the energy acquired by the spacecraft. This works because a craft following a planet moving away from it has a very long time to accelerate. When the probe swings around and whips back the other way, the planet distance increases by its own velocity plus that of the craft, so there is much less time for gravity to slow the object. A spacecraft swinging around a stationary body (relative to the launch platform) would, of course, decelerate on the outbound trip by precisely the same amount it accelerated on the inbound trip. Something similar must be going on here. All the other objects in earth's gravity well must collectively lose energy in the amount gained by the rock, though it is not clear to me precisely how.

The lanasphere's dimensions were constrained only by the amount of lanamite I calculated I could spare for it. Weight, of course, was not a problem. I thinned the lanamite to a paint and sprayed a portion on the sphere. The bulk of the paint was reserved for special cargo being brought offshore by the merchant ship *Chayka*.

I still had enough pull at the Byakonur cosmodrome to pull off the delivery. Naturally, not even Ilyusha (Ilya to everyone else including his mother) was about to ship a Soyuz spacecraft to the U.S. coast just because I asked for one. He has the personal authority to order it and to keep the delivery quiet for a while, but he would have to explain his actions eventually. If the explanation wasn't good he would be arrested. True, this Soyuz was an obsolete model never to fly in the bare bones Russian space program. True also that my promise of vast rewards tempted Ilyusha. But, as so often in my life, something else tipped the balance. Ilyusha always had an eye for me. Perhaps that is what appeals to me about men. They are very predictable. Other women just amaze me when they claim they don't understand men. They are looking way too deep.

The Soyuz was to be modified according to my specifications. The main engine would be removed with the extra space given to more life support. The entire vessel would be enclosed by a titanium steel sheath with simple mechanical louvers front, back, top, bottom, and sides so arranged as to allow maneuvering jets to fire through them when open. "Shielding," I had told Ilya. The object would resemble the classic cigar shaped UFO so often spotted by drunken fishermen over swamps. I did not reveal the existence of lanamite. I didn't order the lanasphere attachment from Russia because that either would have tipped my hand or convinced Ilya that I was insane. As it was, Ilya trusted that I was on to something big; but he surely must have worried that I had just slipped a gear.

The early morning sky was a painfully bright gray. The silhouette of the *Chayka* broke the horizon 13 miles off shore.

"You're kidding! That's a Russki," pointed the skipper of my rented fishing boat as we approached.

A spray of cold salt water stung my eyes. "Just pull up along-side."

"I thought all this cloak and dagger stuff was over. What, is this some sort of smuggling operation? I'm not getting paid enough." He cast a nervous look skyward as a curious Coast Guard aircraft made a low pass.

"Chill out. There's nothing on your boat that's illegal in any clear sense, and you're getting paid more today than you earn in a week."

He glanced back at the huge metallic "balloon" bobbing on its tether above the stern of the boat. "Is it illegal in an unclear sense?"

"What isn't?"

Within minutes, my lanasphere was tethered to a deck bitt aboard the *Chayka* and I was holding onto a rope as crewmembers pulled me up the hull of the ship. My underpaid fisherman hightailed it back to the Jersey shore. It was quite likely that he would be questioned later. The Yanks still keep an eye on Russian shipping. Nothing he could say would make much sense to anyone though.

The spray painting of the Soyuz and the attachment of the lanasphere proceeded quickly. I bought some time for myself by giving Ilyusha his own special technical training session inside the capsule. I promised to reveal to him everything in only a few days. The lanasphere intrigued him, but he agreed to my request not to look inside yet. It would have upset him, of course, to have discovered the sphere was empty. He suspected all this was some sort of stealth technology or possibly a force shield of the Star Trek sort but he wanted to see some results soon. He would.

The resources floating about in space are enormous. A raw nickel iron asteroid one kilometer across is worth well over half a trillion dollars at current prices. The asteroid Psyche measures 250 kilometers in diameter. Since volume increases according to the cube of linear dimensions we have an object worth over 7.5 quadrillion dollars.

Ninety percent of asteroids are rocky silicates with some carbon compounds. Most of the commercially valuable metal rich rocks orbit about 400,000,000 kilometers from earth in the outer asteroid belt. Ancient collisions and interactions have knocked a few into the inner solar system. However, I planned on making the splashier trip to the belt for PR reasons. By opening the Soyuz louvers I could gravitically pull from the front while the lanamite pushed from the rear. It would be a long trip. I would be lucky to average the equivalent 1/100 g, which meant a round trip of 66 days. Time equals the square root of the distance divided by one half the acceleration. Allow for deceleration too.

I sat alone in the Soyuz as Ilya and his team stood on deck watching. The craft had been freed from its moorings by my request.

"Standby, *Chayka*," I spoke into the radio. I always have wanted to say "standby" into a radio.

I flicked the switch, which closed the louvers on the outer hull. My stomach churned as I went weightless. After that there was no sensation of motion. Was I still sitting on the deck of the Chayka? Even a modest weight acting on the craft could hold it in place. A single person would be enough to hold it down. I let a minute tick by. Then two. I began to sweat. At three minutes no one yet was banging on the hatch. I opened the louvers for a quick glance and my stomach jumped again. The Soyuz was well over a hundred kilometers above the clearly curved surface of the earth.

I directed a message to the *Chayka* saying that I would be back in a month or two. Since it was likely they would not hear me I sent a second message to the International Space Station. A rather surprised sounding cosmonaut asked me to repeat my identity.

"The *Mineral Tsaritsa*," I answered. So the name is not elegant. Hey, the man caught me off guard.

I shut the louvers earthside and opened the ones facing the moon. The plan was to approach the moon closely, shut the louvers and then get the extra anti-gravity bounce. In the event, I calculated a bit close and nearly scraped the paint off the ship on the lunar mountains, but the experience taught me a lesson and gave me a very good boost.

It often has been noted that the more advanced the form of travel, the less interesting the trip. Open wagons offer loads of scenery along with more hardship than most folks realize. Car trips make children demand "are we there yet?!" Airliners are so boring that they show movies. A month in a Soyuz is only slightly more entertaining than the same time in a dark closet.

The asteroid belt is not like in science fiction movies and comic books. It is mostly empty space. One can fly through it on a random course with no serious risk of collision. The Pioneer and Voyager probes did just that. Finding any rocks at all, much less an uncommon type, requires serious hunting skills. As any hunter knows, during duck season pheasants walk nonchalantly in front of one's face, while the ducks are off on vacation somewhere. Every rock I turned up was just so much silicate debris. I was about to call it quits, grab anything just to prove I had been there, and head back home when a hard radar signal indicated a nickel iron pellet several meters in diameter.

Even with maneuvering jets the task of capture was far from easy. After laborious jockeying and six near collisions, the rock slipped into the open jaws of the lanasphere. It was time to go home.

Moscow was totally unreasonable. First, they demanded their ship back with the strong implication that a Siberian labor camp was to be reopened just for me. Then when I mentioned that I was a US resident and was prepared to land there, they got all sweet, but their earlier threats were much more credible. Actually, I didn't want to land in the USA. I was sure the Americans would find some excuse to steal this from me. They might think I owed them something for that Princeton business. I wanted to put down someplace where the Russian army could protect me but where it was not in a position to arrest me. Perhaps one of the Baltic states. Oxygen supplies required that I decide soon.

"You have a choice," I repeated. "The future citizens of the galaxy can speak Russian, but it has to be on my terms. My interests must be protected." This nationalist appeal was drivel. I don't care if future Martians speak Polynesian. The only reason I didn't land in Tahiti is that French paratroopers would greet me. But tribalism means a lot to most people.

"ISS to *Mineral Tsaritsa.* Could we have a private word with you please?" Someone had overheard.

It was less of a risk than one might think to share Stolichnaya with the two cosmonauts and one astronaut who currently were on the station. Two were male, whatever their nationality. Tatyana, who was exceedingly quiet, worried me rather more. After the social amenities we got down to business.

"How much do you think you can get for that rock?" asked Alexei.

"$200,000 or so."

"It is really not so much money."

"Yes, I know. The point is that we can make a lot of trips. The bigger stones may even carry gold. The wealth is there for the picking,"

"If they let you sell it and keep the money," added Charles.

"Yes."

"Did I hear you correctly that you worked with warheads back home?" asked Tatyana which was her first utterance since "Hello."

"Yes. That was years ago."

"Is your ship nuclear-powered?"

"Well, yes, in an odd sort of way. It's not what you think though."

"I don't think anything. I'm not a mechanic. Does it use uranium or plutonium?"

"Yes."

"Weapons grade?"

"Yes."

"Do they know down below that you possess that stuff?"

"The Russians probably do. The others may suspect it."

"Well?"

"Oh. I see. You are suggesting nuclear blackmail. How do you know I have any warheads or even enough nuclear material to make them?"

"How do they know you don't? It's all a matter of credibility and you've just established some."

"I'm running out of air, food, power, and water. That weakens my negotiating position."

"We have plenty," said Alexei.

The American balanced greed and patriotism. Greed won.

"Welcome aboard, partner."

Tatyana nodded her head.

Strategic deterrents still work. Once they appreciated our military punch and the risk of our defection to other nations, Moscow became remarkably cooperative. They even are providing all our scientific equipment on credit until we can pay with the riches of the solar system. I was worried during our first supply pickup at our desert landing zone in Mongolia, but the Russians and the Mongolians kept their words and left us alone.

The tokamak came indirectly from Western sources. We made a secret and risky landing for it. I thought it best not to give Moscow too many leads about how to duplicate my work. The machine is small and much simpler than the one in Princeton. We are interested only in the peculiar patterns of pan dimensional geometry it briefly generates.

I insisted on dealing through Ilya. Even over the poor video signal he looked pale and shaken. Whatever cell they had kept him in didn't get much sunshine. When I flew off the *Chayka* he concluded that my lanasphere contained some sort of radical new fusion propulsion system. Silliness about cold fusion still turned up in the news frequently enough to make this seem plausible to him. I reinforced his opinion by denying it. My demand for plutonium and tritium made him sure. He has convinced the rest of the government by now. No one ever asked about the paint even though I sprayed the craft in front of everyone with the explanation, "Reduces friction."

Moscow demanded secrecy regarding our base on the far side of the moon, though it is bound to become news soon enough. They also want sole distributorship of mined materials and a restriction on immigration into our domain by anyone except Russian citizens. There is that silly nationalism again, but it is working for us so I won't complain. It is fine with me if my first generation of subjects were born in Russia.

Ilya set up bank accounts for us in the Bahamas, Luxembourg, and Liechtenstein. I think the lure of wealth makes him more loyal to us than Moscow, but I will remain cautious. The Russians plainly plan to take us over, but they will fail in this. The takeover may go the other way.

Meanwhile Tatyana and I keep each other sane in what we call "the chimp house" here on the moon. She is my prime minister. It will get better soon. My first wave of new subjects will arrive next week. They will build new domes and add more living space. The colonization of the galaxy has begun.

We charged the tokamak with tritium at our makeshift but expanding lunar base.

"All right, Alexei. Detonation in two minutes."

The tokamak powers up. It is now 60 seconds before our cocktail of plutonium and special ingredients detonates. We will soon have enough lanamite for a fleet.

Oh yes. I did say subjects a little earlier. I now rather like my adopted American name. I think I'll keep it. Move over Zsa Zsa. There is a new Queen of Outer Space and she is Svetlana the Terrible.

DEATH'S LITTLE HELPER

Everyone says I'm lucky.

My lucky streak began on my twelfth birthday. I was in the back of a mini-van with four other kids en route to a soccer game. The driver was a neighbor's mom. I never liked the neighbor boy much. He was a bully. About two miles from home an animated cell phone conversation distracted the driver's attention from the oncoming concrete truck. I was the only survivor. Even the truck driver was killed. He had tried to swerve at the last moment, but succeeded only in rolling the truck over on top of us. I happened to be in the only part of the van that wasn't crushed.

My lucky streak continued when my mom's new boyfriend took me out water-skiing with his two boys. He didn't really like me much, but he was trying to play up to my mom by being nice to me. He and his kids were in the boat. My mom stayed on shore. He slowly let the towline tighten until I began to drag forward in the water. Then he hit the throttle. I popped up on the skis. It was fun for a while. Then the boat hit a rock and the fuel tank exploded. No one in the boat lived. I splashed headfirst in the water but was unharmed. My flotation belt did its job. I swam back to shore with my skis. Hey, accidents happen.

In December of the same year my mom put me on a commuter flight to Buffalo to see my dad. A bad weather front pushed in more rapidly than predicted. The plane went down. I was the sole survivor. The FAA blamed ice on the wings and a faulty right engine. I remember the plane shaking violently. Then there was dark and a blast of cold air. I woke up still belted into my seat. My seat was lodged in a pine tree. The tree had a trunk of modest diameter and so had absorbed the energy of my seat's impact. I wasn't even bruised. Just to be on the safe side, however, the EMS workers who fetched me from the tree put me in an ambulance and sent me to the hospital. The ambulance slid on the ice and smashed into a tree. I was the sole survivor.

Yeah, I'm just lucky as hell.

My neighbors and acquaintances dropped like flies over the next several years. Carnage surrounded me as though it were my personal garment. The direct causes varied. There was a lightning strike in the park, a shark attack at the beach, and a tornado that touched down half a block from my home. I was never hurt, but I always was nearby and at least casually knew some of the victims. Then there was that terrible incident at my high school that you might remember from the news. One of my classmates, a nice kid though quiet and a bit of a loner, came to school one day with 2 automatic weapons. He shot up the place and then fired at himself. It was awful. At one point during his rampage I ran around a hallway corner and found myself facing him. I looked him straight in the eye from less than ten feet away. It was as though he didn't even see me. Instead, he shot four students who had run up in back of me to my right and left. I was too stunned to drop to the floor as I should have done. It didn't matter. He just fired all around me.

The pattern continued when I entered college. Some students set the dorm on fire while smoking weed. Seven were killed in the flames and nine more from smoke inhalation. I was on the fourth floor when the fire alarm went off, yet I didn't even cough on my way down the stairs and out the front door. By some trick of airflow, an envelope of good air surrounded me the whole way.

As I sat on the Quad lawn and watched the dorm burn, the sense grew in me that these accidents somehow were connected to me. In some strange way I had triggered them. You might think I would have guessed this earlier, but denial is a wonderful thing. It keeps us sane during hard times.

"It's my fault. It's all my fault," I muttered to myself.

A sooty faced young woman who sat near me asked, "Did you start the fire?"

"No. But it's my fault anyway."

"What do you mean?"

I explained my life to the young woman whose name was Margie. She was a good listener. When I was finished she objected.

"Total nonsense! I mean, that's a horrible story. It's awful that you have been through so much. But you aren't responsible. You aren't some lethal jinx. The world doesn't work like that! Weird things happen sometimes."

"They happen around me a lot."

"It's all just random chance."

"Chance? The odds are pretty clearly against it."

"Well, yes and no. Look, when we say the odds are against something happening, like a plane crashing, we really mean it can happen. In fact, it assuredly will happen if you count enough planes."

"We're not talking just one plane accident here."

"No, but my point is still valid. There are billions of people in the world. Most of them won't ever have much improbable happen to them, but some of them are bound to have odd coincidences in their lives. If you think about it, the math requires it. You're like that woman Back East who won two state lotteries. The odds against that were astronomical. It still happened. There wasn't anything supernatural about it. She isn't likely to win another one though. You've seen or been part of some bizarre terrible things, but you managed to walk away every time. However, there is no reason to believe things will keep on happening around you. You're not guaranteed to walk away from the next accident, if there is one, either. You're like that woman. You've just been lucky so far."

"Yeah. Lucky."

"Stop blaming yourself. Stop feeling invulnerable too. That can be unhealthy. Luck runs out eventually."

Although I was reluctant to admit it, Margie made me feel better. Everything she said was sensible. I needed someone well grounded in my life. Besides, she was cute and cuddly. True to her defiance of superstition, she said yes when I asked her for a date. She didn't fear my company. We became a couple. She helped me through so much. She lifted me out of the daze in which I had wandered after so much loss. She constantly reassured me that the world was full of loss. Such was the nature of things. None of it had anything to do with me.

Margie assured me I was not responsible when we watched our college team's quarterback killed in a freak tackling mishap. She assured me again when the marquee from a movie theater we just exited collapsed in back of us trapping a dozen people beneath. She assured me again the time we entered a restaurant, decided the wait for a table was too long and left; minutes later a natural gas explosion destroyed the place. She even assured me through her sobs after we escorted a girl from her dorm to the bus stop. The girl tripped on the curb and fell under the wheel of the bus as it pulled up.

By this time, I suspected Margie was wrong. One day in a funk of doubt I went downtown and sat on a bench. I suppose I was tempting fate by being present in a crowded place. This arguably was rather rude since the fate I was tempting would befall others, not myself. I sat on a sidewalk bench and waited for the catastrophe I knew would come.

Soon, a madwoman down the block and across the road caught my attention. Perhaps in her 30s, she had dyed black hair, pale skin, black denim clothes, and black boots. She ran along the sidewalk touching person after person until she was directly opposite me. One woman, whom she had touched, almost immediately walked out into traffic and was struck by a taxi. The madwoman turned, saw the scene, and laughed. She ran across the street through the stopped traffic, trotted up to me, and reached out to touch my shoulder. She looked into my eyes and stopped.

"Whoops!" she exclaimed. "I wouldn't want to hurt a fellow elf. The job is much too big for that, isn't it dearie?"

She ran off singing a weird variation on a Christmas song, "I'm making a list, I'm checking it twice, I couldn't care less if you're naughty or nice..."

I got the picture. She was one of Death's little helpers. So was I.

It occurred to me that Margie was in great danger. I loved her too much to be the cause of her untimely demise. That night I saw Margie and broke off with her. She was furious. When I tried to explain she shouted that I was crazy and hopeless and that she gave up on me. She stormed out the door. Less than an hour later she was killed in a senseless mugging for eight dollars.

I should have realized. My close friends and family were always safe throughout my life. My casual contacts were the ones marked for death. By throwing Margie over I had sealed her fate.

I understand the madwoman well now. I want Margie. Without her my personal life has no meaning. I'll dedicate myself to my job instead.

I graduated college last month. I got lucky. Despite the current employment situation, the regional Power Company has asked me back for a second interview for my new job. I'll be working at the Twin Rivers nuclear power plant. It is an older light water reactor, similar to the Three Mile Island plant. I'll keep an eye on the coolant. Yeah, I'll keep a real close eye on it.

BATHORY'S DUDGEON

The good news is that vampires don't exist. The bad news is that they do. How can both be true? Paradoxes vanish when we properly define our terms. So, what are vampires? I'll tell you what I know.

My name is Victor Szabo. Regular readers of *The Mystic Cynic* know me. I have been a contributor to the publication for the past 10 years.

Most media coverage of the paranormal is exploitative, credulous, sensational, and lacking in the most elementary journalistic ethics. The most amazing double standard prevails in such matters. The same newspaper that requires reporters to double check sources and to ignore unsubstantiated rumors when writing about a politician or some crime will happily print without comment any whopper from some local eccentric about a ghost sighting.

Our magazine is different. *The Mystic Cynic* is a magazine with a mission. We investigate the miracles, the psychic phenomena, the ghost sightings, and the UFO abductions that receive uncritical mention in the papers and on the 6 o'clock news. We do so skeptically, but fairly and honestly. Our purpose is not to deceive anyone, least of all ourselves. If we ever actually find a ghost, we will say so.

So far, we have not found proof of any paranormal phenomenon. On no occasion has physical evidence or an eyewitness report stood up to critical examination. Frequently, as our critics are quick to point out, we are unable to disprove claims of paranormal phenomena. Yet, the mystics of the world should not, as they so often do, use these failures as demonstrations that our skeptical views are closed-minded. The absence of negative proof means nothing. For example, prove to me that you didn't rob a convenience store on April 3 four years ago. Odds are you can't. Yet, that is no reason to accuse you of the crime. The burden of proof lies with the person making the claim or accusation. The more outlandish the claim, the better proof we properly require. If a man tells me there are brainy ice toads native to the moon Charon, I cannot disprove his assertion. Until he produces real evidence, however, I am not closed-minded if I disbelieve him; rather, I am open-minded to the odds stacked against him being right. If he tells me he actually met one of the toads, I am open-minded to the probability that he is a liar. An extraordinary claim requires extraordinary evidence.

Not every extraordinary claim or irrational belief involves the supernatural or mystical. Take UFOs. It is in principle possible that earth's swamps are being buzzed by extraterrestrial flying saucers. It is just very highly unlikely. More down to earth are the many secret histories and revelations of dark conspiracies published each year. These have varying degrees of credibility. There really are conspiracies in the world, after all, but how are we to respond to a tabloid assertion that JFK was killed by a conspiracy of Marilyn Monroe fans? Rational belief depends on the quality of evidence. Once again, the more unlikely the claim, the better evidence we require.

There is one advantage to investigating the non-mystical type of story. Ultimately, the existence of the supernatural can be tested properly only by dying, and, as Houdini discovered, it is awfully hard to report back. ESP skills, being somewhat less mystical, can be tested more easily: either the psychic can read my cards without peeking or she can't. True, she can claim she had a bad day or (one I've heard many times) my negative energy interfered with her, but at least I can report the results of my earthly test. Alternate histories, which usually rely upon no mysticism or unconventional physics at all, can be checked against real documents and any living participants.

Our editorial position annoys much of the public. Most people are fond of the lake monsters, black helicopters, aliens, and spiritual entities whose existence we question. Of the hate mail that fills The Mystic Cynic's PO Box in Hartford, much is addressed to me personally. This always has been a source of satisfaction to me.

At first I was reluctant to take on the vampire assignment. The editors of *The Mystic Cynic* wanted me to investigate an urban legend that New York City in recent years had become a battleground of vampires and of vampire hunters. The story struck me as too silly to justify my time or the expenditure of ink. Worse, the assignment would doom me to listen to self-aggrandizing lies of attention seeking drunks. I have listened to far more than my share of such people over the years. There is never a shortage of "eyewitnesses" to paranormal events. I had no doubt that I would hear testimonial variations on the following:

"Vampires? Hell, yeah. I've seen 'em. I was out late drinking with some friends and we hooked up with these spooky dudes who invited us to an underground bar. Where? Uh, it was over on the West Side somewhere. I'm not sure exactly where. Like I said, we were drinking. I figured at first it was some SM place but it was more sinister. As soon as I realized the dudes in the booths weren't necking with their chicks but biting them, I knew what was going on. We were in a vampire bar. Every vampire in there had brought in some regular person like me. They wanted us for our blood. I got out of there when no one was looking, but plenty of other people didn't get away that night and I haven't seen them since. Who? I don't know but I used to see them at my hang-outs and they're not there anymore."

On the follow-up, I would find no vampire bar on the West Side or anywhere else. Although there always are missing persons in New York, there would be no specific identifiable victim. Yes, the project looked to be another big waste of my time.

One of the editors changed my mind when he handed me some news clippings. A very real serial murderer was operating in and around New York City. The killer was the apparent source of the current vampire legend. The first known related slaying was six years ago. The most recent was only a month before my meeting with the editors. In each case the killer drove a stake through the heart of the victim. Police nicknamed the murderer Roman, apparently a graveyard humor reference to Roman Polanski's *Fearless Vampire Slayers.*

This was a story with real meat to it. A live human being, not a drunk's fantasy, was running around impaling people with wooden stakes. It was a good old-fashioned crime story. The vampire angle would suit the editorial position of *The Mystic Cynic* well; the slayings were an excellent example of the dangerous effects of irrational beliefs. A belief in vampires had driven some lunatic to murder. I took the assignment.

The basic facts were these. At least eight young men within a 30-mile radius of New York City had been stabbed in the chest with wooden stakes. Four additional stabbing victims had wounds consistent with the same method. The murder weapon for each of those four had been removed from the scene. It was unclear whether the weapon had been removed by the killer or by some other person or animal; each of the bodies had been undiscovered for a time and each had been disturbed.

If the murderer sometimes removed the weapon from the scene, the possibility existed that even more victims than suspected were connected to Roman. The fractured structure of area law enforcement made proper co-ordination difficult even in ordinary cases. While police in any nearby jurisdiction surely would tie in a staked body to Roman, some "ordinary" stabbings in jurisdictions such as Newark, or Norwalk, or Hempstead, or Somerville might have been treated incorrectly as separate.

A large number of missing persons throughout the region met the victim profile. Of course, the profile was broad. All victims were males between the ages of 21 and 40. All but two were single or divorced. Three of the clearly related slayings were in New York City, three were in New Jersey, one was in Westchester, and one was on Long Island. Four of these had been killed in their own homes. Three of those four were in a total or partial state of undress. Police announced no other connections among them.

My look at autopsy reports immediately revealed another connection. Six of the eight victims had alcohol in their bodies. So did all four of the possible victims. All but two of these ten were legally drunk. Either the police deliberately omitted this information from their press releases or they placed little importance on it. For me it was my best clue.

Bars located near the crime scene were the obvious place to start. Even the sober victims might have been at a bar. They could have been lured away before placing an order, or they might have been designated drivers. I am a light drinker myself and often have spent time in a bar with nothing more in my glass than Coca-Cola; I was there just to be social with friends, or to hear music, or to girl watch.

Because a few of the victims were undressed in their homes, gay bars were my first targets. While an intruder might have surprised these victims at home at bedtime, it was more likely, I reasoned, that the killer was an invited guest. Besides, the police reports made no mention of forced entries. The known personal histories of the victims suggested that all were straight, but many men lead double lives. Perhaps a secret life was yet another connection among them.

Suburban gay bars exist but are rare. Local married couples keep intruding on them, sometimes with children in tow. Therefore I began in New York City where there are hundreds. It turned out only a handful of such bars were near each New York victim's home, which made my initial inquiries simple.

The police, it turned out, had a similar theory to mine. They had preceded me. My questions at every one of the bars elicited "not again" groans. Few patrons would talk to me. Of those that did, none had anything useful to say. No one knew or recognized any of the victims. The bartenders also were unhelpful and uniformly hostile besides. The *Falconer* bartender, a balding middle aged man with a gruff style, gave me the most assistance, although it wasn't his intention.

"No, I don't want your money. The drink is on the house. Just finish it and take yourself elsewhere, buddy. The police annoy everybody here with those same questions at least twice a week. It's bad for business. No one likes talking to police, and I don't like it when reporters like you make my customers worry that they're drinking with a serial killer."

"Maybe they are."

"I don't think so."

"What if you are wrong? Suppose some of your customers are in danger? What if the killer is some homophobe who lures and kills? Maybe the vampire thing is just to throw the police off. Have you thought of that?"

"Look, buddy, this is the last time I'm saying this to you or to anyone else. If any of those victims were regulars here, I'd remember them. I don't. Look someplace else. There is no good reason to focus here. Why not suppose the guys were lured by a woman? Or by a woman with an accomplice? Have you thought of that?"

I had considered a female killer, but ranked the probability as low. Men comprise 80% of murderers — and of murder victims. I hadn't thought of a killer couple though. The bartender was right. I was being too conventional in my analysis. Moreover, if I simply followed in the steps of the police I would reach the same dead end they apparently did.

The suburbs began to seem a better place to nose around. There were fewer bars of any kind in the neighborhood of each crime scene and strangers in them stand out more. Perhaps some kind of witness could be found out there.

I racked up 4,000 miles on my Plymouth driving about the suburbs. I interviewed bar owners, bartenders, and customers in the areas around the slayings in Long Island, Westchester, and Jersey. I found quite a few individuals who knew the local victim personally, but no crime witness in any real sense. No one remembered anything useful about the night of a murder. No one remembered seeing a victim speak with a stranger. No one remembered seeing a victim leave, alone or in company.

I needed a new lead.

As I sat nursing a beer at the *Wicked Witch* bar in Stirling, NJ, I accidentally tore my paper place mat, which had absorbed some spillage. I looked at it more closely. The place mat was a monthly calendar of bands. Every night starting at 10 PM the *Wicked Witch* had live entertainment. An almost whimsical thought fluttered through my mind.

"Jim, do you have a schedule of bands that played here last October a year ago?" I asked the bartender.

"A year ago? Hell, no. I may not have one left from last month."

"Try the paper," offered a patron two stools away from me.

"Excuse me?"

"I work classifieds at *The Daily Record*. The paper prints band schedules at local clubs. Look up past issues and you can see who was playing when."

"Of course. I should have thought of that. Thanks."

Newspaper research is easier than it used to be. Back issues for over a decade are online for most local newspapers. The time, even the day, of death was approximate for several victims, so I chose a window of several days for each slaying. I checked what bands were playing in local bars during that period. A repeated coincidence in the schedules leapt out at me. On all but two occasions *The Heather Field Band* was playing nearby. Was the killer a Heather Field fan? Was this Heather herself in danger?

I looked up current issues of local papers to find her upcoming appearances. I found a listing for that night at *Limericks* in Glen Cove, NY.

Heather was pretty good. A pretty woman of indeterminate age with long black hair, she used her strong and unusual voice to excellent effect. I liked her quirky guitar player too.

I followed the band for the next three weeks. She noticed. At the *Rodeo Bar* in NYC Heather sat down next to me. She ordered a shot and swallowed it. She ordered another.

"I know you are a vampire. I won't let you in."

This was too easy. How had the police missed it? Maybe they just didn't have the time to follow a blues band for three weeks.

"Are you Roman?"

"Virginian."

"I mean, are you a vampire slayer."

"If you aren't a vampire you shouldn't be frightened."

"If I am a vampire you should be frightened."

"You can't hurt me because I know who and what you are. I won't let you in. Actually, I can destroy you and your whole nest and you can't do a thing to stop me. I will too. Want to get a room?"

"I think not."

Heather smiled. She pulled a long cigar and a Bic lighter from her bag. She flicked the lighter and held out the flame toward me for several seconds before lighting her cigar. Heather blew smoke in my face. She got up and left.

I could have gone to the police at once, yet nothing she said was reason enough for them to arrest her. The woman easily could argue she had been teasing me. She even could deny talking to me altogether. Unless the police possessed physical evidence of which I was unaware, I had nothing. I wanted something.

Heather had placed cards on the bar with her play schedule for the next two months. I took one. One of the listed engagements on the card was at a club named *Bathory's Dungeon.* I instantly knew Heather's plan. Heather meant to flick her Bic at this place. The club in Heather's mind surely was a nest of vampires. How could she think otherwise? Heather was sure to know the origins of the name.

Two historical figures are most often credited as bases for the vampire legend. The best known, thanks to Bram Stoker, was the 15th century Romanian warlord Vlad Dracula the Impaler. Rather less well known, despite the sensational aspects of the story, was the 16th century Countess Elizabeth Bathory of Hungary. She was a frightful woman who dabbled in the occult and who indulged a homoerotic sadomasochistic taste for pubescent girls. She is reputed to have bathed in the blood of virgins for the sake of her complexion. This last accusation may or may not have been true. However, it is true that young peasant girls on her lands disappeared with alarming regularity. Those who went to work as servants at the Bathory castle seemed always to have odd fatal accidents or to jump off walls. Despite this, the local peasant families were remarkably sanguine about sending daughter after daughter to the castle. Despite Elizabeth's protected status as a member of the aristocracy, the authorities eventually intervened. She was placed under house arrest in her own castle for the remainder of her life.

I drove out to Morristown, NJ, and spoke to the owners of *Bathory's Dungeon.* The owners are an eccentric young newly married couple named Stephen and Pamela Bathory. Shortly after

their marriage they had opened a two level Hungarian
Restaurant on a down-sloping lot. The upper floor, facing the
street and on a level with it, they called *The Wild Magyar*. It
offered ethnic fare in a colorful but fairly conventional atmosphere. The lower level, with an outer door to a municipal parking lot in the rear of the building, was the pub *Bathory's Dungeon*.
The pub was dark, to put it mildly. The wood surfaces were wal-
nut stained. The painted surfaces were black. Battle axes and
maces graced the walls. A painting of the eponymous Countess
taking a bath hung above the bar. Breaking the atmosphere only
slightly, the pub had a stage lighted mostly with black light.
Bathory's Dungeon featured live music four days a week and com-
edy acts on Sunday.

A background check on Stephen had turned up little other
than that he was a well-to-do young man. There had been a somewhat secretive DEP investigation of him a few years back involv-
ing a small spill of some kind, but whatever the accident was had
not led to fines or charges. Pamela's background was murkier.
She had a record of four arrests on prostitution charges.

The pub's name and ambiance were enough for it to draw a
peculiar crowd. There wasn't a large Gothic element in very suburban Morris County, but virtually all that there was showed up
in this bar. If anyplace could look like a nest of vampires, this one
did.

I nudged up to the bar between a black-haired woman with a
pasty fresh-from-the-graveyard look and a slender man in a black
raincoat who wore wraparound sunglasses despite the near
absence of light. I managed to get the attention of the owners
who were working in back of the bar. I moved to the less crowded far end of the bar. The two owners came over.

"Interesting pub you have here," I began. "Are you related to
Liz in the painting up there by any chance?"

"Yes, a great great great aunt or something," answered
Stephan. "Is that what you want to talk to us about?"

"Not exactly. I want to talk about Heather Field. She is booked
to play here next week."

"I know. I hope she is worth it because she is a royal pain. I
never met her but she bugged us incessantly for a gig. Pam final-

ly gave her one when one of our regular groups went on tour. I don't know why it meant so much to her."

"I do."

"What? Does she have some Gothic theme or something? We're getting quite a reputation with those types."

"So I see. Yes, I suppose she does have a Gothic theme, but it is a lot subtler than anything I see here. It's a lot more dramatic too."

"Interesting dichotomy. How so, and what is your interest?"

I explained to the Bathorys my belief that Heather was Roman, the stake murderer.

Pamela objected. "Do you have any proof of this aside from your chat with her? She could have been teasing you, you know."

"I think she was serious. Besides, there is the coincidence of her band schedule to the murders. I realize that is circumstantial, but she is who I say. She believes this a nest of vampires and she plans to destroy you all."

"All by herself with a wooden stake?"

"Try fire."

"I see. Thanks. We'll handle it," said Pamela.

"That is a pretty cavalier attitude."

"Let's just say that this time she picked on someone her own size. Someone with fangs."

"Is that a metaphor or do you believe in vampires too?"

"Tell me, Mr. Szabo. What would you call someone who sleeps in a coffin, sometimes for years at a time, then wakes up, feeds, has some fun, and returns. Is she a vampire?"

"At the very least."

"I think so too. Here. Have a drink on the house. It's our signature house drink, a Bloody Lizzie. Tell me what you think of it and I'll explain to you what I have in mind for Heather."

The drink was thick and red. I'm not a fan of drinks with tomato juice, but I had one to be sociable. Despite the base color, the liquid seemed to emit a blue glow. I assumed it was an artifact of the black light in the bar. The taste was ghastly. I couldn't imagine the pub sold many of these. I was about to tell Pamela what I thought of her drink when things went a bit fuzzy.

Pamela shook me awake. My mouth was dry. The bar was

empty except for the two of us. The chairs were stored upside down on the tables.

"Wow, how long was I asleep? An hour? Two?"

"Twelve. We'll be opening again in a couple hours more."

"That's ludicrous."

Pamela pushed Wednesday's paper in front of me.

"But it is Tuesday."

"Not anymore. Sorry to do that to you but I was proving a point."

"What point?"

"We have an elixir. A chemist back around 1900 invented it, but that is another story. The point is, it makes you sleep. For days. For weeks. For years, if you like."

"Nonsense."

"What day is today?"

"I get your point, but a lot of Mickeys can knock you out for twelve hours."

"Want to try for a week, if you must satisfy yourself?"

"Uh, no. Let's assume what you say is true for now. What good is it? Why sleep away your life?"

"You don't sleep it away. You don't age while sleeping, you see, so you have as much awake time as you ever did."

"I'm still not clear on the advantage."

"True longevity. Some remarkable breakthroughs are on the horizon. If we can survive until they are made, maybe we can have a lifespan of a few hundred years, real time. Maybe we don't have to die at all."

"Sounds pretty pie in the sky."

"Don't you like pie?"

"You believe what you are saying?"

"Yes. In fact, Stephan and I are going into a long term hibernation soon, but we'll take care of little Heather first just as bit of public service."

"What is long term?"

"A few decades. We can check in then and see what progress is being made."

"Toward longevity."

"Yes. I'll mix you a stronger Bloody Lizzie if you want to experiment on yourself. You have to promise not to give it to anyone for analysis though. If it becomes so widely accessible that every-one goes to sleep, it kind of defeats the point."

"OK, I promise. About Heather, though, I don't think I can let you kill her. The woman is crazy."

"Oh, dear me, I wouldn't think of it. We'll just give her a Bloody Lizzie on the house, a stronger one than we gave you. We'll put some red stains around her mouth. In a few years she'll wake up in a coffin. Trust me, she'll have a whole different atti-tude about the whole vampire thing when she thinks she is one of them."

"What if she doesn't? Or what if she takes to biting people instead of stabbing them?"

"You're the reporter. Leave a warning about her behind for the future. The police may keep an eye on her when she turns up again."

Pamela had appealed successfully to a dark element in myself. I agreed.

This will be my last article for a while. Consider it a warning for the future. Don't bother visiting *Bathory's Dungeon.* It closed last week. *The Heather Field Band* no longer plays either. See you in 20 years. Maybe 30.